ZERO ISLAND

CHRIS BAUER

Severn River
PUBLISHING

Severn River Publishing
www.SevernRiverPublishing.com

ISBN: 978-1-64875-116-5 (Paperback)
ISBN: 978-1-64875-117-2 (Hardback)

ALSO BY CHRIS BAUER

Blessid Trauma Crime Scene Cleaners

Hiding Among the Dead

Zero Island

Scars on the Face of God

Binge Killer

Jane's Baby

Never miss a new release! Sign up to receive exclusive updates from author Chris Bauer.

Join today at ChrisBauerAuthor.com

For granddaughters Teddy and Bea.
I hope you enjoy your sisterhood
as much as Oma and Opa enjoy our grandparenthood.

WARNING-WARNING!
All enemy parachutists and invaders are hereby warned
not to shoot our Hawaiians more than twice.
The third time "makes them mad"
and we will not be responsible for their actions.

—Albert G. Christian, 299th Infantry, c. 1942,
"The Koa Regiment,"
Hawaii Army National Guard

1

Miakamii Island, Hawaiian Islands
Late June

Whup-whup-whup-whup...

The tourist helicopter jerked and made death rattle sounds as it dropped down, down, down, careening sideways, spinning wildly, four thousand feet, three thousand feet, two...

Islander Kealoha "Ella" Waumami, on horseback, could hear each *whup-whup-whup* more distinctly as the aircraft spun earthward, five hundred feet, four hundred feet, slicing into the heavy tree canopy that edged the island's church and school, crashing fifty yards and two livestock pens away from her, her horse rearing up.

She'd seen all of it—the copter starting its descent, picking up speed before flipping and twisting out of control, its blades shearing through the treetops on a diagonal until the canopy fought back, the thick vegetation splintering the aircraft. The flight deck skidded nose down to a stop in the clearing, the blades carving up dirt and scrub and animals in pens: cows, sheep, a wild boar, their bloody carcasses splatting against the island's one-room schoolhouse and tiny church, and crashing through a church window into its interior.

Most alarming, she'd also seen two people jettison from a high altitude, one dropping straight down like a bullet into the Pacific not far from shore, the other riding the air until a parachute opened, then splashing into the middle of the Hanakawii Channel. A cigarette boat picked him up and spun in an about-face to head toward Kauai Island across the channel.

Ella galloped her bareback mare out of the clearing and onto the beach, dismounted, then sprinted on short but powerful legs into the water and swam hard. She knew the helicopter pilot well, a close friend. He was the one in the fluorescent yellow jumpsuit who looked lifeless before he hit the whitecaps.

The second leg of their trip, a flight to Kauai Island's Lihue Airport, was behind them. Thirteen hours total in coach from Philadelphia with a short layover in Denver, Philo and Patrick on board, one half of Blessid Trauma Cleaning Company. A two-week junket. Philo left the business in the hands of former owners Grace and Hank Blessid, who would operate it on a skeleton schedule. The thirteen hours in the air had turned into fourteen hours plus, the plane needing to circle the airport due to an unspecified air traffic issue.

They deplaned a short distance from the gate, emergency vehicles and a fire truck assembled on a nearby runway, their sweeping red lights advertising a crisis. At the gate a cop stood listening to a walkie-talkie chirp a message Philo overheard: "*Missing helicopter located off-island, on Miakamii. All clear on Kauai, over.*"

"Copy that, over," the Hawaiian cop answered.

In shirtsleeves, shorts, and sandals, they entered the single-story airport terminal with eight flight gates inexplicably numbered three through ten. Once inside, it was like someone threw a switch on Patrick.

"Not feeling it, Philo sir," he said, his head swiveling. "Nope. Not doing it for me. None of it. This isn't it."

To Patrick, Philo was always "sir" or "Philo sir." The formality had little to do with Philo's military background, more to do with Patrick's dented, challenged noggin.

Philo Trout. Possessed of enough brown hair to say he wasn't balding, but the two bare skin patches on either side of his tufted rooster comb were staking larger claims. The rest of him cut a hard, angular physique, tall, lanky, but with good guns for biceps. Counter to his tough cruiserweight body, his hair was losing out to his age.

"Thirty seconds off the plane on an island you might or might not have ever set foot on before, and you're already writing it off," Philo said. "We'll be island hopping for two weeks, Patrick. Something might click. Give it a chance. Let's get our bags."

They lost their baggage carts at a drop-off point near the street curb. The two men, two rolling suitcases each, strode toward a row of car rentals. A rush of salty Hawaiian air overwhelmed them, stopping Philo in his tracks.

"Wow. Wonderful," he said.

At any given time, Philo knew from personal experience, a person could smell four things on most of the islands: saltwater, coconut oil, plants after a fresh rain, and…

"Barbecue," Patrick said. "I smell barbecue."

Korean barbecue to be exact, from a street vendor outside the terminal. Upon discovering it, the charcoal aroma became the one thing a person's nose would search for again and again on Kauai.

"Plentiful, Patrick, all over these islands. We'll get some later. Let's keep moving."

Patrick Stakes. Not his real name. A temporary identifier

still in place after more than three years. He'd been a John Doe at the ER in a Philly hospital. Was found bludgeoned and unconscious in a foot of snow in a dumpster near the iconic South Philadelphia cheesesteak joint, Pat's King of Steaks, so why not name him something similar, the ER docs said. The blunt head trauma had lowered his IQ a few points and left him an amnesiac. He was maybe twenty-five years old, his real birth-date and birthplace unknown, and was deemed Hawaiian, or at least Polynesian, this because a female acquaintance of recent infamy, also Hawaiian, touted that as his ethnicity, and it had been confirmed by DNA testing. No matches for his fingerprints or for DNA from the FBI or military databases. It was hoped, therefore, on the part of Philo, Grace and Hank, and Patrick, that this Hawaiian visit would rekindle memories elusive to him from the first twenty-five or so years of his young life.

A rooster scooted from underneath an SUV rental and crossed the road into Philo's path, wings flapping, a cake donut in its beak. It lost its hold on the donut, dropping it onto the blacktop at Philo's feet. A standoff, rooster versus man, or so the rooster's loud squawk intimated, the donut between them.

"Don't go near the donut," Patrick said.

"Wasn't going to," Philo said, retreating a step.

Large for a rooster. Wide, gray, feathery collar, brown body, and pronounced black tail feathers. It picked up the treat in its beak and ran past him, onto a pet relief lawn. An Irish Setter on a leash whimpered when the rooster charged it, the dog's tail curling between his legs. The chicken disappeared into the shrubbery beyond the lawn.

"I see they still grow their chickens big in Hawaii," Philo said.

"They're wild here," Patrick said. "The ones at the cockfights are even bigger. The chickens keep the cats under control."

"Chicken versus feral cat?" Philo said. "Not buying your assessment about the outcome, Patrick."

"Hunger does crazy things on the streets, sir."

Inside the SUV, their bags stowed, Philo pressed the ignition. "Pull up the address for our rental cottage on your phone, Patrick."

"Target acquired, sir."

Philo backed the car out, not particularly careful about any wildlife that might still be lingering underneath. Kauai chickens were, from what he remembered, a nuisance regardless of size because they were everywhere, and they were aggressive. He stopped the car for the traffic light at the parking lot exit, processing the rooster incident in his head. His gaze lingered on Patrick, who stayed serious, his head swiveling at what was, for the moment, non-existent cross traffic. The light turned green.

"You can go now, Philo sir."

"You realize what just happened, Patrick?"

"Yes, sir. You almost fought a chicken over a donut, sir."

"Yes. But I didn't, did I? Because odd as it all seemed, I knew not to even try. Because I've been here before."

"Yes, Philo sir, you were smart. Those chickens are nasty."

"Yes, they are." Philo stayed at the exit, waiting for something to click for Patrick. The light turned red again, their SUV still idling. "You listening to yourself, bud?"

"Sir?"

"You knew about these chickens. You know this place."

Patrick blinked hard, absorbing Philo's words, his eyes darting back and forth until they sank in. He choked out a response.

"I've... I've been here before! The chickens. I remember the chickens!"

Philo's congratulatory squeeze of his shoulder put him on alert. Patrick now tried to absorb every detail of every passing tree and building and sign at every turn the SUV made after leaving the terminal. No other hits for him as they drove the island perimeter, but he was beside himself anticipating new revelations.

This first destination island, Kauai, was an indulgence, Philo looking to check in on a retiring Navy commander he'd served with on more than one deployment: Commander Evan Malcolm, CO for the Hawaiian Missile Training Outpost at Howling Sands, on the western side of Kauai. Philo awaited a return call from his CO buddy to set up their reunion. Howling Sands was a military-use-only airport, not open to the public. But before tomorrow's cross-island stop, they needed to drive twenty miles along the coast to their VRBO beach cottage rental, where they were scheduled to stay a few nights. Close to the cottage was tiny Port Allen Airport, like Lihue Airport open to the public, but with a runway able to handle only small aircraft and tourist helicopters.

The plan was to check in, then rest on a sandy beach for the remainder of the day to handle their jet lag. Tomorrow morning would be more beach time for Patrick, with Philo intending to drive farther west along the coast to Howling Sands. He had a favor to ask his Navy buddy Evan: could they get clearance to visit Miakamii Island from whoever could grant it? For Patrick's sake, to at least rule it out as an origin for him, a long shot considering Miakamii's secretive status and strange history. Two weeks to visit all eight islands. It was ambitious, but that was the plan to give Patrick the best chance at finding his identity and lost early life. Kauai and

Miakamii, the westernmost inhabited islands, would be their first two stops.

"Monk seals, ten o'clock," Philo said. Patrick craned his neck to look past Philo, out his window. They splashed out of the water and onto a small beach as they drove past. The seals were prevalent on Miakamii and Kauai both, Philo recalled. "They do anything for you, Patrick?"

"Sorry, sir. Not remembering the monk seals. But they're really cute."

Miakamii Island, a.k.a. "The Prohibited Isle." Where time stood still for 1,230 inhabitants per the 2010 census. During the last decade the census count became suspect, both from heavy attrition and closer scrutiny. From a practical perspective, no one knew the real year-round population, save maybe for the island's ruling family. Conspiracy types questioned if there was anyone still actually living on the island, considering so many had migrated to Kauai to lead "normal" lives.

One visit might be all that was needed to eliminate Miakamii from consideration. Philo's Navy buddy Evan would hopefully provide an introduction to the Logans. The family had a long and very storied history dating back to the mid-nineteenth century, when Catherine McDougall Innes, Scottish farmer and plantation owner by way of New Zealand, bought the island from Hawaiian King Kamehameha V with gold and gemstones worth about fifteen thousand dollars. Among the caveats about the purchase was the agreement that the new owners and their descendants would preserve the island's culture and lifestyle in perpetuity, including a good-faith promise that the family would only visit, not live on, the island. That promise had been kept generation to generation, most recently by Douglas Logan, aging great-great-grandson of Ms. Innes, and his family, the island's current caretakers.

Philo's personal attachment to Miakamii was as a Navy SEAL. The Navy used the island for training and defense, something the Logan family had supported for decades dating back to WWII, and later on with SEAL tactical maneuvers front and center in its interior and on its shores.

"Can I go with you tomorrow, sir?" Patrick said.

"To the Navy base? Negatory, Patrick. If the Navy agrees to make a pitch to the Logans for us to see if they'll let us visit the island, it wouldn't be tomorrow anyway. They'd need to schedule it."

Philo's cell phone chirped. He left traffic and pulled onto the shoulder.

"Commander Malcolm. Hey. Just talking about you. How are you, bud?... *What?*... My God, Evan... Sure, anything... oh-eight-hundred hours tomorrow. See you then."

Philo's phone hand dropped to his lap after the call ended, his straight-ahead look vacant, mystifying. The SUV interior turned pin-drop quiet, Patrick waiting for him to come out of his trance, traffic whooshing past them like racecars passing the pits.

"Philo sir, what's wrong?"

Philo spoke without fully processing the news, trying to make sense of it. "Evan's fiancée. She's *dead*."

They had no attachment to the fiancée other than Philo expected to meet her during the trip and have Evan tell him about his decision to get married again. Friendly banter, meet the fiancée, camaraderie, and commiseration re their respective retirements, Philo's a few years in arrears, Evan's coming up at the end of the year. A pleasant reunion. Plus the request that Evan cut through some Miakamii visitation red tape for Patrick's benefit.

"Dead from what, sir? An accident?"

"A home invasion." Philo swallowed hard. "Her cleaning lady found her. She was disemboweled."

"Disem-what?"

"Her internal organs were missing."

Philo blanked his face, then spoke into the windshield. "Evan wants us to look at her place after the scene's released by the police."

He faced Patrick, now more in control. "It seems you'll get to see the base with me tomorrow after all. The base, then her house. If you want to, bud."

The news of the murder had stiff-armed the air out of Philo. He suffixed his offer to Patrick with a *please* that was soft on supplication, heavy on maudlin.

3

His body was manageable in the water, pockets of air caught inside his bright yellow flight suit. Ella swam on her side, pulling him along, had to keep moving, her fingers under the back of his helmet, her sidestroke and her legs fighting the channel's sea chop, thankfully light. Once she got closer to the Miakamii shore the breaking waves helped. She dragged her large friend out of the Pacific and onto the sandy beach, his body the deadest of weights now that there was no buoyancy. Ella strained as she pulled him as far onto the beach as she could, away from the tide, onto dry sand.

She'd kept her emotions in check for the hundred or so yards of hard swimming on her way out, and for those same hundred harder-fought yards on her way back. Coughing from the effort to catch her breath, her gasps were now supplemented with a good cry.

"Chester. My goodness. Oh, Chester..."

No reason to try CPR, or chest compressions, or turn him over on his side to expel seawater. Chester Kapalekilahao's throat was sliced open in two places, the blood and seawater glistening on his dark Miakamiian neck. The oozing blood drained off his skin and into the sand, turning it a purplish-red and then a dull gray, with the sand staying that way until the evening tides would move in to wash away all traces of the gore.

She undid his chinstrap, removed his helmet. Wavy black hair, chunky face, dead man's stare from his black eyes. He and Ella shared the same date of birth a year apart, which meant they went through much of their Miakamii schooling together because of the island's negligible enrollment. Those many decades ago he was her crush when she was only a *keiki*, a young girl who finally settled down with her eventual husband Benehakaka ("Ben") after Chester's decision to leave the island. She and Ben were now married more than thirty years.

"*Auwe!* My dearest Chester," she said, pacing, sobbing. "Who did this to you, love?"

Ella gazed across the Hanakawii Channel at Kauai, the direction the cigarette boat had taken. Yes, who out there could do such a thing to this wonderful, proud man, and why? He'd been a success story by Miakamiian standards. An inspiration.

Her horse shook her mane, trotted closer to Ella, nudged her shoulder, and neighed. "I know, Kumu, we need to go back. I'll get Ben to bring a boat."

She cupped her lifelong friend's cold, wet cheek, sobbed again. "I have to leave you here for a little bit, Chester. Ben and I will return to take you back to Kauai, back to your family."

She rose, stood over the body. Her horse nudged her again. Ella climbed onto Kumu's bare back, patted her neck.

"This is a sad, sad day, Kumu. And I'm afraid sadder days are coming."

Horse and rider galloped off the beach onto a path through the surrounding thick and prickly scrub brush.

They wrapped the body tightly in boat canvas and laid it lengthwise in the bottom of the skiff. Ben piloted their seaworthy outboard, at one time a lifeboat, back out into the water through the low-tide risers on a calm, late-afternoon sea. He and Ella and the body of Chester Kapalekilahao headed across the seventeen-mile channel that separated Miakamii and Kauai, the sun to their backs. As Ben guided them around the Kauai surf for their push into the bay at the edge of Howling Sands, Ella raised her binoculars. She called over her shoulder to her husband in her native Miakamiian, letting him know that she could see the police chief on the pier.

"Roger that," Ben said in English. "I'll bring us in on the sand next to it."

Closer to Kauai's cell towers Ella found a cell phone signal. A 9-1-1 call had engaged the island police. Ella's second call went to Mr. Logan, whose silver Range Rover was now arriving. He parked it next to one of four police cruisers.

After the tears that Mr. Logan—Douglas to Miakamii's resident islanders—and Ella had shared on the phone, he'd heard Ella explain in a calm voice about where the tourist helicopter, one of five copters the Logan family owned, had crashed in the island's interior. The wreckage would need remediation that wouldn't come until after scrutiny by the Kauai police and the National Transportation Safety Board.

"It killed some of our cows and sheep, Douglas," she told him, "and the church, it... the church, Douglas! It's damaged..." With Douglas Logan, she hadn't had to go into detail about the livestock loss and what it meant. He knew the hardship this would cause. The Logan family had been supplementing the island's food needs through times of hardship that often lasted years. But damage to the small island's only church had made the cut to Chester's throat seem even deeper, crueler.

"Ella, you needn't worry about any of it," he said. "We'll get through this. I want to see my good friend Chester first. We'll talk about the damage later."

Chester had left Miakamii at age eighteen, went to work for the Logan family on their cattle ranch in Kauai. He attended flight school at Douglas Logan's expense, learned to fly helicopters, and had stayed in the family's employ ever since, handling tourist sightseeing. The bond Douglas shared with all Miakamii islanders was real, but the one he shared with Chester was special, like father and son, and not unlike the love Douglas also had for the island of Miakamii itself.

But the Logan family was in a financial tailspin, Miakamii the cause of it. Their ventures—a cattle ranch and a sheep farm, the shell leis made by island craftspeople, a robust Hawaiian honeybee and honey business—had all taken a hit lately. The ranches and farms and the honey business had been shuttered, with the cattle ranch resurrecting itself on Kauai but costing the Logan family a fortune to transition it. Adding to the family's financial miseries was their impact on the Miakamiian people, whose jobs relied on these ventures. The island's poor prospects were sinking the Logans in debt and throwing the native inhabitants into poverty.

Which put the island's ownership in question, and this in turn put the island in play as an available property. There'd been a long-held opinion that the state or federal government could and should claim eminent domain, this due to the island's strategic military location as an early-warning site in the Pacific. Losing its viability as a privately held commercial enterprise also made it a prime acquisition target for someone who could make it financially healthy again, maybe resurrect its cattle farming and honeybee businesses. Miakamii's stewardship by the Logan family, in place for more than 150 years, was in jeopardy.

A new player had emerged, much to Douglas Logan's dislike: another well-heeled family that claimed its interest wasn't in owning the island. A certain consideration could help the Logans climb out of their mountain of debt: the island's shell lei business. They wanted the Logans and the island residents to allow an indigenous family to manage it. Miakamii shell leis were like gold and rare gems, coveted worldwide. An important enterprise for sure, some of the leis bringing more than ten thousand dollars each on the open market because of the rarity of the shells. The mollusks that produced them were, to anyone's knowledge, found nowhere else on the planet, and the unpolluted water gave the shells an uncommon luster.

Ben motored the skiff parallel to the thin pier jutting from the beach, the pier empty of fishermen or other foot traffic, the police having chased everyone off its fifty-yard length. He steered the skiff through the sea foam to the beach's edge. Four Kauai police officers met them near the "No Boat Landing or Launching" sign and helped pull the skiff onto the sand.

Police Chief Terry Koo legged his way down the pier in time to join Mr. Logan in his trot from the parking lot. The two were soon walking side by side through dried seaweed, Chief Koo slowing his gait to remain alongside the shorter yet trimmer Douglas, determination etched onto their faces. Their footsteps sank into the dark, wet sand.

"Douglas," Chief Koo said in acknowledgment.

"Terry," Douglas said, breathing hard.

"Let us handle this, Douglas."

"No issue, after I see Chester."

Blue-eyed and with thinning hair, the Douglas Logan that Ella knew could be both ornery and polite inside the same exchange, a benevolent employer, and very much a Christian. While under the Logan family's tutelage, Miakamii residents were expected to always behave in a Christian manner, and they had done so dating back generations. Douglas steadied Ella after she climbed out of the skiff onto the sand and leaned into a hug as tight as one he'd give a grieving child. Douglas also gathered the rugged Ben in his arms, the three of them suffering through a hard cry cut short because of the task at hand.

"Let's get him out of the boat, then we'll take him where his family can be with him," Douglas said.

Chief Koo interrupted. "The medical examiner needs to see him first, Douglas, to pronounce him and then determine cause of death. This isn't negotiable."

"Look, Terry. Ella explained what the wounds look like, what she saw before the copter went down. Let the M.E. meet us at the funeral home. His family will be there—"

Ella stepped between the two men before past bad blood could surface. She raised her chin to Douglas, spoke compassionately to her dear employer, patriarch, friend, and ally, with the common sense required to get Chester's body where it needed to go as soon as possible.

"It will be all right, Douglas. His neck—no coroner will be able to get past those wounds as cause of death. The autopsy should be quick."

Chief Terry Koo chimed in. "My guess is that the M.E. won't need more than a day, Douglas. Let's let everyone do their jobs so we can get the bastard who did this, okay? Don't fight me on this."

"Language, Terry," Douglas said.

"You know what I mean, Douglas. Sorry, Ella. We'll get this

done as soon as possible so he can be turned over to his family without a significant delay."

Douglas acquiesced. The four police officers removed Chester's wrapped body from the boat and laid him on a medical stretcher for the short trek through the sand to the coroner's vehicle just arriving.

"Hold it," Douglas called, Ben and Ella bringing up the rear. "I need to see him before he goes. It's—I just need to see him, please..."

Chief Koo halted his men. "I'll make you a deal, Douglas. I need to get some people onto the island to see the helicopter crash site while the NTSB does its work. You can take a quick peek if you promise not to argue with me on that. Deal?"

Ella held her breath a moment. Douglas had never been keen on allowing people onto their precious island other than current and former Miakamiians and the U.S. Navy, plus paying safari participants for controlled commercial hunting trips.

"Deal," Douglas said.

"Fine." Chief Koo gestured for his Kauai officers to lower the stretcher to the sand. "Make it quick, Douglas, please."

Douglas, Ella, and Ben caught up. "I did the wrapping, so let me undo him," Ben said.

Ben undid the clips along one side of Chester Kapalekilahao's canvas-clad body, then unwrapped the top section to expose his upper torso and the barbaric wounds on his neck. From the looks of it, the two wounds in combination had nearly decapitated him.

"Lord have mercy," Douglas said, his eyes widening, but with no gasp. He placed his hand on his friend's chest. "Chester. I am so sorry, son. May you rest now, dearest Chester."

Chief Koo's cell rang. "Koo. Fine, got it. Douglas, we have

to get him to the morgue right now. I've got another crisis. My officers are needed elsewhere."

Chester's hands had been gathered together and placed near his waist, in a coffin pose. Douglas patted one, lifted and kissed it—"We'll find who did this to you, Chester"—then laid it back down. He stepped away from the body and Ben rewrapped it.

Chief Koo addressed his men. "Officers, after we load up Mr. Kapalekilahao, one of you needs to call the dispatcher. Probable home invasion near the Navy base. One dead…"

4

Hawaiian Missile Training Outpost
Howling Sands, Kauai

Philo was first in line inside the visitor center. "Tristan Trout, with Patrick Stakes, to see CO Evan Malcolm."

"How's everyone doing today?" the guard said, Seaman Long per her nametag. A rote question. The greeting held no cheer and was unsmiling, her blank eye contact an indication that the outpost's mood was grim. The murder of the commanding officer's fiancée could do this to an installation.

"I'm a close friend of the CO," Philo said, feeling the need to mention this. "I'm aware of his loss."

She nodded. "A sad day. You're on today's list, Petty Officer Trout. Show me some personal ID and info on your car, please. I'll process you first, sir, then your associate."

Tristan "Philo" Trout, Petty Officer First Class, Retired, dropped his driver's license, car rental agreement, Uniformed Services ID card, and permit to carry a concealed weapon onto the desk blotter in front of the seaman.

"Are you carrying your firearm today, sir?"

"Not today, Seaman. Not on my person or in my car."

"Good." She checked off a box, passed it to an associate at a desk behind her. "Very well. Please stand over there. Seaman Kerry will wand you, then take your picture. Next, please."

Patrick presented his official State of Pennsylvania ID card to the seaman, the only form of ID he had.

"No driver's license, Mr. Stakes?"

"No, ma'am, just that. I have dissociative amnesia. Someone helped me get the state ID. There's nothing else. I'm, uh, here in Hawaii..."

Patrick eyed Philo eyeing him. Philo's nod said, *You're doing great, Patrick. Stay with it.*

"I'm here in Hawaii because I hope to, um, I want to—"

You got this, Patrick bud...

"I need to know who I am, ma'am. These islands... they might tell me who I am."

"Hold a minute for me, please, Mr. Stakes, while I confirm the protocol."

She punched some numbers into her console, spoke quietly into her headset. A nervous Patrick moved from foot to foot, Philo's wink doing little to calm him.

Seaman Long listened to instructions, held the ID away from her face, and toggled it in the reflective light. "Yes, it has a hologram, sir," she said into the mouthpiece. "Yes, sir. Mr. Stakes?"

"Yes, ma'am?"

"You're good to go. Stand over there. Seaman Kerry will wand you." To Philo: "After your friend's picture is taken, we'll issue your temp IDs and vehicle pass. Have a nice day, gentlemen."

They returned to the SUV, their passes on dog tag chains around their necks. Time check: they were due in CO Malcolm's office on the south end of the U.S. Navy's Hawaiian

Missile Training Outpost at 0800 hours, thirty minutes from now. One more checkpoint to negotiate before they'd gain entrance to the outpost itself, three miles away.

The range was both a naval facility and military airport located four miles northwest of Kekaha, in Kauai County, Hawaii. Philo knew its attraction to the Feds as an installation: it was isolated, with an ideal year-round tropical climate; the environment was encroachment adverse; it contained the world's largest instrumented, multi-dimensional testing and training missile range. It was where submarines, ships, aircraft, and space vehicles could be tracked simultaneously, the only place in the world like it. Plus the location gave it eleven hundred square miles of instrumented underwater range and 42,000 square miles of monitored and controlled airspace. It also used the nearby island of Miakamii for remotely operated surveillance radar and helicopter flight training. The deal the U.S. Navy had with the island's owners, however, was not all-inclusive. Extraordinary or unplanned access to Miakamii was not automatic, always requiring permission. Philo hoped his Navy commander buddy could secure this permission, but with the news about the CO's fiancée, today's visit would take a more gruesome, somber tone. As the SUV cruised the Kauai coastline on the way to the last gate, Miakamii was visible on their left horizon, seventeen watery miles away.

"There she is, Patrick," Philo said. "The Prohibited Isle of Mee-ah-*kah*-mee." He enunciated the syllables loud enough to overcome the road whine, the SUV's windows open. The winding coastal road paralleled the mysterious private island. They were alone in enjoying a great view; this was not a well-traveled road.

"Miakamii is loaded with, dare I say, all the modern conveniences that nineteenth-century Hawaii had to offer, despite enjoying U.S. statehood since, what year was it again, Patrick, that Hawaii became a state?"

A niggling inside joke.

"1959, sir."

The year kept coming up, the topic of Patrick's persistent dialogue with Grace and Hank Blessid when he started living in an apartment above their garage in the Germantown section of Philadelphia, after his homelessness. The police and a few medical professionals had originally labeled him as Alaskan Inuit or Eskimo. It took a crime scene cleaner with mob ties—Hawaiian mob ties, the organized crime family resurrecting itself in Philadelphia—to clear up this misconception. The amnesia left him with only small swatches of memory, one of them the year that his birth state had earned its statehood, though that date was shared by both Alaska and Hawaii.

Additional DNA results for Patrick from Ancestry.com were due while they were away for this trip, a vacation to what Philo, Grace, and Hank expected was his birthplace. Would names of family members surface? Aunts, uncles, cousins, close or distant? Ancestry.com just might come through with a storybook ending.

"So Patrick—did you know Miakamii actually voted against statehood? The only Hawaiian island to do that."

"No, sir. That sure is interesting, sir," Patrick said.

A rare snippet of sarcasm for Patrick. Philo could sometimes be one big ol' fountain of trivial bullshit, except this wasn't one of them.

"I learned some of the island's history while I trained there, bud. Or what passed as history. Mostly legends and oral accounts, although the statehood voting thing is a matter of record."

"Really good info, sir."

"Wise guy."

Philo slowed the SUV, pulled up behind another car waiting at a tall iron gate separating them from the part of Kauai that housed the military training outpost.

"We're here," Philo said. A Marine guard validated their temp passes in the system and a second Marine ran a mirror around the SUV's perimeter and undercarriage while visually checking the interior. The iron gate slid open for them.

They followed signage at each intersection to CO Evan Malcolm's office in a one-story building. Palm trees, blue sky, and low humidity surrounded them as they exited the car. Another beautiful day in paradise, except for the murder they were about to address.

Inside the building the CO's secretary greeted them in an office adjacent to his. Female, a lieutenant, mid-fifties, Caucasian, graying hair wrapped in a bun sitting just above her starched white collar. Career Navy.

"I'm Lt. Bingham, gentlemen. Nice to meet you. Petty Officer Trout, a word if I may." She motioned him away from Patrick, to outside her boss's closed door.

"Commander Malcolm needs to not be here today. I can't get him to go home. He told his captain he's heading home but he won't go. He's insisting he escort you. Talk him out of this visit to his fiancée's house. Pick another day. It's too soon."

Philo shook the lieutenant's hand, called Patrick over. "I need to talk with him alone first, to try to call this thing off for today. You need to hang out here."

Inside, Philo strode into a hearty hug with his husky friend, his dark, somber face above Navy khakis, the hug's front end busy with SEAL and other verbal military platitudes, the back end filled with teary-eyed regrets and a tighter hug because of Evan's shocking personal loss. The installation's commanding officer tucked his large frame into a chair behind his desk, his commander's hat resting an arm's length away, its oak leaves and acorns—"scrambled eggs"—perched in a single arch on each side of the bill, embroidered in lustrous gold bullion. Evan extended a welcome for Philo to sit.

"So. Scatman." Philo treaded lightly here with the nickname, forcing himself into a timid smile. Early in their friendship, twenty years and fifty pounds ago, the nickname worked, Evan's sleek dancer's frame the reason, reminiscent of a famous black actor. A tightly trimmed black mustache offset the current frog-like bulk of Scatman's bald head and flat, broken nose. "We're here to help any way we can, Evan, but I think today's not a good day to start."

"Appreciate the sentiment, Philo, but neither you"—Evan glanced at his door—"nor my lieutenant get to make that call."

"Right. But your captain does. And he did. Go home, take a few days off, we'll hook up another day."

"His wasn't a command, Philo, it was a suggestion. Finding the bastard who did this needs to start right now..."

"Yeah, but the police—"

"The police are on it, Philo. And you and I will be, too."

"You realize," Philo said, measuring his words, wanting to deliver them without an ounce of insinuation, "who the number one suspect will be?"

"You think I give a shit? The hell with that husband-boyfriend shit. I'll go it alone if I have to, damn it..."

"Not implying—"

"Fine. I've got something to offer you in return. You want access to Miakamii. It might be a stretch under the circumstances, but we made the request." Then, with Evan fighting for composure, "Having you help with Miya should be easier to manage. The police chief is a friend, and you're in the business, so..."

The crime scene business. Gruesome murders, messy suicides, meth labs, hoarding, chemical cleanups, other human and non-human detritus needing remediation... this was Blessid Trauma's wheelhouse.

"... maybe you can make sense out of it, Philo. A slaughter..."

Philo reached across the desk, grabbed his friend's fisted hands, and gripped them hard.

Evan stayed melancholic. "So warm and caring a person. I never thought I'd find someone to love like that again..." The commander choked back the hurt; in a moment he regained control. Fire rose behind his eyes, and he became the man Philo knew from shared military missions past. A man to be feared.

"The person who did this," Evan said, seething, "when I find him... maybe he gets terminated with extreme prejudice."

Evan pulled open a drawer, lifted out a holstered forty-five, placed it atop his desk. His Navy issue Colt. Out of his chair now, he strapped the sidearm around his waist, settled it on his hip.

"What circumstances?" Philo asked.

Evan unholstered the handgun, checked it, confirmed it was loaded. "What?"

Philo was now also on his feet. "You said getting access to the island was a stretch 'under the circumstances.'"

A hard rap at the CO's office door. "Hold that thought, Philo. Come in," Evan called.

Lt. Bingham entered. "I have some answers for you, Commander, but I still think—"

"Look, Lieutenant—Mary—I know you're worried about me. I can't not do this investigation now. Tell me how you did."

The lieutenant's jaw tightened. *A lot of good you did,* her glance at Philo said. "But sir, a person needs time to grieve—"

"Lieutenant..." Evan's voice was stern.

"Fine, then. You're allowed on the scene, Commander, sir. The police and the NTSB said okay. So did the Logan family."

"Thank you, Lieutenant. Have our detail assembled by fourteen hundred hours please. I'll have our guests back by then."

She did an about-face, spoke under her breath.

"No, you're not going, Mary," Evan said in response. The door closed behind her exit, the hard close a statement.

After trimming up his cap on his bald head, Evan announced their plans.

"I have a van with a driver outside. We're going to Miya's house. The cops wouldn't let me in until last night. Are you aware of the copter incident that caused the air traffic issues yesterday?"

A huge local news story that had quickly gone viral. Something Philo learned after they landed. "Yes. It, ah, cost us over an hour in the air."

"Also cost the copter pilot his life and turned one of the helos the Logan family owns into a crime scene." He ushered Philo toward the door. "The Logans asked the Navy to look at it. I already added your names to the official detail. Your ticket to visiting Miakamii, Philo. But before that, my fiancée's place. Introduce me to your associate, then let's get the hell out of here."

5

The driver of Wally's gold Escalade limo pressed the talk button on the tarnished metal box on a black pole at window level. The outdoor speaker was thick and heavy-duty, a replica that looked tougher than the ones that hung from poles at 1950s drive-in movies. Two stories overhead, a rough-hewn, wooden yoke crossbar connected the left side of the fencing to the right, and boasted in etched concave letters that they were about to enter the Logan Ranch. Beyond the silvery aluminum pasture gate stretched a thousand or more acres of private Kauai ranch property. Plenty of head of steer, no buildings in sight.

The speaker emitted a disinterested squeal. "Who is it?"

"Mr. Lanakai to see Mr. Logan," the limo driver said.

Ten seconds of silence, then the tinny female voice returned. "Please stay in your car until your escort arrives."

An incredible day—low humidity, cloudless sky, slight breeze, mid-eighties, another of Hawaii's endless summer of incredible days. The Escalade's tinted window powered closed, Wally and the three occupants remaining stoic and pin-drop quiet. Wally Lanakai, his light business suit custom-tailored to accommodate his girth, some of it newly acquired from his crime family's lucrative relocation to the U.S. mainland, was contemplative, his expression uncompromising. His focus was on the distant horizon, below the dome of an azure blue Hawaiian sky, where someone who wasn't thrilled to see him awaited his arrival. The limo's escort would arrive momentarily.

Dust kicked up. A few hundred yards from the gate two horses and their riders emerged, a cloud trailing them from disturbed prairie soil mixed with volcanic ash dust, the sunlight leaving mini rainbows in their wake. One galloping *paniolo* in a sombrero reached the split rail fencing and pulled up on the left. The second *paniolo*, also in a sombrero, took a position on the gate's right. Pancho Villa throwbacks, with bandoliers across their chests, the bandoliers far from affectations, with semi-automatic gun magazines instead of individual bullets. The pasture gate opened electronically. The Hawaiian cowboy on the driver's side barked orders at him.

"Ten miles per hour." It wasn't a request. The driver nodded. The automated gate rolled back to a full stop behind the split rails.

The cowboys giddy-upped their horses to trot alongside the limo while they followed the long entrance road to the Logan residence. A grazing twelve-hundred-pound steer glanced with disinterest at the passing limo. Wally eyed the cowboys and their crisscrossed bandoliers much like he'd done on a prior visit, unable to see where they kept their handguns, on their persons somewhere or on their horses—he didn't know which, maybe both, but they were never visible. He knew this hidden hardware was a Miakamii thing, mostly because the Logan family forbade the island's inhabitants from carrying firearms on the island itself, forbade firearms on the island, period. The affectation persisted once they'd left Miakamii for the other Hawaiian Islands, including here on Kauai, even though it was understood they would at times carry weapons while providing security for the Logans' ranch.

Escorting a convicted crime boss, Wally knew, was one of those times.

At ten miles per hour it took them five minutes to reach Douglas Logan's sprawling home. The cowboys dismounted, stood like sentries while Wally and his protection disembarked the limo. The driver stayed with the car in the circular driveway. The front door to the ranch home was already open. Mr. Douglas Logan, face pinched while sizing up his guests, blocked their path.

"Thank you for seeing me, Mr. Logan," Wally said, extending his hand.

Douglas Logan's hands stayed at his side. "Let's get this over with." He beckoned Wally and his bodyguards forward. "Follow me. Try to keep up."

Logan showed them his back and quick-stepped through a large foyer into a long hallway. Wally's troupe fell in line behind them, and all were silent for the hundred or so feet it took to arrive at an office. They filed inside, their host closing the door behind them, two more of Logan's bodyguards already there. Muscle faced muscle, all the same ethnicity, Polynesian-Hawaiian, Wally included, except for Mr. Logan.

"Sit," Logan said.

Each man's bodyguards crowded the room as its occupants settled, Wally Lanakai's men in tailored suits and Douglas Logan's men in denim. The crowding begot nothing worse than benign knuckle-cracking and deadpan facial expressions.

Logan launched into it.

"The judicial system says you paid your debt, Lanakai. I'll accept that. But I'm not your friend. I respect you only because of the violence you're capable of. Tell me why you're here." He steadied his lean face, went straight-lipped after having scowled through his speech.

Wally would allow this rudeness, was able to control himself around it if it made good business sense, but only to a point. In this instance, he knew what the loss of the Logan helicopter and its Hawaiian pilot meant to Mr. Logan, because Wally had made it his business to learn everything he could about this proud *pipi'i*, the Caucasian owner of an island he coveted.

"To offer my condolences, Mr. Logan," Wally said, "and to reinforce what my associate told you on the phone. I'm not responsible for the loss of your helicopter, or the loss of your dear pilot friend. Not me, not anyone associated with my family. I wish you only good things, Mr. Logan. My offers to you have been sincere, with no plan to ever intimidate you or your enterprises into accepting them. You have my word on this, on all of this. It was not me."

Logan harrumphed. "Your word. The word of the head of a crime family."

"Please, Mr. Logan, don't insult me. I only want to help."

"How about this, then. A question for you. You own a cigarette boat? Ever charter a cigarette boat?"

"In days past, yes, before I left the islands. Years ago. Not since my return here. No."

Logan measured the response, drilling his eyesight into Wally's head, Wally's soul. Wally knew the territory, something all good businessmen learned to master over time: recognizing tells, searching the faces of one's competitors and detractors for lies. In Wally's case, Logan could find none because there were none.

Logan moved on. "I thought Ka Hui was dead. It turns out your family businesses are thriving half a world away in Philadelphia. Go back to Philly, Lanakai. Eat a few more of those belly-bomb cheesesteaks, they seem to agree with you. Hawaii's doing fine since you've been gone. Miakamii is still not for sale, nor are any of its ventures."

Wally's custom-made dress shirt suddenly felt tight around the collar. He didn't need his bodyguards; he could gut this skinny little loudmouth by himself. The hell with Logan's bodyguards, too; his knives could take care of them just as easily.

But Douglas Logan was grieving. Lanakai's poking had uncovered the father-son closeness that Logan shared with the copter pilot, a transplanted Miakamiian, and Wally had made it a point to learn all there was to learn about, and swoon over, Miakamii and its inhabitants. He would allow Logan his anger, and his grief, and his rudeness; Wally Lanakai wasn't an animal. What he was, was practical. And patient.

"My interest in the island is not the only reason I'm here. Again, I had nothing to do with the loss of your pilot friend. I'm here to say I will see what I can find out about it. Are there any leads you can share?"

Aside from the cigarette boat mention, intentional or not, which Wally tucked away.

Logan stood. "I don't need your help. I don't need you. But I'll give you one thing: I believe you're telling the truth. The problem is, aside from you, I have no idea who could have done this. No motive other than your interest in Miakamii. And that's all that the police, and the U.S. Navy, have as a motive, too. They know Ka Hui's back in the islands, and they don't like it. I don't like it either."

Wally, standing now: "Well, they're wrong, Mr. Logan. I have a few personal things to look into, and I'm looking to reacquaint myself with someone who might have returned to the islands, but these are temporary interests, nothing to keep me here permanently. Rumors of Ka Hui's resurrection have been greatly exaggerated. Ka Hui is extinct. My former business associates and I are leading a quiet life on the east coast of the U.S. mainland. But I'll leave you with this.

"I have nothing but the best of intentions regarding Miakamii and the folks who still live there. Their way of life, their culture, their long-term financial and physical health, their artisanship. And I have the best intentions regarding you and the Logan family, personally, as well. I simply feel it's time to return the land and its commerce to its native people, to those who can best steward the island into the future, but you already know my feelings on this subject. I remain hopeful you will eventually see it my way."

Logan spoke, his head shaking his answer. "That island and those people are a part of my family. We will weather this temporary hardship. None of it is for sale."

***

The gold Cadillac Escalade exited the ranch gate, the two *paniolo* escorts and their horses leaving amid additional clouds of volcanic ash rainbow dust visible in the rear view.

Wally grabbed a bottle of guava juice from the limo's bar, tossed the cap, sipped, then drilled a stare into the man sitting next to him.

"I need to know what happened, Magpie."

Magpie Papahani was a big man. Polynesian-African descent, his was a nickname earned not because of his ruddy onyx skin. It came from his ruthlessness in getting what he wanted, for his boss and for himself. The dramatic, self-inflicted departure of Wally's first in command, Olivier

'Ōpūnui, had left big shoes. No one else on Wally's remaining staff had bigger shoes, or balls, than Magpie.

Magpie returned the stare. "This ambush, if that's what it was, the copter crash, came out of left field, but we're asking around about it, boss."

"I want that island, and I want the Logan family to want me to want that island, for a fair price, after all this drama is over." Wally softened, sipped more guava juice, spoke the next question to Magpie calmly rather than bark it.

"You found any leads on her yet?"

"Her" was Kaipo Mawpaw, ex-Ka Hui mob cleaner and fixer who recently left Wally's employ on the U.S. mainland. A contractor. By day, hers was a lucrative personal training business. But her business cards for her after-hours work could have read *Have industrial pressure cooker, will travel, with lye, electric saws, tarps, and hazmat suits*. Ice in her veins. Need a body to disappear? She was your man. Was ex-Ka Hui based on her terms, not Wally's, which did not sit well with him or the rest of the Ka Hui enterprise, and for more than one reason. Kaipo Mawpaw was a rare gem of a woman, exquisite, a true original, and a beautiful love interest of Wally's, but the feeling wasn't mutual.

"We found her pressure cooker behind Icky's center city Philly restaurant in a dumpster, then we found her van abandoned in North Philly."

"Anything inside the cooker?"

"Spotless. Nothing helpful in the van either."

"She's good," Wally mumbled. "Too good."

"That's why she works for you."

"*Worked* for me," he said. "I just never thought she'd run, never thought she'd leave..."

Me was how Wally wanted to finish the sentence, but he didn't, leaving an awkward silence.

Magpie filled it. "Still checking East Coast airport passenger lists, boss, when we can get our hands on them, day in, day out. A crapshoot, but we're doing it. She hasn't kept any of her mainland personal training client appointments since, you know, the night of the bareknuckle fight. And if she's no longer going by Kaipo Mawpaw, if she has a new identity—or if she's doing drugs again, if she *wanted* to disappear, it's a great big world out there, boss—"

"Shut up. Shut the hell up. Find her. Just... do something and find her."

Wally knew he never really had her to begin with. He'd tried, but she'd rebuffed him. Treated her like a queen. Coveted her. Most importantly he'd cleaned her up, got her sober, groomed her, had his Ka Hui thugs monitor her extracurricular activities until she was able to function alone, this after a few relapses. Relapses that forced Wally to maintain a scorched-earth approach regarding dealers in Hawaii, then again in Philly: if you give drugs to Kaipo, your head will end up in a bag on a doorstep on Christmas Day, or shrink-wrapped among the packaged lettuce at the grocery store, or in a trash can at a carwash, the latter detached from a body Kaipo herself had been brought in to remediate, a gift from Wally that she didn't want. She'd stayed sober because she'd gotten with the program, accepted that she needed to, accepted the gravity of her addiction—quit, or die from it— but also because she had guardian angels eliminating many of her sources of temptation.

Guardian angels wasn't quite accurate as a description. More like grim reapers, in the person of Ka Hui's soldiers.

She was on his arm that last night, for a lucrative illegal bareknuckle bout he'd arranged in Philly. Then she ran.

His limo was now on its way to Lihue Airport. Wally had hired a private helicopter to take him up, wanting to see if he could get a view of the helicopter crash site on Miakamii, maybe learn something more than he already knew.

He looked up from his phone to catch the big man grinning, a barely noticeable event similar to all the man's grins, which made him more sinister. "What are you happy about, Magpie?"

"You can make it so she'll come to you."

"How?"

Magpie leaned forward, folded his hands between his knees, and spoke with self-assurance, his eyes half-lidded.

"First, there's already been an incident on the island. The copter crash. Wherever she is, if she's seen any news lately, she knows about it."

"Go on."

"She's Miakamiian. She left the island as a teen. You should put the word out, start a whisper campaign, make your contacts on Kauai and elsewhere more aware of your interest in the island. She knows you, knows what you do. Knows your new business venture. She'll hear about it somewhere."

This was one of the things that had sent her packing, not being able to square herself with Wally's newest undertaking: illegal organ trafficking. If he made inroads with gaining partial or full ownership of the island, he'd have access to its inhabitants. They were far from Third-World backward, but they did suffer from lack of experience in the modern world, lack of marketable job skills, and therefore lack of funds to survive in it, even on the island, needing significant subsidies from the Logan family. Desperate people sometimes found organ donation an easy way to make large sums of money. Wally knew this from the undocumented immigrants he continued to exploit on the mainland.

Cheap raw materials, huge profit margins. The same blueprint he was using in Philly.

Cha-ching.

Minimal risk, and little of it borne by Ka Hui, most borne by the donors. If some of it went the same way—south—as it occasionally did for donors in the Philly organ-harvesting model, it could keep Kaipo in business as a mob cleaner, too.

"At that point," Magpie said, "she'll make the same mistake Logan did, blame you for the crash. Things would change for Miakamiians if you became responsible for them; maybe she wouldn't see the good in it. Maybe she'd decide to come back, to try to talk you out of your interest."

But some of this new work was not going the same as with the Philly model. These people were different, this because of where they lived. Different because of what surrounded them in the water off Miakamii. Shells. Specifically, the mollusk shells they collected for use in making their expensive leis. Something special about those shells, something... medical.

Research, all of it recent, by the pharmaceutical industry, had surfaced an anomaly. Not the known oddity of Miakamii having been the only Hawaiian Island to escape polio in the 1950s, nor the only one to never report a case of AIDS. But the newest discovered abnormality was that in all of modern medical history, and in all of the island's oral history, as far as could be researched, none of the island's current or former inhabitants had ever shown symptoms of senility, dementia, or Alzheimer's. Not one.

Rumor had it that it was because they and all their ancestors spent lifetimes handling the shells. Rumor only, but rumor, word of mouth, and innuendo managed to fuel the organ transplant industry, legal and illegal.

Illegal transplant organs were expensive. Via word of mouth, organs believed to come from a Miakamii native could break the bank, and so far, some had. Business in the islands since he had returned was robust.

"I want Kaipo, Magpie. And I want that island."

"Understood. But one more thing, boss. The ice chest."

"What ice chest?"

"The one waiting for you under your table near the pool today."

Wally's eyes got wider. A Styrofoam container at his reserved space poolside at his hotel this morning; the cabana help claimed to know nothing about it. In it, a full human liver in dry ice.

"It was viable as a transplant organ," Magpie said, "and it's already in play."

A gift worth hundreds of thousands of dollars. Unprompted, mysterious, and so far, untraced. Someone knew about his new venture, but Wally didn't know who that someone was. He loved the gift, but he was furious he was in the dark about who had provided it, and why. What the hell did this person want?

"Tell me more," Wally said, "like where the container came from."

"A cheap disposable. Available at Walmart, Target, anywhere. It's not likely we'll have any luck—"

"There's a dead body out there missing this organ, Magpie. Find out who it belonged to."

6

Spreading left and right of the house's center entry were long, single-story wings that curled around a green front yard like two outstretched arms. Philo and Patrick were at the deceased Dr. Miya Ainaloli's residence with Philo's Navy buddy Evan.

"They released Miya's house as a crime scene this morning," Evan said. He unclipped the crime scene tape stretched across the entry's threshold and swept it out of the way. "They also told me they didn't clean up after themselves."

"Most cop jurisdictions don't," Philo said. "They get in, process the scene for evidence, get out. It's what keeps crime scene cleaning companies like mine in business."

"If you say so." Evan paused and pressed a palm flat against the doorjamb to steady himself, then took a deep breath and exhaled. "Miya was so proud of these front doors..." An impressive flea market find, he said, their antique French colonial glass panes puttied into place individually and stunning in the sunlight. Except with her, Evan had been more pragmatic.

"Her argument was Kauai is low crime, she had a security system, with cameras and alarms and a quick-response arrangement with the security company. Plus she had Betsy, her Boston Terrier. But this old French door entry, with these glass panes—"

His finger poke found the empty space that once held a pane of glass, the one nearest the door handle. One tentative poke only, to confirm the glass was missing.

"... they rendered it all worthless. No deterrent whatsoever, the alarm service only good after the fact, after she was..." Evan's mouth moistened, him swallowing the pain. He cleared his throat to compose himself. "After she and her dog were gone. I should have argued harder with her."

"They killed her dog, too?"

"Don't know. The cleaning lady told the cops Betsy wasn't in the house when she arrived yesterday. The dog's still missing."

Only one pane of glass in the door was broken; all that was needed. Evan could reach in and open the locks from the inside but he didn't, instead using the front door key on his keychain. All part of the denial, Philo knew. All part of not wanting to normalize what some murdering monster had done. Evan's pragmatism had been validated, sure, but there would forever be the other side of it: rats always found a way in.

The front doors opened wide, letting them into the two-story section of the home. They were hit with a blast of cold air, almost cold enough they could hang meat in there. A sentiment Philo thought better unmentioned.

"Air conditioning's still on high," Evan said, "the way Miya liked it."

The way the cops liked it, too. Helped preserve a crime scene, reduced odors, kept blood and other liquids from evaporating. More info Philo kept to himself.

The open concept living and dining areas had a mock

French chalet look inside and out, heavy on finished wood, plus what appeared to be an expensive tile floor. Circular black metal stairs led to a second floor.

"Watch your step," Evan said. "Broken glass."

The glass crunched underfoot, Evan stepping only a few feet more before pulling up. Philo and Patrick stopped alongside him.

"She loved her home," Evan said. "Such a nice place." A pensive declaration filled some with melancholy, some with exasperation, all of it veiled in hurt.

"Very," Philo said.

Inside, the far wall, tan stone embedded with rough-hewn timber, rose to the second floor. Nothing overt by way of damage in here, as far as they could tell. They wandered past the circular staircase and entered a hallway that took them to the left wing. Abstract paintings hung on one side, the other tall, panoramic glass windows showing the sprawling front lawn with mature tropical flowerbeds in oranges and neon blues.

"I know, Philo, you're thinking more ground-level windows. These are thermo pane, a little sturdier than that hundred-year-old tinker-toy crap in the front door. But still, a single woman living alone, and it's only glass."

Evan rubbed his temple as they walked. "A wonderful, quiet neighborhood, but we decided to live at my place after we were married, a gated community on the water."

He stopped them in front of a door, gulped some air, then released it slowly through puckered lips to settle his nerves. Breathe in, breathe out...

"Here we are. Her bedroom."

He swung open the door. The first smell to hit them was a blush of sandalwood, the scent coming from a king-size bed's ornately carved massive headboard and equally impressive footboard, plus other bedroom furniture pieces carved out of the same wood. Knockoff heirloom furniture that someone might build a house around, its carvings intricate depictions of Hawaiian ritual coronations with all their tropical pomp and circumstance, the wood pleasant and still aromatic as hell, like a burning candle.

"This bed had a right to be called king-size," Evan said. "It's a replica of a piece from Hawaiian royal family history that predated colonization of the islands. Miya said the set cost her three months' salary."

Philo mentally checked down part of that info: Miya was a doctor. Three months of a doctor's salary meant it had to be one hell of an expensive bedroom suite.

A second smell came from the bed's mattress, standing on its end against an armoire, out of the way. Not a pleasant one. Philo knew what it was: the sweet, metallic pungency of dried blood. Confirming this odor was a dark brown stain, the blood not only on the mattress's quilted surface but also inside its tufts, through broad slashes hacked into the material, exposing the padding and coils. How Evan could now be in the same room with this monstrosity—the bed on which his fiancée's murder took place, and no doubt where they had made love—Philo couldn't fathom, having seen the outcome of similar acts before, violent and gruesome, as a crime scene cleaner. Not something Evan would have run across as a citizen, or as a Navy commander, maybe not even something he would have seen as a SEAL, either.

"These fucking animals—"

"Let's take a break, Evan." Philo draped his arm around his friend's neck, pulled him into a shoulder squeeze. "We'll leave Patrick to evaluate what needs to be done in here. Any beer in this house?"

He about-faced Evan and they exited the bedroom, leaving

Patrick to get a feel for the remediation effort required, and to maybe see what others sometimes didn't see, even the police.

In the kitchen, each man held a beer bottle by its neck. Philo leaned back against a countertop. Evan paced.

"I'm lost, Philo, just... lost. This person, this lovely woman... Miya and I dated for a year. She became my best friend, Philo. Big shoes to fill, I know, and no offense, but you bailed on me."

Philo's cue to respond. "You prefaced it with 'big shoes to fill' so you're good by me. But a person's retirement isn't bailing, right? Always just a phone call away. So tell me more about Miya."

Evan's eyes welled. He took another pull from the bottle, let his beer hand drop to his thigh again, stopped pacing. He launched into it.

"Witty, lovely, caring. A gifted researcher. We met at a function the Navy and the local state representatives hosted for donors for the naval museums on Oahu, and the veterans, and some other causes around the islands, that kind of thing."

"Pearl Harbor memorials stuff."

"A lot of that shit, yes. Benefactors out the fucking ass, wanting to show their patriotism and support. I do support it, of course. It just gets overwhelming some days for me and the other COs around the islands."

So much for maintaining a Douglas Logan-inspired PG-rated discourse. "So we're off the clock now, language-wise, Evan?"

"Fuck it, I can't help it. And crazy enough, I was introduced to her by none other than Mr. Douglas Logan himself, a goddamn saint, and I call him that with reverence and respect both. The old guy played matchmaker from the start. Grizzly and ornery, but he means well. He's always been good to me...

"Miya's grandparents, they talked her and her family into

leaving Miakamii when each of them felt it was right, said Miya should follow her dream and go to a good med school...

"She picked Johns Hopkins, went into medical research, genetic mutation work, came back to her beloved Hawaii to conduct it. Breakthrough stuff. She was married once before, to someone from the mainland, but he died. Early-onset Alzheimer's."

"Huh. How old?" Philo asked.

"Young. In his fifties. No children. She stayed a widow, stayed married to her work, met me, this because Douglas Logan made sure our paths crossed. I owe the man, Philo. And I know he's as devastated as I am about Miya."

Evan surveyed Miya's kitchen as if just now remembering where he was. His dark face got puffy again. "I already feel like I don't belong here anymore..."

"Mr. Logan sure does get around, doesn't he?" Philo said, opting for redirection. "A pain in the ass during my SEAL training. Him and his rules, his protectionism. No profanity in his presence. Ultra-Christian, always walking the straight and narrow. I can't see him being nice to any non-Hawaiian without a long courting process. And yet he matched you two up. You passed muster. You need to feel good about that, Evan."

"He likes me, likes the U.S. Navy. The federal government, not so much. And he most definitely loved Miya. He's good to people of color; the marginalized. And he loves everyone and everything associated with that pristine island of his."

"Miakamii? So she was a native?"

"Yes. The clock stopped on Miakamii sometime mid-nineteenth century, Mr. Logan still living up to his family's end of the bargain from when they bought it generations ago. Miya's grandparents, parents, brothers, and Miya herself, they all decided to emigrate when she was a teenager, and they all now live here, on Kauai." He paused, corrected himself. "All of them, but now, one less."

Philo watched Evan's jaw tighten, saw a scowl forming, his unblinking eyes glazing over. Evan needed to be relieved of his empty beer bottle before he did something stupid with it. Philo drained his own, put his hand out. "You want another one?" he asked his host.

"Yeah."

New bottles in hand, long pulls at them followed. Philo continued to probe, Evan answering questions about Miya's research.

"It took on new emphasis when her husband died, she told me. Her background, her husband's death from it, somehow made her uniquely qualified to run her team. She and two other research doctors, always on a mission. But you gotta love them—her—for it. I, ah"—a swipe at his eyes—"I adored that woman, Philo." Another swipe, another deep sigh, then a return to the task at hand. "How do you think your teammate's doing?"

"Patrick knows where we are. Let's let him stay on task." A new redirect. "I appreciate you getting clearance for our island visit. It could mean a lot for him. Life-changing, maybe."

"Sure." An auto-response, Evan's eyes down again, a reflective moment. "The Logan family and the Navy... they go back eighty years. Back to the beginning of dubya-dubya-two before, you know, the siege. But you knew all that."

Yes, Philo did know. The Miakamii Siege. A great moment in American patriotism, but it was also accepted in part as a catalyst for the U.S.'s abysmal handling of Japanese-Americans during the Second World War. A difficult time in U.S. history...

. . .

December 7, 1941, in the channel between Miakamii and Kauai.

Tamenani "Tom" Imakila snorkeled for spiny lobsters from his skiff. He heard, didn't see, the airplane with its failing engine out in the distance, in gray clouds to the east, hanging heavy over the Hanakawii Channel. He'd seen a number of planes overhead over the years, just wasn't used to hearing any engines buzz this close to his island, and worse yet, this close to him. The clouds finally spat the aircraft out, the engine sputtering with smoke that trailed from underneath the fuselage and one wing. It had to land somewhere or it was going to ditch in the channel...

Whirrr (cough)...

Whirrr, whirrr (cough)...

Still airborne it coasted toward his skiff, moving west but way too low, staying parallel to the surf. It reached the beach before the engine gave out, the plane gliding above the island's scrub flora lining the dust field behind the sand. It skipped across the treetops, severing one wing, which spun the plane in circles until it crash-landed on its belly tail-first in a clearing.

Tom didn't know much about airplanes, didn't know much about anything that went on around the rest of the islands in real time, or elsewhere, but he did know what this aircraft was: a Japanese Zero that had sputtered so close to his head he could have reached up and rubbed its emblem. He rowed ashore and hoofed his way through the break in the tree line, into the clearing.

Three-quarters of the aircraft sat intact and horizontal on its fuselage, one wing missing, smoke rising from underneath, the severed landing gear somewhere in the trees.

Tom picked up a large rock, tucked it into the crook of his arm, and climbed onto the wing. He lumbered up to the glass-enclosed cockpit, got eye-level with the unconscious pilot. The pilot's head was slumped forward, visible in the smoke-filled cabin.

Tom muscled the rock overhead in both hands.

He brought it down hard, as hard as he did on spider crab shells. *Crunch.* The first blow sent spindly cracks across the cockpit glass that blurred his view of the pilot, but it didn't breach the plane's interior. The second and third blows did, cracking open the compromised glass, the pilot fully visible again and now within arm's reach—a Japanese man in goggles, leather helmet, jacket, gloves, and a white aviator scarf turning crimson around his neck.

Tom reached in, grabbed the pilot's handgun loose in his lap, and tossed it out of the cockpit, where it landed in the scrub grass. Smoke now wafted from the interior, was met with smoke rising from under the fuselage. Blood trailed down the pilot's face from his scalp to meet the blood coming from his nose and mouth, the pilot still slumped while Tom punched out more of the cockpit glass with his bare hands, had to hurry, the smoke getting thicker inside and out. He unclasped the unconscious man's harness and fit his arms under his shoulders. He lifted and dragged, and a few grunts later Tom lay on the wing, the bleeding pilot draped across his lap. He lowered him to the ground and hopped down. Flames flared from beneath the fuselage, rose quickly into the cockpit, lighting it up like a bonfire. Tom dragged the man across sand and dirt, out of harm's way, and propped him against a tree while some of the plane's aluminum skin ignited. The rest of the plane went up like gasoline-drenched charcoal in a fire pit, the lone remaining wing left intact.

Out of breath and seated next to his new charge, Tom watched the fire. The pilot's eyes opened behind his goggles, the dancing flames reflecting off the lenses, terror overtaking him, his shrieking protests in Japanese. He groped at a breast pocket in his aviator jacket, his hand not behaving, him unable to unbutton it. Tom did it for him, the pilot protesting, a weak attempt at resistance until the battered man drifted into unconsciousness again. Tom lifted out the pocket's contents, some yellow papers. He unfolded them.

The markings were in Japanese, unreadable to him, but there were maps. Drawings of Miakamii, the rest of the Hawaiian Islands, and the other Leeward Islands leading west from Kauai. Small depictions of numerous U.S. warships docked in what Tom knew as Pearl Harbor on the island of Oahu.

These were the pilot's orders. They detailed his mission, in Japanese and pictorially.

Goodness... he was returning from a bombing run...

Tom's wife entered the clearing, called then ran to him.

"No, stay back, Lani," he shouted in Miakamiian. "This man may be dangerous. His gun is over there. Bring it to me, then go back into the village. Find someone who can speak Japanese. And we need a stretcher. For now he will be our prisoner. We need to find out what happened to the places marked on these maps." But he already had a pretty good idea what that was.

Lani did as told. Tom removed the pilot's leather helmet, unzipped his flight jacket, and aimed the gun at the sleeping man's head while he waited for him to regain consciousness.

Help arrived by way of their islander friends and someone who could read and speak a little Japanese. What would come to be known as The Miakamii Siege, an event that terrorized Miakamii's small native population, began when a Japanese sympathizer on the island liberated their prisoner. Tom and Lani Imakila ended it with a late-night ambush, Tom hurling the pilot into a stone wall after taking three slugs from the pilot's gun, to the groin, the stomach, and the upper leg. Lani pounced, bashing the pilot's head with a rock. A wounded Tom finished the pilot off by slashing his throat.

Two suicides followed, both islanders of Japanese descent who had provided the pilot hospice. The pilot's body was dumped into the channel. The islanders cannibalized the rest of the plane, spiriting away anything usable, including one aerial machine gun and its ammunition taken from a wing unaffected by the fire. When the U.S. Navy finally came to investigate, there was little left of the wreck to recover.

Internment camps opened in the islands and on the U.S. mainland shortly thereafter.

———

"Any chance someone was trying to get at you with this hit, Evan?"

Evan's stern gaze met Philo's similar countenance. "No. Hell, I don't know. I don't think so." He shook his head, but Philo could tell he believed himself a little less as each second passed until he returned to the same resolve. "Better fucking not be that. No."

On the closest Miakamiian mountain ridge, the U.S. Navy's fully functioning unmanned radar early-warning system went through its paces 24/7, watching the skies, maintaining an all's-clear signal. And if it ever wasn't all clear, the installation was there to send a different message, whereby the U.S. could open its war gates of hell in response. The system was CO Evan Malcolm's responsibility as part of the Kauai military outpost until the end of this year, when he was due to retire. North Korea, China, Russia all seemed less friendly toward the U.S. day after day. The closest physical threat to Hawaii—Japan—was now a U.S. friend, although some second- and third-generation Hawaiians would forever remain skeptical.

Patrick exited the hallway fresh from his assessment of the bedroom, spoke to Philo.

"Need a deep clean under the floor beneath the bed, sir, might even need to replace the plywood and the underlayment, maybe a blast of enzymes in the crawl space below it, too. I can get into it and take a look, sir."

"Thanks, Patrick. Evan, we'll look into who carries environmental cleaning supplies in the neighborhood, make some calls, scour the internet. Okay with you?"

A weak nod from Evan.

"And Philo sir?"

"What?"

Patrick held out a small, cloudy plastic drinking cup. "From the bathroom, sir. See, ah, I found this there—"

Philo and Evan looked inside the cup. "What are we looking at, Patrick? A big mothball?"

"Um, no, sir," Patrick said. "Dry ice."

A low fog surrounded the white-gray dry ice chunk, making the bottom of the cup look eerie. Too big for a mothball, Philo knew now, his nose in the cup. Didn't smell like a mothball either. Didn't smell at all. Extremely cold. A hallmark of dry ice, the solid version of carbon dioxide, was no smell. Frozen water had a smell; frozen CO_2 did not.

"Why didn't it melt?" Evan asked.

"Dry ice doesn't melt, it sublimates," Philo said. "Transitions from solid to a gas, no liquid form in between. Might take more than twenty-four hours to fully sublimate, depending on how large the piece or pieces were, and if there was any insulation. Any reason Miya would have dry ice in her bathtub, Evan?"

"No idea."

"The bathroom, sir," Patrick interjected, "it's a mess. Something happened in the bathroom."

They reentered the bedroom, marched to the master bath, to a door that wasn't open during their first pass through the bedroom. "You open this door, Patrick?" Philo asked.

"Yes, sir."

White porcelain slipper tub, standalone shower stall, toilet, a counter with two elevated basin sinks, fishhook spigots that leaned over them, his and hers mirrors above it all. Pastel blue-green walls, white wainscoting halfway up. The tile floor, also white, had black shoe scuff marks between the tub and the door. The three of them stepped inside, the bathroom spacious. They were immediately drawn to the tub, red stains draping the inside of the porcelain. Soon after hovering over the tub, their interest went to the window, the lower frame closed but empty, the glass gone.

Philo checked the frame for jagged glass, found none. He poked his head outside, surveyed the jungle-like overgrowth that started fifteen feet or so from the house, beyond where the green grass ended. Directly below the window, on the grass, the glass shards sparkled.

"Broken from the inside out," Philo said.

But inside, the floor tile crunched under their feet. "Then what's this?" Evan said, lifting his boot.

On the white tile where they stood, a splotch of yellow, the tile it covered feeling gritty underfoot. Philo got down on one knee, stuck a finger into the dried stain, rubbed it, raised it to his nose. "Urine. It crystalized."

"Betsy was in here," Evan said. "Her dog."

"Sirs?" Patrick redirected them to the tub, to the blood stains there. "See—more dry ice chunks." A haze surrounded two more pieces of dry ice the size of baseballs sitting on the tub's drain.

"Almost melted," Evan said.

"Like I said, it sublimates directly to a gas. CO_2. The tub is tilted so water drains out of it," Philo said. "The dry ice slid toward the drain because of the tilt, not because it was melting."

Philo crinkled his nose and leaned sideways, now looking for the origin of another smell. He checked out the space between the freestanding slipper tub and the back wall.

A large, single, tootsie-rolled dog turd lay there, hardened. "It seems Betsy left another gift."

Evan said it first. "They locked her dog in here with her."

Philo closed the bathroom door so they could get a look at the back of it. It was scuffed with nail marks and bite marks, and chunks of the white wood were ripped out.

"Probably locked the dog in here first," Philo said, pivoting for another look at the window, "but the dog wanted out."

"Wanted to protect Miya," Evan said.

Philo couldn't stop himself from a reflexive glance in the tub's direction. Chances were at some point it was more like Betsy was protecting Miya's dead body. "Yes," he said, "before and after."

The toilet seat, next to a hamper, next to a vanity, next to the window, was the path the dog took. "Then Betsy went through the window, the only way out."

"The cops," Evan said, incredulous, "why didn't they mention any of this to me?"

"I don't know. Still working the case, not in a sharing mood maybe. Let's have a look outside for the dog."

———

Behind the house Evan called for her, getting no response other than a heightened cacophony of birds, insects, and animals. The three of them fanned out, wandered ten yards or so into the jungle, wild Hawaiian flora reaching at them as they walked. Philo pulled up, stopped calling for the dog, shouted to Evan.

"Any water nearby? Rivers, lakes, a pond maybe?"

Evan answered, kept walking. "Yes. A pond, another twenty yards. Why?"

"Evan, I didn't mention this back there, but—"

"Philo sir." Patrick's voice came to them from up ahead, slightly right. "Over here, sir."

Philo and Evan swept away eye-level tree branches as they trudged through the thick, frondy vegetation brushing their legs and ankles, soon converging on Patrick. Buzzing flies feasted on something at ground level in front of him. Evan got into a crouch.

"Sweet Jesus. Betsy sweetie..."

He swiped at the flies on Betsy's cold nose and those hovering near it, blood caked on the dog's forehead, but the mark was only slight, not more than a scratch, certainly not a mortal wound. "What happened to you, Betsy..."

Philo laid his hand on his friend's shoulder. "Evan. Evan..."

Evan, now distressed: "*What*, damn it?"

"I'm surprised she made it this far, bud. She wasn't attacked, Evan; they left Betsy in that bathroom, in there with the dry ice and Miya. The sublimation... it was suffocating her. CO_2's heavier than oxygen, will stay near the floor until it builds up. My guess is this is why she left her dead mistress's side and bolted through the window. Lightheaded, woozy, she was trying to stay conscious, maybe looking for water..."

Evan raised his head, faced forward, Philo and Patrick doing likewise. The pond was less than thirty feet ahead of them. Evan finally lost his shit, his sobs turning malevolent as he bellowed at the insects gathered on the corpse, swatting at them, brushing them off, stomping them into the dirt, no other wounds visible on the dog and yet there she lay. He now pulled at her body, started dragging it toward the pond—

"I gotta give her a chance..."

"Evan. No. Evan, c'mon now, bud..." Philo crouched, put his arm around his friend.

Evan pulled back, dropped ass-first onto the forest floor, buried his head in his hands, his shoulders rising and falling in waves. He suddenly calmed himself, like he'd been stiff-armed to his face.

"Why... the fuck... was there dry ice in that tub?"

When Philo didn't answer right way, Evan tilted his head, analyzing the hesitation: "What is it? Tell me, damn it!"

Philo and Patrick shared glances. It would be Philo's place to spell it out, as a crime scene cleaning pro, but more so as Evan's close friend.

"Chances are they brought it for the organs. For transport."

7

Incognito on Tahiti, the status of one Kaipo Mawpaw. A status presently undergoing interruption in French Polynesia, the South Pacific island collective.

She needed to leave Tahiti behind for a bit after hearing the drumbeats from the north. More like word-of-mouth omens, drifting twenty-four-hundred miles south on the warm sea winds that occasionally brought a few of her home-island's former inhabitants to her newly adopted residential paradise. The message: trouble from the U.S. mainland had breached Kauai and was about to spread.

She boarded a plane in Papeete, the collective's capital, on Tahiti-Nui, the bigger portion of the island. Her new home was Iti in the southeast, connected by an isthmus. Smaller, less developed, much less populated, it was the sharpest of contrasts to the U.S. mainland, the violent world she'd left behind. Tahiti was a place for her to rest, a place to hide, a place she could return to after she dealt with whatever the threat was up north. She'd cobbled together an itinerary, the first leg overland, the second in the air to Lihue Airport, Kauai, Hawaii.

"*Now boarding rows eighteen through thirty-seven,*" the agent said through the loudspeaker.

Her bag went into an overhead bin. She took her seat in Economy. Eight and a half hours in here. God help her and her leggy five-ten frame. Sunglasses, with a navy-colored baseball cap that covered her black cornrows: a new look for the native islander. New because it had to be.

Tahiti's black sand beaches propped up its reputation as a paradise, with only a few roads, mostly dirt, between the populated areas. How much infrastructure did a person really need, had been her argument with herself. She had freedom, distance, and anonymity, which went a long way toward all but guaranteeing her safety, at least in the short run. But she had no livelihood. That's why she spent four days a week on Bora Bora, another part of the French Polynesian islands and more of a tourist magnet. An expensive commute, but necessary. Bora Bora was where people with money congregated for their South Pacific vacations, to include customized services that were her wheelhouse: massages, personal training, and sometimes, as pleasing as she was to the eye, as an escort.

Good reasons, all three, to get to know her, but she was no longer anybody's piece of ass in this business. Too impractical —customers talked, and bad reputations could sink business —but the other reason was she refused to fuck anyone for money ever again. Staying ahead of her drug addictions meant she no longer had to.

She'd worked a deal with one of the Bora Bora hotels: they gave her space in a luxurious hut over the water, where she provided her wellness services to a wealthy clientele four days a week in exchange for providing personal training for the hotel execs on staff, all of it on the up and up. She had a steady stream of income to supplement what she brought with her from her former employment on the mainland. Her stash was substantial, and it allowed her to decline training and massage work whenever it didn't feel right.

New to Bora Bora, and new to where she preferred to call home, Taharuu Beach on Tahiti, she lived quietly with a new identity: Aiata Hauata. Aiata, or "woman who eats clouds." A Polynesian name she'd liked from past visits. For her it had additional, transcendent significance: *eating clouds* was drug parlance for smoking and eating opium, something Kaipo had been doing heavily not too long ago after her pill habit had accelerated. Which was before the Hawaiian crime family Ka Hui had taken an interest in her and her expertise: crime scene cleaning, the kind that made crimes look as if they'd never happened. The drug habit nearly cost her her life. Ka Hui fixed all that. But staying with the crime family would have relegated her to trophy status on the arm of one Wally Lanakai, which would have cost her her freedom and her identity as something other than Wally's woman. She'd left Philadelphia to rid herself of Wally, which meant she had to become a ghost.

Hauata, her chosen surname, she'd picked from a list of Tahitian names on the internet; she had no idea what it meant. The fake passport and identity had cost her thousands. A cheap price to pay for independence, to not be owned by anybody.

This plane ride from Tahiti to Kauai was unrelated to her Tahitian work gig. A rumor kicking about the transient hotel help had found her: the Ka Hui crime family had returned to Hawaii and brought with them their private, legally suspect organ transplant business. Some risk for those who donated, most often the indigent, but, rumor also had it, with a big-money payout as the enticement. Heavy interest in Hawaiian donors with Miakamii island roots, products of a healthy, pristine, disease-less environment. It was a venture she considered cannibalistic, and a line she could never cross again, the losses too personal from both sides of the equation: one dead boyfriend, an organ donor, and one dead mother awaiting an organ transplant that never came.

Her intention: insert herself into the mix. Spread the word among the native islanders about the danger. Become the argument against donating. It might mean sacrificing her individuality, and possibly her freedom, while she got the word out. Could she do that? She was about to find out.

For Kaipo, the Hawaiian mob Ka Hui had been a mixed blessing. A lot of pluses and minuses, the last minus being an overture about marriage. On the ledger's other side, the pay had been fantastic—enough that it allowed her to relocate here on a whim. It had afforded her protection, invisible as it was, as a single female in Philly providing in-home personal services in an urban environment. And Ka Hui's crime family had also wrestled into submission the monkey on her back. Correction, they had killed it, many times over, by eliminating every drug dealer who had ever sold to her, first in Hawaii, then on the U.S. mainland, in dramatic fashion. But in some cultures monkeys had multiple lives. How many lives did hers still have?

At least one. People in recovery were told to never forget that. There was always one monkey left, never more than one taste away.

"Anything from the bar, miss?" the flight attendant asked.

"No, I'm good."

She'd gotten lucky: both seats next to her in Economy were empty. She could stretch out, could recline rather than sleep sitting up.

The plan was to remain in the shadows on Kauai. She'd

stay off the radar of one Douglas Logan out of apprehension, and one Wally Lanakai out of self-preservation.

How could she help her island? Other than word of mouth, she didn't know yet, but she knew the islanders weren't aware of what was on the horizon. She, however, was, and she didn't want them to face it alone.

8

The airborne copter had a slight forward lean, was now crossing the Hanakawii Channel like it was on a zipline. Evan, helicopter-rated, was not piloting. His Navy brass had insisted on this before letting him take Philo and Patrick onboard for their ride-along. Miakamii, the Prohibited Isle, soon overwhelmed the width of the copter windshield. An azure blue lagoon gained in definition, with white beach sand edging it on three sides and green scrub beyond the beach, and beyond the scrub, tall trees. Steep cliffs rose up to the right, where higher elevations led to a mountain ridge. Just off the coast of the island, the rim of an ancient volcano dominated the view.

Evan spoke into his headgear intercom, worn to better the chopper's deafening blade noise. "You're about to meet Douglas Logan, Philo. He and Miya were very close. He doesn't need to know any more about the crime scene at her house than he already knows. It will only make him more upset. You copy?"

"I copy," Philo said, wearing similar headgear. "But you gotta ask the police about the dry ice. Give them a chance to explain."

"My assistant is checking on that."

This was a struggle for Evan, obvious to Philo, the three of them plus their pilot strapped in tightly aboard the Navy Seahawk. Evan was intense, but he was also grieving, at a loss about the disturbing nature of the attack. Yet Philo knew Evan well. He would carry out his CO duties, would do his job, would put other necessary people in place for them to do theirs, too, so they could all get some answers.

"I'm impressed, Evan," Philo said, the intercom chirping his comment.

"About?"

"Getting approval for us to hitch this ride."

"Extenuating circumstances, and you guys are in the crime scene remediation business. That's how I sold it. I also stressed that none of us would be armed, per Mr. Logan's protocols. The Seahawk will hang out near the radar package on the northern tip of the island and wait for us to finish up."

"Copy that."

Over land now, the copter followed the coastline. Two heli-ports served the island, one for its infrequent tourist drops, one exclusively for the U.S. Navy. The pilot chose neither, instead found a small open space nearer the crash site, flat enough for them to land.

Whup-whup-whup-whup...

Dust and sand and loose scrub swirled as the copter touched down. The blades slowed their rotation, everyone remaining seated until the pilot gave the all-clear. They removed their headgear. Evan slid open a side hatch but wouldn't let them exit yet. Visible now was another helicopter sitting silently at the end of the clearing.

"NTSB is here, too, still working their investigation. We'll have to hoof it a hundred yards or so to the other side of those trees." His tone turned somber. "You guys need to understand something about Mr. Logan and this island."

"Fine. Where is he?" Philo said.

"Where we're headed: the crash site. It's visible from the beach, but not from where we needed to land." He gestured for them to huddle up. They leaned in.

"You'll be seeing parts of the island that are off limits. Mr. Logan never lets tourists into any of the populated areas, wants to maintain his family's hundred-fifty-year-old promise. I believe we'll see the church and the school because of their proximity to the wreckage. Do not get pushy if you have any questions. They need help—we all do—understanding what happened, but it won't be at the expense of badgering him or any of the people who live here. And please, *please*, let's all use our Sunday school language for this. We clear?"

"Shouldn't be a problem," Philo said. "Right, Patrick?"

"No shits or fucks, Philo sir."

Evan led, Philo and Patrick maintaining stride alongside. They crossed white sand, then entered an open section with a heavy layer of volcano rubble that funneled into a wide dirt path with thick tree canopy overhead. In the wide expanse on the other side were two people in dark blue NTSB uniforms, one male, one female, plus another male Philo assumed was a plainclothes cop or detective from Kauai. With them Douglas Logan, short and wiry, just as Philo remembered him from SEAL training decades ago, but with less hair, which was now all white. A tied-off yellow kerchief, a la John "Howdy, Pilgrim" Wayne, circled Mr. Logan's neck.

In the far left corner of the clearing sat a tiny steepled church in gray-white clapboard siding. A few hundred paces from the church, and closer in, was a one-room schoolhouse, also gray-white. Solar panels highlighted both roofs. In between the wood frame buildings were large, mangled pieces of colorful helicopter, the copter's nose planted in the dirt like an amusement ride gone bad, the windshield blown out, the interior exposed like a cracked egg.

"Not what I expected," Evan said. "It looks like the flight deck split, but otherwise it survived the impact. No fire. Lucky, for the investigation at least." He gestured at the wall of trees next to the clearing, the canopy thick and jungle-like. The diagonal path the copter and its rotating blades had taken to the ground had sheared the canopy, clearing the way.

Gathered copter pieces were strewn across portable folding tables. Hacked carcasses dotted the animal pens spread out between the two buildings. The blades had redistributed portions of the slaughtered animals in all directions, leaving behind dried blood sprays and large fleshy chunks that had slapped against the school, with other parts taking out one window of the church.

All of it—church, school, vegetable gardens, crumpled helo parts, animal carcasses, and the beach—were within shouting distance of each other, fully validated because that was what Mr. Logan was doing now, shouting in the direction of a man and woman at the water's edge. Both were on the same bareback horse, their horse standing just out of reach of the crashing surf. Philo could only assume they were indigenous to the island and, judging from how close they sat to each other, they were a couple. Mr. Logan's shout to them had followed a quick, acknowledging glance at Evan and his guests arriving.

"Ben and Ella," Mr. Logan called again, "come over here, please."

The horse cantered with its two riders aboard, arrived alongside Mr. Logan. He eyed their bulky burlap satchels strapped like saddlebags across the horse's rear haunches. "Goodness, Ella. That's a good catch for today."

"You're welcome to have dinner with us, Douglas," the woman said. "Ben is making his huli-huli chicken to go with the lobster."

"Thank you for the offer, Ella. We'll see. I need some time with these people."

He addressed Evan. "Commander. I'd like to say it's a pleasure seeing you here but we both know it isn't. I need the Navy's help in dealing with the NTSB, but why this visit to the island had to be by you in person escapes me." He laid his hands on Evan's shoulders and pulled him in. "I am so sorry, son, for your loss," he said into Evan's ear. "God gets an angel, we lose one."

"Thank you, sir." Evan's lips quivered, but he stayed serious. "We're all still processing this." He cleared his throat. "I'm glad you let me bring along some additional expertise." A hand wave beckoned Philo and Patrick into the conversation. "I'd like you to meet—"

"I knew who he was soon as I saw his name in your text, Commander. I expect he wouldn't soon forget our island. It's Frogman Trout, isn't it? Tristan, I believe?"

"Yes, sir. Retired now. Going by Philo nowadays, sir. Philo Trout. Long story."

"I see." The island owner sized Philo up. His hand went out, Philo accepted it. "Well, I'm still Douglas Logan. Same as yesterday, and I'll be the same tomorrow, God willing."

"Copy that, Mr. Logan, sir," Philo said. "And this is Patrick Stakes, my assistant."

"Hello," Patrick said.

How many SEALS had trained on Miakamii, Philo didn't know. They might number in the thousands, the training arrangement in place with the Logan family for decades. He also didn't know why someone from the family would remember him in particular, yet there it was.

"So let's get down to business, Commander," Mr. Logan said. "You're here to brief the NTSB on what goes on around here, and on my deal with the Navy." Mr. Logan moved in closer to him. "And to see if there could be any connection to Miya. So let's get to it."

He segued into his introductions of Evan and friends to the folks huddled near the helicopter's front end, the aircraft split in half from the crash, the flight deck here, the tail with the rear rotor twenty yards away. The NTSB agent suffixed their exchange with a patronizing facial expression and a "don't touch anything" verbal admonishment.

"Gas tanks been emptied?" Evan asked her, eyeing both tanks behind the flight deck, their compartment splayed open beneath the blades.

"What do *you* think?" she said, her tone sarcastic.

"Just checking," Evan said.

He put a question to the group. "Has it been confirmed there were only two people on board?"

A good place to start in Philo's mind, too. The small-talk responses among them offered a few yeses, but they were still only speculation.

Evan eyed the plainclothes cop off by himself taking photos of the flight deck with his phone. Open-collared button-down shirt, shorts, deck shoes, and a backpack. Japanese-American. He could have passed for a tourist. Evan leaned into Philo, pointed. "Go ask the detective that same question."

"Me? Why not you?" Philo said.

"Just do it, Philo, please." Evan's jaw tightened. "It won't end well if I talk to him now. His last name is Ujikawa. Uji for short."

Philo accepted this was not a debatable request; he called to the cop. The man was bent at the waist, still pointing and shooting with his phone. "Detective Ujikawa. Excuse me. How many were aboard?"

"And you are?"

"Philo Trout. Blessid Trauma, a crime scene cleaning service. I'm with Commander Malcolm."

The detective straightened up, put his phone away, and retrieved a bottle of water from the backpack. "Manifest says only two on board. No indications anyone walked away from this. It also matches the eyewitness account. So I'm going with two. Ella, Ben," he called to them on their horse, "good to see you folks again." He returned his attention to Philo.

"Ella's the eyewitness. So yeah, one of the two persons jettisoned from the helo, per Ella, was picked up in the channel by a cigarette boat. Nothing on the Kauai end yet about it. Checking cameras wherever we can find them. Ella retrieved the pilot's body. Quite a superhuman effort." The detective raised his chin her way in admiration, then retrieved his phone again—"so if you'll excuse me"—and began taking more photos.

Philo, back with their small group, reported to Evan. "Official cop assessment, two aboard. You're welcome."

Mr. Logan rubbed his forehead like his head hurt. "All of this is so... senseless. I, ah, I just don't get it..."

Philo and Patrick slipped out of the discussion and moved back in the direction of the debris field, localized between the church and the school. The metal, glass, and plastic pieces meant little to either of them, Philo having been a passenger on military copters more than once, but certainly no expert on the aircraft's composition. But what he felt he could say with certainty was, after looking over the front deck half and the parts catalogued on the tables, it appeared there'd been no midair explosion. No holes punched through the metallic skin in either direction, from an interior explosion like an onboard bomb, or from an exterior source, like an air strike. All this damage seemed to have come from careening through the trees and slamming into the island after falling pilotless out of the sky.

A similar story for the tail half, severed by the trees. Its shredded skeletal remains with rear rotor sat a distance from the flight deck after a different path into the dirt.

No midair explosion made sense; the pilot's throat had been slit. More than reason enough for the crash. And this short but powerful-looking woman here—Ella—had recovered the body. Philo agreed with the detective's assessment that hers had been a heroic effort.

He and Patrick wandered away from the debris and entered the tiny church through a side door, intact save for one tall window caved inward, its glass shattered, the wood frame dangling. It was the window nearest the church's pulpit. Something had jettisoned through the glass and its wood crossbars, hit the floor, and skidded against the pulpit itself, and was now covered in flies: the head and neck of a boar with tusks.

"Poor Pumba," Philo said.

"Sir?"

"Bad joke. Forget it, bud."

They wandered through the church's interior. A familiar arrangement: pulpit and altar in front, wooden pews facing them, row after row leading to the rear, could hold maybe two hundred people. The paint on the walls and ceiling was peeling, and dust swirled in the shafts of sunlight that connected the pews to the windows. Dust had settled on the pews, the tables, the pulpit, the altar, everything. They wandered down the center aisle, toward the back, the small church steeped in shadows. Wainscoting with ornate carving and tangerine-colored stain graced the bottom half of the rear wall. A door in the back wall opened outward into the congregation, its keyed lock affixed eye-level, securing it to its frame. Safe space, Philo surmised, maybe for church artifacts and holiday decorations, the door wide enough for a lawn tractor or something larger to fit. Philo tugged at the lock, but it didn't give.

"It's Philo Trout, isn't it?" A female voice startled them from behind.

Ella's call to him was from the altar area. She continued her quiet entrance, passing the pulpit, moving up the center aisle, her face stern. They hadn't heard her enter the church.

"Sorry, but yes. And I guess we're snooping, ma'am. A hazard of the crime scene cleaning business. Another set of, you know, eyes after law enforcement leaves. And you're Ella. They tell me you're a hero."

Ella and her stern expression stayed a course down the center aisle, soon reached him and Patrick. "Far from a hero," she said. Round head, narrowed, smoky eyes, and the whitest of unsmiling teeth. She'd spoken to them with her chin raised, because she'd needed to. But her tough countenance soon faltered.

"Chester, the pilot, he, um…"

She choked up, tears forming, her aggrieved face softening. "He was a close friend. I did what I had to do, but he was *hala* already…" Her scowl returned. "More than gone. Murdered."

She wasn't tall enough to turn this into a stare-down, her head barely reaching Philo's shoulders, but she was doing her best despite the height disadvantage. "Why are you here, Mr. Philo Trout?"

Direct. Skeptical. Parochial. He admired her when he first saw her on the beach, she of indiscernible age, best guess forties-fifties, and he liked her even more now. Fiery personality, fireplug physique. She could no doubt both start fires and put them out.

"Like I said, my company cleans up after nasty events like this back on the mainland, in and around Philadelphia. Messy, hazardous situations, some accidents, some not. We mostly handle crime scenes after the cops are gone. Hardcore stuff. We try to make it like it never happened."

"I got that, but the damage is in the front of the *hale pule*."

"The what?"

"The church. Why are you back here?"

A fair question. "Sometimes there's more damage than people realize, in places they don't notice. And when we clean crime scenes, we sometimes find things people overlook."

He didn't pry, like ask her why she was skeptical about their wandering. Her right to be, of course; they were trespassers, all of them, plus it might also be cultural. A natural, healthy skepticism, from the island's hundreds of years of isolation.

"How old is this church?" Philo asked, his eyes panning the ceiling, the windows, the walls.

"Eighteen-nineties," Ella answered, then focused more on Patrick, watching him give a hard pull at the lock on the tall storage door before moving to the far aisle. He followed the aisle toward the front of the church, got a closer look at another side window, on the same wall as the one blown out by a boar's jettisoned head. Patrick ran his hands over the clear glass panes and the window's puttied edges, the putty ancient, cracked, and missing in spots. Ella's stare was now less stern, more curious. "Your friend. His look, it's like he's a lost *keiti*."

"A what?"

"Child."

"He's in the zone, in investigative mode. He's also an amnesiac, from a brain injury. He's Hawaiian, but he has no memories of himself prior to a few years ago. We're here in the islands on vacation to see if anything looks familiar to him." Philo raised his chin, called to Patrick. "Anything interesting, bud?"

"No other breaches I can see here, sir," Patrick answered from aside the destroyed window. "Nothin' else neither, sir."

The "nothin' else" related to Patrick's search for his identity, shorthand to mean he had no latent memories of this place.

"You need someone to help board up this window, ma'am?" Patrick said.

"That won't be necessary. My husband Ben will have someone take care of it. But thank you. Kind of you to offer."

Philo absently ran his hand along the top of a church pew, a reflex. He came away with a layer of dust, looked at it, then brushed it off his fingers. Ella didn't miss the gloveless white-glove inspection.

"That was rude, Mr. Trout. It's volcanic ash. It's tough for the island to stay on top of it, there's always so much. Centuries of it. Resettles everywhere. You're wearing out your welcome in here, sir. Outside now, please."

Ella marched them back to the group congregating near the helicopter remains. A sporty aircraft, the flight deck seating was finished in soft, camel-colored leather, like a luxury car upgrade, all except for a smudge of blood on the pilot's seat caked brown and black in the hot sun and confined there, not enough for it to run elsewhere. Mr. Logan, Evan, and the police detective were finishing up with the NTSB folks when Ella delivered Philo and Patrick to the discussion. She retreated, rejoining her husband alongside their horse.

"... so that's it, then, Mr. Malcolm?" the NTSB agent said; she finished scribbling. "Your CliffsNotes version of Mr.

Logan's arrangement with the Navy?" The agent clicked her pen, lowered her clipboard. She removed her aviator sunglasses, squinted at Evan and Mr. Logan both.

"In a nutshell, yes," Evan said. "In place since the fifties. I'll send over some declassified documents tonight, plus other peripheral info, some of it redacted. A little more than what the media already has. I know your superiors won't be bashful asking for more if they need it."

The five of them—Evan, Mr. Logan, Philo, Patrick, and Detective Ujikawa—walked the perimeter of the fenced animal pen in observation mode, ogling the copter's front deck pieces, blades, twisted bulkhead skin, and at the far end of the rectangular animal pen, the rear section including the tail rotor.

"You feeling anything here, Philo?" Evan asked.

"Nothing more than wondering what the NTSB's going to do with these chunks of helo, how they intend to cart it off, and to where. A planes, trains, and automobiles solution to the max."

"Some bigger Sikorsky military-grade copters," Evan said. "Forklifts, maybe a small crane to either move it onboard or tether it underneath for a cable ride across the channel. I'm waiting for orders."

"I can vouch for that," Detective Ujikawa said. "It's getting airlifted to a small warehouse at Lihau Airport. Chief Koo's already gotten clearance. This isn't only an air disaster, it's a murder investigation. The Kauai police get to sink their teeth into it, too."

Philo crouched down outside the front passenger side of the flight deck, positioned himself for a clear view across one bloody seat to the other. "To the naked eye, there's blood where you'd expect it, on the pilot's seat—"

His pointer finger was in motion. "... and here you can see

droplets splattered around the interior. Originating from the victim probably, from the centrifugal force of a copter starting to spin out of control. And there..."

He directed them to the pilot's door. "A bloody left hand-print, pressed against the inside bulkhead. The pilot trying to steady himself, after he'd been attacked maybe. And right here, if you look closely—"

His finger swept its way from the bulkhead to the joystick. "His bloody right hand held onto the controls until he no longer could, which was until—stay with me—"

Philo pointed. "Until the passenger dragged him across the interior, across his own seat, and out of the helicopter with him. See? More blood. A left-to-right bloody skid mark on the seat cushion, a smear I figure is from dragging the pilot across it."

The detective dropped to a crouch next to Philo, his facial expression noncommittal, his head taking its time swiveling everywhere that Philo had directed them to look. When he rose from a squat he retrieved a notepad and pen from his jacket pocket. His nod was slow and pronounced, affirming. He addressed Philo.

"I like it. I like all of it. And I liked it just as much when our investigators arrived at the same conclusion. But one part of that scenario is problematic."

Philo, out of his crouch, ran a hand through his rooster-comb hairline, coming up empty on a response.

"Time's up," the detective said. "The issue with that scenario..."

"I got it!" Patrick said from the fringe. "There was, um, no need to drag the pilot out of the copter after his throat was slit, sir, because, you know, he was already gonna die."

"Exactly," the detective said. "Yes. So here's what happened, based on an expedited autopsy by the coroner, and something you guys couldn't know: his throat was cut in two places. The first thrust of the knife caught his aviator helmet's chinstrap on the way to cutting into his neck. Not a mortal wound, so it probably only pissed him off. Unfortunately, the second wound was. Mortal, that is."

Philo, seeing it now: "The second wound came after he was pulled from his seat."

"Bingo. They might have even struggled some after they both exited the copter. Chances are there's a knife or some other sharp instrument out there in the channel, or maybe it's somewhere on the island. Either way the body, and this spectacle we see here, is enough to tell what happened to bring the aircraft down." He clicked his pen, flipped open his notepad. "Gimme some contact info on you and your associate, Mr. Trout. Maybe we can talk later. Name-wise I have Philo Trout, and it's Patrick... what did you say your last name was again, Patrick?"

A newly distraught Douglas Logan turned away, found a seat on a bench outside the church, and dropped hard onto it. Ella and Ben sidled up alongside, comforting him. Detective Ujikawa finished his notetaking, then checked for a phone signal, eventually finding one. Philo, Patrick, and Evan converged on Mr. Logan at the bench but kept their distance.

He waved them forward, finished sniffling into the large yellow kerchief raised from his neck. "So this is the young man you were talking about."

"Yes, sir," Evan said.

Mr. Logan stood, took measure of Patrick, a visual scan north to south and then north again, Patrick cooperating but uncomfortable at so close an inspection. His face, his coal-black Polynesian hair, they were similar in color and texture to Ella's. Mr. Logan's squinty scrutiny stopped just short of gripping Patrick's chin like a rancher does livestock.

"The short answer is many families have left the island with their young children and moved to Kauai over the years. The timing could have been right. But no, I don't recognize him as one of them. Ella, Ben?"

Heads nodded in agreement, their comments to the same effect. These were not no as an answer, more like only probably no.

"Tell you what, Frogman Trout," Mr. Logan said. "I can check my records back home, on my ranch, if you'd like. Some hard-copy info we're in the process of cataloging for a database. You, your friend Patrick"—he glanced at Evan—"and you too, Commander, you're all invited to my ranch where we can go over whatever we find. I'll check my records regarding your friend more closely. Please call my secretary."

He handed Philo a business card, hesitated releasing it, then did. "You don't remember, do you, Mr. Trout?"

"Sir?"

"What happened during your SEAL training when you were with us?"

"Well, I—"

Philo sensed Douglas Logan had found a happy place to blunt the pain of losing Chester Kapalekilahao, the dead copter pilot. A moment that apparently gave the island owner comfort, as short-lived as it would be, something that made him proud. For Philo, it was a moment in his SEAL career that was less than flattering.

"Your capture." The warm smile spread across Logan's face like a grade-schooler telling tales.

"Do you know about this, Commander?" he said to Evan. "I don't expect Mr. Trout would have told you about it. It was during one of the exercises the Navy puts you SEALS through. What Miakamiians call 'Hide and Seek.'"

Philo knew where he was going, made no attempt to short

him on reliving the glory he was about to re-bestow on one of his island charges.

"A SEAL team in training entered one of Miakamii's jungles in full gear," he began, "for an overnight stay. They were expected to make hidey-holes for themselves. A survival exercise. Sole purpose was to stay camouflaged, hidden all night until they could all be rescued in the morning, simulating their retrieval after a mission. Except one frogman was captured that night—"

Mr. Logan's smiling eyes shifted from Evan to Philo. He awaited a reaction, was being cute—and inclusive—by letting Philo join in the warmth of the anecdote.

A sheepish Philo raised his hand. "That frogman... was me."

Mr. Logan nodded. "And to add insult to injury—"

Philo finished it for him. He knew the impact Mr. Logan was going for. "The person who found me was a teenage girl."

Mr. Logan's smile broadened, stayed close-lipped, but his eyes now showed appreciation for Philo having played along. "You were a good sport about it back then, and you are a good sport now. No shame to be had here, Mr. Trout. Let me just say she was an extraordinary kid, very resourceful, cunning, fearless. Not a wallflower. And like other islanders she also had an acute sense of smell, her other senses heightened as well. She's someone who captured more than one SEAL during the Hide 'n' Seek exercises the Navy approved over the years. I hope you learned something from it."

Philo's answer was only half tongue in cheek. "I did. I changed to unscented soap."

The group shared a chuckle that petered out when the detective rejoined them, announcing he was leaving as soon as his ride arrived. Ella and Ben's reaction was simultaneous, like a reflex: alert to the point of agitation, both with furrowed eyebrows and a laser-beam focus at a break in the trees that lined the clearing.

"Your ride is here, Detective Uji," Ella said. "The outboard just beached."

Uncanny; something Philo hadn't heard. Impressive.

"Detective—" This was Evan. The cat no longer had his tongue. "Mind if we walk with you?"

They paid their respects to Mr. Logan and friends and waved to the two NTSB employees still busy investigating the wreckage. Once through the trees, out of listening distance from the crash site:

"Chief Koo's your boss, last I remember, right?" Evan said to the cop.

"You know he is," the detective said.

The beached skiff's pilot in shorts and shirtsleeves leaned against the boat, his arms crossed. The lagoon's turquoise water rippled over the sand, a sea breeze catching Philo's hair, Philo wanting to drink in this vista and blank out all the chaos they'd just seen—today's gore, and all the gore of recent memory...

"Great." Evan stepped directly into the detective's path and got up into his facial shit as close as he could without assaulting him. "You tell that motherfucker—"

Philo leaned in to stop Evan from doing something he'd regret. Evan pushed Philo out of the way, got nose to nose with the detective again.

"I wanna know why—the fuck—the Kauai police didn't share with me what they found in my fiancée's bathroom. Why I had to find that mess myself a whole day later with my posse here, no mention of *any* of it to me beforehand. Why the cops didn't find my fiancée's dead dog asphyxiated by carbon dioxide, from dry ice, damn it, thirty yards from her house.

And why no one is returning my assistant's calls! You get your fucking boss on the phone right the fuck now!"

To the detective's credit he stood his ground, withstood the verbal onslaught without flinching, and best of all, Philo thought, he did not retaliate. But he also didn't retrieve his phone.

"Commander—"

"Call him!"

"I don't need to. I drew your fiancée's case. Me. I was one of the detectives who processed the scene."

Evan, seething, stayed in close. "Then you better talk to me, Uji."

"You want me to talk to you, Commander, take a step back."

The man from the outboard, also a cop, had already hustled alongside Evan opposite Philo, the two of them bookending his aggrieved bravado. Evan gave ground. Somewhere other than this island, there would have been four guns in close quarters by way of two cops, a Navy captain, and a Navy SEAL. Chalk one up to Douglas Logan for his no-guns-on-the-island regulation.

"It was info we held back. To help with the investigation. To rule out the crazies on the tip line."

"But you released the scene—"

"An internal screw-up. It should have been handed off internally before they released it. A crew is probably onsite as we speak, something we never do, working the bathroom and replacing the glass in that window. To keep that information hush-hush."

"And removing the leftover dry ice," Evan said.

Detective Ujikawa swallowed hard one time, the only comment to rattle him so far. "Yes. The dry ice... he left the body in the tub for someone to find. Murdered in the bedroom, moved her to the bathroom, left her in dry ice."

Philo spoke up. "So your cleaners will remediate the bedroom, too?"

"Cleaning the rest of the place will be the owner's responsibility. Always is."

"The homeowner *is fucking dead,* Uji!" Evan screamed, spittle spraying. Philo was quick to insert himself between them, successful this time in backing his friend away.

"Right. Sorry, Commander, my bad. Again, please accept my apologies…"

Evan's look was pained, incredulous, but mostly he looked lost. He pushed away from Philo and stormed off, talking to himself while he marched up the beach. On the horizon, a Navy Seahawk started its descent to the island's military installation a half-mile north, a radar tower glinting from the installation's perch.

Philo and Patrick had to hustle to fall in behind him on foot along the coastline, their destination the Navy's Miakamii radar installation to catch their ride back.

9

"So this is one of the land parcels," Wally Lanakai said to the surgeon. Wally eyed the panoramic view from Dr. Umberto Rakoso's second-story office. It stretched far to the north, the distant horizon overwhelmed by the wraparound Pacific Ocean, all blue, all heavenly.

"Yes," the doctor said.

They were seated at a desk facing the doctor, Wally in a comfy side chair, one of two, the other chair barely containing Wally's oversized associate Magpie Papahani. Dr. Rakoso, a native Kauaiian, sat with his hands folded on his desk.

"This property was deeded to you as a Rakoso family descendant?" Wally said.

"Yes."

"A half-acre."

"Yes. It's one of many parcels that total eight-plus acres owned by descendants of the family."

"But not for long, you say."

"That is the present concern. If no one does anything about it, we will lose all eight acres at auction."

Which was why Wally was here on a recruiting run, sent

by another Hawaiian surgeon strapped for cash for a reason far less noble than Dr. Rakoso's: exorbitant gambling debts owed to Wally. The referral came from someone onboard with Wally's organ transplant business, but also aware of the doctor's real estate squeeze. Wally had decided on a stable of two doctors in Kauai to start. Stealth was of utmost importance considering the risk.

The doctor and more than two hundred native islanders were in the legal fight of their lives. A mega-billionaire was sinking hundreds of millions of dollars into acquiring northern Kauai property, much of the north shore sugar plantation town of Kilauea in particular—where land passed from generation to generation with the ownership largely undocumented, which meant property taxes often didn't get paid. The megabucks person was looking to make his seven-hundred-acre beachfront property more private. But the islanders weren't into selling, which meant the billionaire was into suing. In the balance were the rights to auction off the eight acres to the highest bidder, a foregone conclusion as to whom that highest bidder would be.

The doctor and his family needed money, lots and lots of money, for legal fees to protect their rights.

Enter Wally Lanakai. "I see your family has quite a number of crowdfunding pages."

"Yes. Each parcel holder has one. We're desperate."

Wally nodded his understanding. "Hence my reason for being here. If you'll let me, I can contribute."

The intimation was Wally would make cash donations to the doctor for his surgical services, in amounts small enough to stay below the radar.

"You are a liver specialist, Doctor?"

"I am a transplant surgeon who specializes in the liver, but I perform other organ transplants."

Wally began. "I'll pay you per transplant. Handsomely. Outgoing and incoming. I provide the donors, the recipients, the facility, and the support staff. You supply the scalpel. Magpie, your help here, please."

"Sir?"

"Please pull up our operation on your phone and show the doctor."

Magpie hit a few keys, a significant achievement considering how meaty his dark hands were. He reached across the desk to show an image to the doctor. On the screen was the picture of an exterior storefront in a strip mall, the marquee showing shadowy evidence of a sign for the prior occupant's business, a local health services company. The tall windows were papered over except for the real estate "For Lease" sign in one corner.

"One of a few around the islands, Doctor. Short-term rentals from retail space lessors desperate for cash flow. Magpie?" A few swipes by Magpie's paws brought up pictures of the empty interior.

"I'm renting it. As a warehouse for my planned Kauai import-export medical supply business." Wally's sardonic smile and air quotes betrayed the lie. "It looks quite different inside now. This one's proximity to the airport sold me. Convenient for well-heeled clients who want easy and discreet island entry and exit. So let's head to my car, Doctor, where we can talk about the specifics of the surgeries. Have you cleared your schedule for this afternoon?"

"Yes."

"Excellent. Let's head to Lihue so I can show you the operation, shall we?"

Wally being a good host, the ride south along the coastline in the backseat of his limo included snacks and beverages. Magpie drove, the window between the front and rear seats open so he could participate in the conversation if needed. Wally popped the cork on a bottle of champagne, filled a glass flute, and offered it to the doctor.

Dr. Rakoso hesitated—"Your celebration is a bit premature, Mr. Lanakai"—but after Wally's second attempt to hand it to him, he accepted. Wally launched into his pitch.

"An operation small enough not to draw attention to itself. This one can handle the surgery on both sides, donor and recipient. The recipients are pampered. We treat the donors well enough, but not like my paying customers."

"Then let's talk about the recipients first," Dr. Rakoso said. "I assume they're on transplant lists somewhere."

"Ha. Why yes, yes they are, and I'm tapped into them. But once I talk with them, they're added to the only organ availability list that will get them results in the time they want, or need: *my* list. Very exclusive. One my group manages itself."

"I don't understand."

"You will in a bit. Let me start by explaining that my transplant recipients are extremely wealthy, Doctor. They're typically older and have led indulgent, visible lives. Many of them have lost a step or two, but not all of them. They travel in the best of circles in all walks of life. Industrialists, entertainers, politicians, financiers, former athletes, and interestingly enough, some are doctors like you. The only real requirements I have are they must be able to afford the cost of the transplant without financial assistance, and they must remain discreet."

"So they're recipients who are bypassing their health insurance. That sounds like their surgeries are elective."

"For most, yes," Wally said. "But a few are too sick to wait on hospital-curated transplant lists."

"So they go to the black market."

"An oversimplified explanation, but close enough."

Dr. Rakoso studied the bubbles as they rose in his champagne glass while he assessed Wally's answers. He took another sip, then set his half-full flute down in a cup holder, out of the way.

"No more with the twenty questions, Mr. Lanakai. Give me all the details start to finish in one summary. Whatever you think I need to know to get me to sign on."

"Fair enough. First, call me Wally. May I call you Umberto?"

"I'd rather you stick with 'Doctor' for the time being. So tell me what this is all about."

Wally stayed on the recipient side of the equation to start. He, Wally Lanakai, had created a clandestine market for liver grafts, for people who would die without them, but also for indulgent people with a different agenda.

"The living-donor liver replacement approach," the doctor said, familiar with the procedure. "The donors give up only a portion of their liver."

"That is correct, Doctor. In this model, thirty-three percent of the liver is all we need. The donor's liver will regenerate itself and return to its normal size. The alternative, full liver transplants, would leave the donors quite dead, if they weren't dead already. This increases my pool of available livers. So aside from donors who suddenly check out, the ones in my business are all voluntary, and I pay them very, very well. And I would do likewise to the doctors performing the surgeries."

The human liver. Also known as the human chemical factory for its ability to change internal substances into other substances that the body needed, by filtering the blood coming through the digestive tract. It also neutralized substances that the body needed to avoid.

"The recipient patient is taking a helluva chance," the doctor said. "Grafting onto an existing liver doesn't always work."

"And in many instances," Wally said, "there's nothing wrong with the recipient's liver."

"Grafting onto healthy livers with other healthy livers? A big risk. Why do that?"

"It's a risk worth taking for these people," Wally said, about to drop the bomb. "Here's why."

No Alzheimer's or other dementia, no polio, no measles, no mumps, no chickenpox, no AIDS. Pandemic-proof and disease-proof, generation after generation, Wally explained. The most enviable medical legacy on the planet in one small package, the human liver, as long as the liver graft came from someone native to one oddly idyllic Hawaiian island: Miakamii. Either from native islanders still living there, or from natives who emigrated elsewhere.

"Miakamii's generational seashell thing," Dr. Rakoso said. "I've heard it all before. A wonderful old wives' tale. I admit the statistics are compelling. But medicine is far from embracing—"

"Medicine doesn't need to embrace it," Wally said, annoyed, "only my customers need to, and so far the reception has been outstanding. The statistics don't lie, Doctor; the research bears it out. These organ donors don't have these diseases, and they convey their immunity to the recipient. Apparently none of their Miakamiian ancestors had these diseases either. That's what my customers see. And best of all..."

Dr. Rakoso sat transfixed. For the organ recipients, people who had money to burn, perception had become reality.

"... these livers can reverse age-related cognitive decline."

"That's preposterous. Cure patients of their Alzheimer's?"

"You betcha."

"Show me."

Wally called to the front seat. "Pull over a moment, Magpie. Send me the list."

Wally read from Magpie's email. Four names, all prominent people who were highly visible: one old-money female socialite, one aging rock 'n' roll diva, one retired senator, one actor. All had been on the slippery slope dementia-wise, well documented by family members. Over the past few months alone, all had come to Hawaii when called by Wally, and all left with partial liver grafts. "I have their contact info. I can get any of them on the phone. They will each vouch for their progress, or they have people who will do so for them."

Dr. Rakoso studied the names. He knew these people. Media darlings plus other people who were very visible. Below the line were more names. "You have a waiting list?"

"Yes. Like I said, my own list. Separate, and very exclusive."

The doctor counted the names; more than thirty, most of them public figures.

Wally pushed. "I can keep you as busy as you'd like, Doctor. I could become your biggest financial crowdfunding supporter. This is cutting-edge stuff. Sometime after this business gets its legs, the medical community will learn about it, embrace it. At that point there will be no reason for physician anonymity. On the contrary. The doctors performing these surgeries might even get heroes' welcomes."

They crossed into Lihue's town limits, passing through plantation farmland once ripe with sugarcane but repurposed into grazing lands for roaming livestock, the local sugarcane industry gone. The cattle huddled under a few trees to keep out of the sun, grazed while their tails swished, were disinterested in the passing limo. Dr. Rakoso mirrored their disinterest, remaining quiet.

"Tell me what you're thinking, Doctor."

"I'm doing the math."

Wally had a good idea what was in his guest's head. What it would take to accomplish a goal. The number of surgeries, price per, etc. Plus the risk.

"One other aspect to help you with your decision, Doctor, after we work out the financial details. If anything goes south—cops, loss of a patient—your response to law enforcement and the medical community would be that Ka Hui forced you into this arrangement. And we would validate that assertion. You have my word."

Dr. Rakoso retrieved his champagne glass from the cup holder.

The doctor might have thought he was still on the fence, undecided, but his sips from the glass, embracing his host's hospitality, told Wally his pitch had connected.

The Escalade claimed a parking space that faced a storefront window papered over from the inside in brown, like an overnight package. They exited the limo, straightened themselves out, and entered the shade of the overhang. The storefront was wider than it appeared in Magpie's cell phone photo, looked to be about the size of...

"An urgent care facility?" Dr. Rakoso said.

"A pain management clinic. Hell, why bother with the charade, it was a pill mill. A few sensational ODs by former patients put them out of business. Before we go inside"—Wally's congenial expression turned serious—"tell me here and now that what you're about to see, you will share with no one."

"A verbal non-disclosure? Sure, no problem."

"Too cavalier. You must remain discreet, Doctor. Otherwise..."

"Fine. Dire consequences otherwise. I get it. You have my word."

They pulled at the glass-door entry and filed inside the single-story building. Two large men worked the lobby's front desk, their attire casual: loose-fitting tropical shirts, gabardine trousers, boat shoes. How much of what the clothing covered was girth and how much was concealed weaponry was indistinguishable. The men nodded, their expressions blank; they returned to their phones.

"Nurses' station, coming right up," Wally said.

The station functioned as a nerve center, its three walls cloaked with medical supply parts hanging on pegboards, standing oxygen tanks, shelved respirators, and more, outfitted to look like a parts desk at a warehouse yet it still performed its original duties.

"'Sup, gentlemen?" A tiny, elderly Hawaiian woman in a pink smock over nurse scrub pants looked away from a desktop computer. She rose to greet them from behind the counter.

"How is our patient doing today, Nancy?" Magpie said.

"One day into post-op. Our associate madam justice is doing splendid. And at her age, mind you," Nancy said, beaming. "She leaves tomorrow for the medical spa. No signs of organ rejection, and she's convalescing well. Her children are beside themselves at how much more coherent she's already become. And she's stopped having lengthy discussions with her deceased husband. All appears well."

Dr. Rakoso's eyebrows rose. "Am I supposed to believe you have Supreme Court Justice—"

Wally held up his hand. "No names. You may believe whatever you want, just don't share it with anyone. Let's move on. I'll show you the operating theater, then we'll come back out here and talk."

He stopped them with a raised hand in front of a set of swinging doors. "All surgeries are performed here. It's a sterile environment." He pointed to bins on a table next to the entrance. "Gloves, masks, footies. Let's suit up, Doctor. Nothing is in session, but keep your hands to yourself when we get inside."

What was once a spacious meeting room had been repurposed with operating room essentials, intensely bright lighting, and two sets of everything. Wally gestured left, then right.

"A simple arrangement," he said. "Donor surgery on one side, recipient surgery on the other."

"Screening?" the doctor asked.

"For recipients, it's based on family physician statements and recommendations. The donors are prescreened at another Kauai clinic. A standardized evaluation process including a psych eval. They're one hundred percent voluntary."

One very noticeable machine sat in a corner. "A hotdog cart?" Dr. Rakoso said. Transplant surgeon parlance for a heart-lung machine. "You're doing other transplant surgeries here?"

"Exclusively livers, but shit happens. As circumstances present themselves, the surgeons may need to improvise."

"Which means you've lost patients," Dr. Rakoso said, his wince noticeable, "and you've harvested other organs."

"Yes. So far, not here. On the mainland, in Philly. The nature of the beast, Doctor. You know that."

The doctor moved onto a different topic. "Tell me about post-op care."

"Some patients receive it right here, on site, from a few surgeons beholden to me. Most patients prefer getting it from their own doctors, privately, elsewhere on the islands."

"The donors?"

"Paid for by the organ recipient, even lost wages. A week at a special health spa with medical oversight. No heavy lifting for—"

"Six to eight weeks. I know."

More stops, at a scrub room, a kitchen with a freezer, and a rear storage room with access to an alley, then came Wally's redirection as host and tour guide: "Let's head back out front so we can talk."

Wally's arm found its way around the doctor's shoulder as they walked. He made a final push.

"I won't ask you what you think, Doctor, I already know. The site is basic, the equipment minimal. The clientele, however, is impressive. You are intrigued, you like the trail-blazing surgical procedures aspect, the potential long-term medical community recognition you will receive, but you're still apprehensive. So let me make this simple." A friendly shoulder squeeze. "I will pay you a hundred grand for each surgery, donor or recipient. You do both ends of the transplant, that's two hundred K in donations for maybe eighteen hours of surgery, tax-free. That should put a dent in your legal fees. Sound good to you?"

They emerged from a hallway, passed tiny Nancy at her nurses' station, and reentered the lobby secured by its two casually dressed guards who perked up at their entrance. Wally put his hand out there for the doctor to take, confident a deal was only a handshake away.

Dr. Rakoso accommodated him. The doctor's congenial

smile became a straight face. "This isn't a yes, Mr. Lanakai. I'm going to need more time."

They were sharing a moment, their hands pumping, the guest trying to remain gracious, the host doing his best to remain calm after not having closed the deal. An ear-piercing car alarm blared—*honk, honk, honk*—ending the mood. Magpie hustled to the front door and jammed his face into the slice of sunlight visible through a separation in the paper. In his line of sight was Wally's gold Escalade, in the parking space fronting the store.

"The hood of your car, boss... someone left something on it..."

Magpie blasted through the entrance door with enough bad intent it should have left its hinges, his handgun out of its shoulder holster. His head swiveled as he scanned the perimeter, soon resettling his focus on what sat on the car's hood: a cheap white Styrofoam cooler.

Wally and Dr. Rakoso followed him outside, the three of them staring the cooler down. Magpie holstered his gun, then pulled the cooler off the car. They surrounded it on the blacktop. Wally grunted an order at Magpie. "Open it."

The loose lid aside, inside was pretty much what Wally expected would piss him off: dry ice, chunks of it, enough to protect its contents. The edge of a clear plastic zip-lock bag poked through the top layer, the contents submerged. Magpie lifted the bag out with a bare hand, quickly laid it on top of the dry ice. They leaned in.

"A human liver," Dr. Rakoso said. "Complete, not a partial."

Magpie drew his handgun again, used the barrel to check through the dry ice chunks to see if there were any other gifts inside. He found a yellow envelope clasped shut against the side, nothing else.

"Give me the envelope," Wally said.

Magpie complied. Wally slid out a single piece of paper and read the message aloud. "*TYPE O. UNIVERSAL DONOR. TWO HOURS FRESH. HAVE A NICE DAY — Y.*"

This secret-admirer-organ-donation bullshit had run its course for Wally, with him being a beneficiary now two times over. "Who the fuck is 'Y,' goddamn it!"

On cue his phone chirped. He read what was on the screen in silence.

"What is it, boss?" Magpie asked.

"A news story and a text. This SOB took out someone in Kapaa," Wally said. "This is his liver. The bastard's taunting me, Magpie. He's got my phone number and is playing me..."

Magpie pulled up the news story on his own phone. "A street performer. The story's an hour old. Someone tossed his body out of a moving car"—Magpie paused—"outside a restaurant. The report says he's a native islander from—"

"Miakamii," Wally said. "The text says he's Miakamiian." He exploded, throwing his phone with severe malice against the asphalt, its plastic frame splintering. When it stopped bouncing he jammed his heel into it, crushing what was left.

Magpie read more of the story. "Already the news people are making a connection, boss. '*Second Miakamiian murder in three days.*' '*Miakamii bodies are piling up...*'"

"Get me the transplant list, damn it. Pull it up and give your phone to me..."

"But promise me you won't—"

"Give me your fucking phone!"

Wally scrolled down a list of potential recipients on Magpie's iPhone, looking for their proximity to Wally's chop house. He found one name, then a second. One full liver could accommodate two patients. "Her. Get Shirley M.'s people on the phone. She just finished a play and is in town. And she's AB. Do it."

"Type O donor, Type AB recipient," Dr. Rakoso said, interjecting. "The donor's liver can go anywhere, the recipient's liver can come from anyone. You're lucky she's on your list."

"Screw luck, I know my shit, Doctor." Wally drilled a questioning look into his prospective freelancer, then addressed his unsolicited comments. "What the hell is it to you anyway, Doc, unless...?"

"If your secret admirer is telling the truth," his guest said, "you've got maybe nine, ten hours to find homes for that liver." Dr. Rakoso retrieved his own phone, scrolled through it, and checked his calendar.

"Breakthrough medicine appeals to me. If you find a patient, I'll scrub in."

10

Kaipo deplaned at Lihue Airport in sunglasses and a different baseball cap, this one University of Hawaii green. She exited baggage claim and found her way to a short line of airport limos waiting curbside, her destination a friend's house in Pakala Village on the southwestern shore of Kauai. Thirty minutes later the limo stopped at the end of her friend's driveway. "We're here, miss."

A newer-looking ranch home with vertical wood siding in pastel yellow, the small three-bedroom occupied no more than a quarter acre. A rental, her native Hawaiian friend Vena had told her. *"A single career girl can afford only so much on these islands."* True that, Kaipo knew, even for someone like Vena, whose resume included current full-time employment as a contractor at the Navy's Kauai missile outpost and dual degrees in maritime and military sciences from the University of Hawaii.

Kaipo handed the driver the fare plus a healthy tip. "Give me a moment," she told him.

Her sunglasses off, she scanned the surroundings. The street was empty of traffic, a residential neighborhood of single-story homes on small lots under a cottony blue sky unobstructed in all directions. Kaipo powered down both windows, their tinted glass disappearing, the afternoon's hazy heat creeping inside. Two neighbors in their front yards tended their lawns, their flowers, their porches, each with no more than a glance at her idling airport limo. A plane soared overhead, and a bubbly Vena waited for her inside her home, framed by the house's front picture window, barely able to contain herself. Yet contain herself she did, told not to leave the house until Kaipo texted her an all-clear.

"Are we good, miss?" the driver said, a polite attempt to hustle her up. He popped open the trunk.

She reacted, her tone sharp. "No. Close the trunk." She supplemented her bark with, "I need a moment, please. This will be a tough visit." That sounded good as an excuse and it was true, but for reasons more consequential than it implied.

A car turned onto the street a few corners past Vena's house. Black BMW. It slowed to a stop one house away, parked curbside across the street, facing the limo. Kaipo focused on it. Seconds passed, the car idling, no one exiting. One occupant only, looked to be male. He remained in the driver's seat, no handheld devices in use as far as she could tell, no phone to his ear, no binoculars, no camera, his lips not moving. Just him staring ahead at Kaipo's limo, interspersing this interest with side glances at her friend's house. After a minute the black car pulled away from the curb at normal speed, closing their distance. Kaipo powered both windows up, put on her sunglasses again, and pulled her green ball cap down. The limo's tinted windows and her dark sunglasses should serve as protection from prying eyes, but more extreme protection needed to come from her backpack on the seat. She felt inside for an aluminum case fresh from airport baggage claim, already unlocked. A one-button press snapped the case's clips open. Her hand found the Glock, kept it out of sight inside the backpack.

The BMW drifted past, the driver holding up a phone, videoing the drive-by, the house and Kaipo both, her gun hand sweating. He was Asian, not Hawaiian, Kaipo giving him the side eye, the car continuing past. She craned her neck to follow it down the street, the car and its heat shimmer leaving her view multiple blocks away.

"Okay, I'm good," she told her driver. "Let's get my stuff." She texted her friend, told her she was on her way in.

An animated Vena emerged from her house and bounced up the driveway to meet Kaipo, her arms opening wide. "Girl, what have you been feeding yourself?" Vena said, leaning back from their hug. "A steady diet of steroids? You look like you're at your college weight. And those cornrows. Très chic…"

"Let's get inside, Vena, and I'll tell you all about it."

At a round kitchen table behind tall lemonades, and after Vena's additional kudos about her hair, Kaipo quickly filled in her friend about her businesses as a personal trainer and massage therapist, her lack of a love life, her chemical addictions, and what those addictions had done to her physically. How they had broken her down, nearly killed her. How she needed to build herself back up, doing it the old-fashioned way with martial arts, boxing, running, hard workouts, and her sobriety: in recovery two years, four months, and twenty-seven days. How she had help in her struggle with these bad habits from a questionable source.

"Ka Hui," a knowing Vena said, frowning.

"Yes."

"They're back, Kaipo. Here in Kauai."

"Yes. The reason I'm here. But where are they? And how'd you hear about them?"

"At work. You want something to eat?"

Tortilla chips and cheese appeared front and center on the kitchen table along with napkins, plates, and salsa. Vena settled back into her chair, sipped her lemonade, and watched a hungry Kaipo dig in.

"Chatter at the Howling Sands installation," Vena said. "Navy outpost personnel talking about gambling, or lack thereof."

Statewide, Kaipo knew, there was no legal gambling of any kind in Hawaii. No casinos, no state lottery, no scratch-offs. No horse or dog racing, no sports betting. It made Friday night social poker games attractive to those who craved the action.

"Card players from the mainland in social games get pulled aside by someone who knows someone and are asked if they want more action. Whispers about high-roller poker games. Strictly taboo, too risky, too potentially compromising, so no one at work does it. But they know about it."

Ka Hui's M.O. From the old days here in the islands, before the Feds eliminated them, and one of the businesses the resurrected family soon put in place on the East Coast, in Philly. And now they were back. But illegal gaming wasn't the only business Ka Hui brought back with them.

"You know anything about organ trafficking?" Kaipo said.

"How'd you...? Never mind. Yes, I do know something about it. Something's going on. Word has gotten around. Here. Look."

Vena picked up her phone, pulled up an advertisement online. She offered the phone to Kaipo, then pulled it back. "Do *not* judge me, Kaipo. Got that?"

"No judging. Cross my heart."

Vena was logged into a personals website, with extremely explicit profile photos of men and women, some of the men very big boys.

Kaipo's eyebrows rose, but only slightly. "So they're main-streaming porn in personal ads. Tell me something I didn't know."

"Okay then. It's just that, you know, I had kind of a chubby, choir-girl image going for me way back when," she said. "Not saying I can vouch for any of these hookups, mind you. Hell, I guess I can vouch for some of it. Two or three of them..." She snickered. "Or ten maybe. No more than ten. But let's stay on target. See this ad here?"

Vena zoomed in on the ad so it took up the whole screen.

"*DONORS WANTED. Ages 18-40. Indigenous Hawaiians. Not heavy drinkers, not overweight. Non-smokers preferable. For a medical study control group focused on the human liver. Blood type O ideal. DM your contact info here...*"

"So here's the deal," Vena said. "A girlfriend of mine looking for some extra money to make ends meet messaged these people. They're looking for organ donations. Livers. Partial livers, actually, because giving up a full liver could be, you know, hazardous to your health."

"Donations? As in not paying for them? Because, you know, selling organs is illegal, Vena. She knows that, right?"

"Yes. The donors get reimbursed for their, um, expenses."

"Let me guess. Their expenses include pain, inconvenience, lost wages, other incidentals..." Kaipo trailed off, her shoulder shrug saying she of course wasn't buying it. She finished with, "Which, she said, can all add up."

"Hey," Vena said, "this isn't an 'I've got this friend' kind of scenario here. It's not my gig, it's hers."

Kaipo went limp, felt her blood turning cold. How bold a move was this as an approach, should this be who she thought? "Tell me she didn't go any further. Tell me you talked her out of it."

"If she goes no further, I have no info," Vena said, dripping with snark. "Of course she went through with it. And I never knew any of this until after the fact. Chances are it's Ka Hui, Kaipo. She did the deal and walked away. With fifteen thousand dollars."

"Let me guess. She's a Miakamii native."

"Yep."

"How did they pay her?"

"The expense reimbursements were in cash. Other amounts came in donations to a crowdfund page she set up for herself. A rent party fund, or grocery funds for the indigent crowdfund, something like that. They suggested she create it. Total payments to her over a few days came to fifteen thousand bucks. Slick, in my opinion."

Her remarks hung out there, Kaipo moving past what she already knew: Wally Lanakai was a smart operator when it came to collecting and handing out payoffs.

"You said she walked away, as in she's doing fine after the surgery?"

"Back on her feet already, slinging drinks and food at Love Your Lava Beach Club in Kapaa."

Vena elaborated, answered more questions about who, what, and when, finally getting to the where. "She said the surgery was in a shuttered healthcare facility, the donor and the recipient on site at the same time. It took about seven hours. Clean, professional, comfortable. She wasn't able to eat or drink for a few days, and the staples came out a week later. She spent time in post-op care somewhere, a week I think it was, in a spa, received pain meds, has a little scarring, but no other aftereffects. Her words."

Fucking Wally. Kaipo often wondered what he could have done with his life if he'd gone legit instead of all-mobster; gone corporate instead of criminal. But asking that about him meant she had to ask the same question about herself.

What she'd done for him, how she'd cleaned up crime scenes after him and his mob folks... how close she'd come to killing people herself...

She stopped her introspection.

"Vena. Listen carefully. Ka Hui—Wally Lanakai—is organized crime—"

"No shit."

"Wally murders people when his survival instinct dictates it, also murders them when it doesn't. Murders them when they don't give him what he wants. Murders them when things go wrong, like with some of these surgeries."

Kaipo lifted her backpack to the table, unzipped it, and took out a thick aluminum case. She flipped open the cover and removed a cushioned tray, in it a Glock 17. She laid the tray with the handgun in it flat on the table between them. Vena didn't take her eyes off it.

"What the fuck, Kaipo."

"I've seen the aftermath. I now carry this, even have a license for it. Tell your friend, and have her tell her friends, and you tell your *other* friends, to not get involved in what's going down with those surgeries no matter how much money's offered."

Vena's glances stuttered between the handgun on the table and Kaipo. The dead air remained unstirred until—

"Why are you here, then? You bolted him once and went into hiding. You've got a new identity..."

"All true."

"So who are you again? Your new name? *Aiata...?*"

"Aiata Hauata. Nice to meet you, Vena Akina."

"Whatever. Seriously, why do this? Why come back to Hawaii? Wait... the copter crash on Miakamii?"

"Not the reason. Something's not right about that crash, but that's not why."

Vena absently tugged at a piece of jewelry on her wrist. Kaipo's mind drifted, keyed on Vena's bracelet as a sweet, shared remembrance of theirs. One similar to Vena's was in Kaipo's suitcase.

"You still have it," Kaipo said, smiling.

"Sure do. I love my special momi snot."

"I love my special momi snot, too," Kaipo repeated, a tender response to a tender comment.

Momi, or Hawaiian for pearls. Snot, specifically snail snot, was the shell itself. Snot on a half shell, snot with a hat, snot that walks: Miakamii nicknames for the tiny colorful mussel shells strung together that graced Vena's wrist. Stripes on some of the shells, starry dots on others. Tans and reds and iridescent blues. They'd made them for each other when they were in their teens. It was what BFF girls did on Miakamii.

"Someone murdered that pilot, Kaipo. The news says it was a tourist. Or someone posing as a tourist. Ka Hui comes back and bingo, the Logan family loses a helicopter and its Miakamiian pilot and some livestock, and the island church gets damaged, too."

"The Logans ever lose a copter before?" Kaipo said.

"Not that I'm aware of."

"That's the part that doesn't work." Kaipo tapped the side of her nearly empty lemonade glass with her nails, thinking. "The Hawaiian mob and the Logans coexisted on Kauai for a long time, didn't interfere with each other. And they're in the organ harvesting business now. The shells, the mollusks—the disease immunities—Wally wouldn't lose good, transplantable Miakamiian organs to the ocean. If he wanted the pilot dead he'd have had him killed on land, then he would have taken his liver." She poured herself more lemonade, sipped. "He won't kill the goose that laid the golden egg. Plus I don't think he'd do anything to hurt that island."

"Well someone did. You see the news coverage?"

Vena pulled up news reports on her phone. Photos taken from the air by Kauai news stations reporting on the crash, their own helicopters and planes hovering over the site before the Navy scrambled their helo gunships to chase them off. "The livestock pens took most of the hit. There was no damage to the school, but see there, the church... something took out a window."

In Kaipo's mind that was a shame, but no big deal. She worshipped in that church, as did all natives born and raised there. But the church and school weren't getting heavy usage nowadays, or so the drumbeats were saying, a declining population and all that. A disappearing way of life.

"Back to why you came back, Kaipo. What do you plan to do?"

"What I'm doing now, with you. Have you give me some leads. Spread the word. In person and below the radar, naming names where necessary. Hoping you do the same. A whisper campaign that says stay away from them. Plus, if it comes to it..." She dropped a hand onto her aluminum gun case. "Protection of the innocent by whatever means necessary. I have something for you."

Kaipo made space on the table, lifted out a second tray from the case. "Here. Keep it in the house."

Vena shook her head. "I... no, I don't think I can..."

"Yes, you can. It's light, it's easy to operate. A quick lesson and you'll be good to go."

Looks passed between them, Vena finally getting it. She picked up the gun from its tray, got wide-eyed while she held it.

Kaipo would drive the seriousness home. "Look, Wally might think he's doing good here, putting money in the pockets of people who need it, but it's too risky. He's ruthless, and that makes him dangerous. I'll spend a few nights here with you to get a feel for things myself, then I'll head back, guns and all. I promise not to eat much."

She held up the empty chip bowl, gave it a playful shake. "But you need to keep the chips and salsa flowing."

The gun back in its tray, Vena's expression lightened. Her phone rang. A FaceTime request. No new tortilla chips on the horizon for Kaipo.

"Let me take this call. It's from my Love Your Lava Beach Club girlfriend who's suddenly fifteen grand richer. Hold on... Hey, sweetie," she said into the screen. "What's up?"

Vena suddenly pulled back, shocked by an image. Then came the recognition. "Oh no. No, no, no..."

Kaipo moved behind her, leaned in for a look. Flashing red lights from police vehicles lit up the screen's background, their sirens gaining strength. Her friend was streaming footage from the front of the restaurant. She began speaking in a panic. *"You seeing this, Vena? I'm on my break... oh my God... do you see this?"*

The streaming image zoomed fifty or so feet closer to focus on the restaurant's circular driveway. A body lay on the blacktop, an adult male in remnants of a clown outfit, thrown from a moving vehicle. The blanket covering him had unraveled when it hit the asphalt and rolled. The body was now face up. The video footage zoomed farther in. The chest and abdomen were eviscerated, the holes packed in gauze tinted scarlet that hadn't stayed in place. Restaurant customers were starting to gather, the police were arriving, and Vena's friend stopped talking, started gagging...

Vena shouted at the screen. "That's Ichigoo! He's a street performer who works that restaurant. Oh mymymy..."

"A friend of yours?" Kaipo said. She helped herself to the phone, taking it from a distressed Vena. The footage was sickeningly gruesome, but a little less so for Kaipo, considering her avocation. The man's entrails were exposed on the blacktop.

"Everyone on Kauai knows him," Vena sobbed, "but I know him personally. He's from the island…"

Miakamii again.

"I… I think I need to show you something else." Vena grabbed her phone back, started keying. "Look."

She'd pulled up a news story. "Another murder, only days old. A research doctor dead from a home invasion."

"What's special about her?" Kaipo quickly scanned the post, saw no mention of missing organs.

"She was the Navy outpost CO's fiancée. I don't know the details, but she's another Miakamii native. What the hell is going on?"

11

Ella pulled her bicycle out of the tool shed next to their horse barn. A 1970s Schwinn, the bike was greased and oiled in all the right places, with only a little rust on the spokes of each wheel and the frame, and one of the foot pedals missing a rung. A mechanical marvel based on age alone, and maybe the most useful tool they had on the island, quite acceptable as a transportation supplement to their horses. She climbed onto the seat.

Seven a.m. It promised to be a warm day, prompting her to load her water bottle with ice from the solar fridge before filling it with water from the depths of their well, preparing for her ride with Ben. A spin around the island took two hours. Ahead of her on the path, Ben waited in front of their house with one foot on a bicycle pedal, one foot flat on the dirt. She pedaled up the short incline to reach him at its crest, the two of them in shorts and sleeveless tees made from homespun cloth and thread, the exposed parts of their bodies bronzed from decades of soaking up the Miakamii sun.

"Did you bring water for yourself today, Ben?"

"I most certainly did, love," he said, patting his backpack.

"Let's go, then. We'll tend to the honey when we get back."

They pushed off, leaving behind their utilitarian two-story A-frame, its weather-beaten siding in a soft white, its shingled roof covered in solar panels, and two gas-powered generators hardwired to the house. They let their bicycles coast slowly down the winding path, needing to use the brakes to control their descent. They passed a tiny cornfield that surrounded their farm's two beehives on three sides, the hives in boxes the size of steamer trunks, sitting waist-high atop stacked cinder blocks. Houses of similar minimalist construction with smaller beehives lined the road, their windows beautified with white café curtains that were hand-stitched, Ella knew, in reds and blues and yellows. Near each home was an adjacent shed or barn or both, or multiples thereof, all the properties quaint and rustic, all well-kept. Older thatched houses, or *halepili*, rounded out the residences they passed, dotting smaller properties in between the larger ones.

"We must remain vigilant," Ella said to her husband, needing to raise her voice only slightly, their ride quiet, serene, idyllic, no one else on the path at this hour.

"We do, love. Our *helua*," he said, meaning self-defense, "remains primary."

"We appear so vulnerable to the mainlanders, Ben. Like children."

"And to those on Kauai and on the other *pukoo*, too. And to Douglas as well."

"All our *na mea kaua* need to be at the ready, dearest. I feel a storm is coming."

"The island's knives and spears," he said, "our bows and darts, our swords—they're in fine condition, Ella. Always have been, always will be."

"Fine weapons, but no match for firearms. Someday Douglas will see the need..."

To change the ban, Ella finished in her head, and let them have guns on the island. It would not, however, have made a difference those many decades ago, the outcome of a certain memorable Japanese "siege" on the island that went the natives' way, belying that they had only rudimentary weapons. But firearms could likely make a large difference going forward, should there be future incidents.

The path bottomed out, and they pedaled to a shuttered house, stopping at the front gate. They laid their bikes down, faced the house head-on, its roof overgrown with vegetation, its lawn a collection of short weeds. Here was Ella's grandparents' home, abandoned after their deaths. Her grandfather Tom Imakila, a WWII Medal for Merit winner and a Purple Heart recipient as a civilian, had been shot in three places during "The Siege," yet he'd still managed to kill his assailant, the Japanese Zero pilot, with his bare hands, his wife Lani assisting. Heroes. Both gone for decades, their home was a shrine to them and their wartime efforts. Ella and Ben made the sign of the cross, then stood solemnly side by side as they paid their respects, Ben's arm around Ella's shoulder.

They rode farther along the path, reached an opening in the tree canopy. Ahead of them, a large, barren field. "Here we are," Ella said.

In front of them a trough of barren, arid soil bunched up like it had been scraped by an earthmover. Here was the path the wounded WWII Zero had taken after it hit the ground, the warplane's slide still noticeable eighty years later. The skeleton of the aircraft lay for years at the end of the furrow, a metallic mastodon rusted and craggy, its ribs picked clean. Nature had tried to absorb the carcass, tried to pull it under and swallow all the remaining jagged, sun-bleached metal pieces whole, had had decades to do so but failed. It finally lost out to museum experts and war historians who photographed the remains where they lay, then carted them off to reassemble them in an aviation museum on Oahu.

Their next stop would be the only other crashed aircraft site the island had ever experienced, where Chester's helicopter had come to rest after his murder. They remained on the fringe, the NTSB people still engrossed in analyzing the copter's wreckage. Again they prayed, this time for Chester.

They rode until they found a deep-bellied cut in the scrub overgrowth along the coastline that gave a good view of the ocean. A tourist helicopter buzzed the shore, a different sight-seeing operator, not Douglas Logan's. It followed a school of dolphin breaking through the whitecaps, jumping over each other, frolicking, enjoying life, the copter's occupants treated to a spectacle that would make their vacation highlight reels for sure. Ben and Ella headed back inland, toward their village.

A voice crackled through their citizens band radio when they opened their front door. "*Ella and Ben. Douglas Logan here. Come in, Ella. Come in, Ben...*"

Ella sat at a desk in their small, wallpapered parlor, grabbed the CB radio's microphone. "I'm here, Douglas. What do you need?" Ben stood behind her.

Douglas spoke through the static, began with, "*I have news from Chief of Police Koo...*"

A cigarette boat similar to the one Ella had seen, the one that made the ocean retrieval of the skydiving passenger from Chester's helicopter, had been found at a Lihue boat rental dock not far from the airport.

"*White with red stripes across the bow. Sound familiar to you?*"

"Yes."

"*It was rented that morning for the day but returned within three hours of putting out into the channel. A cash transaction, with a hefty deposit that was left uncollected. The person who rented it had what proved to be a fake boating license..."*

The renter wore sunglasses and a hip-hop beanie, Douglas told her. The name he gave the establishment owner wasn't traceable anywhere. There was security camera video inside the rental office and on the dock. Two people left the dock for the charter, three came back.

"Maybe Polynesian, maybe Asian, maybe even white according to the person handling the transaction. He couldn't be more specific because of the head coverings and sunglasses. The security video was too indistinct. And Ella?"

"Yes, Douglas?"

"Chief Koo ruled out one aspect, that it had anything to do with Chester personally. They checked him out, found nothing. Straight and narrow, that was our Chester. Simply a case of wrong place, wrong time for him."

Ella had assigned no blame for this horrific tragedy to their childhood friend; it hadn't even been a consideration. But this confirmation left a gaping hole in the investigation: no motive.

"But Douglas..." Ben's hands rested on Ella's shoulder as she spoke. She gave one of his hands a squeeze, and he squeezed back. "Who will the police look at next? Hello? Douglas? Can you still hear me?"

"I hear you, Ella. I think they will look at my family. Something to do with the island maybe, or its finances"—he paused—*"or me."*

12

Philo and Patrick motored into another Kauai neighborhood on recon. Koloa Breeze's ground-level sign fronted a manicured shrubbery entry. All homes were single residences, mostly single-story, some modest, some gaudy, no structures older than ten years, was Philo's guess. They came out the other side, at an intersection busied by a pokey street sweeper washing mud from the curb, the stirred mud turning the blacktop brown. The SUV idled, Philo needing to give the bright green truck and its swirling orange brushes the right of way as it crossed in front of them.

"C'mon, hustle it up, how dirty can these streets be," Philo said, impatient.

"Mud from flooding," Patrick said. "It moves downhill. Be glad it's not lava, sir. It wouldn't be good if it was lava, Philo sir."

"Yes, I get it, bud, lava would be worse."

"This thing here is new, sir," Patrick said.

"What thing? The mud?" Philo looked at Patrick, expectant. "What's new?"

"This far out. Not the mud, the sweeper. Big as a trash

truck, and big orange brushes. New, sir." Patrick coiled his lower lip, turned around to check out the group of houses they'd just driven through. "No sweepers out here, because there were no houses. These houses all look new, too, sir."

It was clear to Philo they were newer homes. Patrick deducing the same wasn't a stretch, but how much was deduction, how much was from memory?

Moving again in the SUV. "If we go this way," Patrick said, indicating a right turn, "we'll hit downtown Koloa, sir. Restaurants, pizza parlors, dry cleaners, hotels. If we go that way"—he indicated left—"we'll find where the old sugar plantations used to be. And behind us, that was..." He squinted, a memory materializing for him. "That was all overgrown. No one lived out here."

"You know this because?"

"I played here, sir, in this forest, when I was little. Where these houses are now. Rode bicycles through here, played in treehouses and forts. Used ATVs, too, and three-wheelers." Patrick blinked intermittently, recoiling like someone had flicked water at his face, into his eyes. "This... this is it, sir. I remember this. I grew up around here. I remember being a kid here, when this was all part of the jungle."

Patrick covered his mouth with his hand, the realization kicking in, his eyes pinching out tears that rolled onto his fingers. "I'm... I'm home, sir. Here, on Kauai. It was my home..."

Philo stopped the car, gripped Patrick's shoulder, squeezed it. "Bring it here, son." A congratulatory shake turned into a hug, Philo speaking into Patrick's shoulder. "So very happy for you, Patrick. Wonderful, bud. Now, the question is—"

They swiped away their tears, composed themselves. Philo finished his thought. "Do you remember your address?"

Patrick slowly shook his head, his answer no. "But I could

walk to these hills, sir, when I wanted. It wasn't far. I came from that direction." He pointed right. "Go this way, sir. I want to see the streets. The stores. Maybe there's something about the stores, Philo sir."

A few intersections later, they had another winner.

"See that car, Philo sir? That black Lexus?" Patrick's eyes were laser-focused on an older Lexus sedan, a luxury model idling out front of a dry cleaners. Philo guessed it to be anywhere from a 2005 to a 2010.

"I remember one just like that while it drove the streets, me sitting in the back seat with a Nintendo Game Boy, playing video games."

"Great. Anything else? Any of these stores look familiar?" Philo asked.

"I thought maybe this dry cleaners store was, but no, not this one. Keep driving, sir. Up ahead maybe."

They stopped at a traffic light. Behind them in the rearview, midway up the street, a Honda Pilot SUV slowed and then stopped, double-parked with its flashers on. In a scene right out of Philly or the Bronx or Detroit, or any other inner-city area where drugs and prostitutes and money might all cross paths on the same street, the driver got out, leaned against his door, folded his arms, and waited. His Matrix Neo sunglasses absorbed the surroundings, his meaty head swiveling slowly atop his thug body. Moments later a short, chunky guy exited a mom-and-pop grocery across the street from the Honda, in orange shorts, sandals, and a white shirt unbuttoned far enough to show a lot of chest hair, and also in sunglasses. To Philo, a player. His hanging shoulder valise gobbled up the long brown envelope he tucked into it as he waited for traffic to clear.

Patrick was focused on the intersection ahead of them; Philo didn't call his attention to the deal going down behind them. Not so much a deal, more like a shakedown. The chest-hair guy climbed into the back seat of the Honda. The flashers went off, the car put on its turn signal to enter traffic, then did a U-turn, no muss, no fuss, and headed back down the steamy Hawaiian asphalt.

Gang activity, or maybe mob-related. Gender of the players, both male. The ethnicity Philo couldn't be certain about because of their sunglasses. Whatever. It didn't involve him.

"Did you see that, Philo sir?"

"Huh?"

"What happened back there, behind us. The man in the orange shorts. Did you see him, sir?"

Patrick's peripheral observation skills were sharp, had always been. Something at odds with his traumatic head injury, but another reason Philo listened to him and his ramblings at their cleanups, crime scenes included.

"I did, Patrick. What do you make of it?"

"A protection payoff. Someone—a man—makes stops along the way, every few blocks. Store owners paying someone to keep them safe, sir, like back when I was ten maybe."

"Sorry, Patrick, you slipped yourself in there. Like when you were ten *what*?"

"Ten years old, playing Nintendo. In the car. He'd toss envelopes into the back seat."

"Who? Your dad?"

"Dunno. Yeah. Maybe. He was driving. He'd toss them onto the floor. No, into a blue pull-string laundry bag opened on the floor, behind the driver's seat. I'd pick up the ones that missed and put them in the bag. They were filled with cash."

Their red light turned green. They were on the move again. Philo was mesmerized.

Patrick, son of a mobster?

"How old were you again?"

"Ten. No, nine. No, younger. I dunno. A kid. Lots of different ages, sir. I went with him more than once. The bag had lots of envelopes in it. Then, um…"

Patrick squinted, was trying to squeeze out more of the memory, and it was hurting him. "Then he, um, stopped taking me on his rides, just like that. Yeah. I was around ten when he stopped."

Patrick's dad: in organized crime parlance, he was a bagman.

"And we moved. To a nicer house. A really nice house. With a pool. On a different island, sir."

"Can you see your dad now in your head, Patrick, what he looked like? Your mom?"

Patrick went silent, swallowing hard while tears formed. "I… no, I can't, Philo sir. I can't see them."

"It's okay, bud, it's okay. You're doing great. Let's concentrate on these stores—"

"There, sir." After a few swipes at tears on his cheek, Patrick's analytical side returned. "That bar on the corner. A different name now. Never been inside, but I remember it. An old woman used to sit outside the bar knitting, under a short palm tree. Not that tree, that one's fake. A real palm tree, in a big tin wash bucket."

Philo had a memory of his own flash past him. He knew the bar, too, KonTiki something, a different name now. He remembered the palm tree, the real one, and he knew why it was gone. Drunk patrons like himself leaving the bar at closing and soaking the shrubbery after realizing they still had to piss really bad. So sophomoric, getting hammered after the rigors of daily SEAL training, the occasional near-death experiences, "occasional" meaning nearly every single day, needing alcohol as a release at night to calm themselves.

Smart move, replacing the live tree with a plastic one, plus a new name for the bar. No old woman sitting on a chair outside; no chair. More to the point, no double-parking of a Honda Pilot after seeing it only a block away doing collection services a few moments ago. This bar had escaped the shake-down. Things had changed. The people in place had changed.

Who was in charge had also changed, and that was the answer. The organized crime family. Philo's Philly connection to Hawaii. Wally Lanakai. Wally's family was gone, eradicated from the islands by the Feds. But not really gone—relocated to the mainland. Someone else was here. Someone with different clients, a different network. But that didn't change one thing that now looked more realistic with each of Patrick's recalled experiences: his past attachment to someone in organized crime. To Wally? If that was the case, why didn't Wally lay claim to him back in Philly? Some of these dynamics, Philo just wasn't able to see.

"Sir? Hello? The light's green. We can move now, Philo sir. Can we get some lunch now, sir?"

———

They met Evan for tacos at a restaurant called Da Crack, a local favorite. Mexican food, indoor-outdoor, with a walk-up counter next to the beach. One look at Da Crack's cartoon logo and the name of the restaurant made more sense: a chubby sombreroed troubadour viewed from the rear, the tops of his ass cheeks visible. Plumber's crack, Mexican-style. Yet the place was perfect for carrying food and beer to picnic tables where the patrons could watch the breakers while eating. Pet friendly, but more so because it was open-air dining. Dogs, cats, geckos, other pets all welcome, as long as they were on leashes. Not so welcome were the roaming feral chickens.

"Yes, there are animal fights occasionally," Evan said. He

was dressed in his Navy khakis, the three of them tucked into a table, their food in baskets in front of them, their beer bottles chilled. "The chickens carve out their territory, pick out their tables, and patrol them. You feed them, your funeral after you stop feeding them. They get belligerent, think they own you. Miya's favorite Mexican restaurant on the island. We eat lunch here"—he caught himself—"*ate* lunch here, a lot."

There were no updates from the police on the attack, per Evan. Her body had been released to her family, with Evan a part of them now even though he and Miya hadn't yet married.

"The service will be small and closed to the public. Three days from today, after her cremation. I need to ask you something, Philo. Do you know a Wally Lanakai?"

Philo sipped at his beer to delay his response. "You asking me means you already know I do. What about him?"

"I saw you on a scratchy YouTube video. Something one of the sailors said I should check out after he saw your name on the outpost's visitors list. What the hell, Philo, bareknuckle boxing in Philly? In an abandoned grain elevator?"

Everybody had a camera nowadays, damn it. "A long, involved story," Philo said. "Too long, and too crazy."

An animated Patrick nearly choked on his burrito, trying to swallow what he'd bit off so he could speak up. "I can tell the story, sir. You should have seen him, Commander Malcolm, sir. What a great fight..."

"Patrick—"

"He knocked out some big guy, an Army Ranger..."

"Enough, Patrick..."

"But during the fight the grain elevator blew up, with us in it! We were cleaning it, getting it ready for demolition—"

"Patrick, stop, damn it."

"He did it for Grace, so she could get new lungs from Wally Lanakai..."

Philo grabbed Patrick's face, pulled his chin in, got face to face with him. "You need to shut your piehole right now, bud. Let me explain it, okay?"

"Okay. Sorry, sir."

Evan heard Philo tell the rest of it. Illegal boxing for big money. A fire in a grain silo in South Philadelphia from an explosion. Its collapse into the Delaware River. People patronizing the fight going into the water. Not all of them climbing out.

"I boxed bareknuckle in my twenties, made a lot of money under the table. It's where I got the 'Philo' nickname. I walked away from it, but it found me again, after I retired from the Navy. Too many swingin' dicks and criminal types involved. People with long memories, and grudges that never quit. It's all settled now, all behind me."

Evan took a long draw from his beer, studied Philo, finally spoke. "You didn't mention Wally Lanakai."

"So you know him."

"Don't know him, know of him," Evan said. "Hawaiian mob guy from way back, kicked out of the islands. I heard a rumor he's back."

Not what Philo wanted to hear. "Doing what?"

"Whatever he was doing before, I suppose."

Which meant gambling, women, loansharking, Philo hoped nothing else. But there was a good chance there was.

"And you mentioned nothing about new lungs, Philo. Hearing your friend mention Lanakai's name and new lungs in the same discussion, you need to be telling me more."

So Philo waded into it. Why he now owned Blessid Trauma Cleaning. Grace Blessid's dire need for new lungs. Wally Lanakai's black market organ transplant operations, the guerilla surgeries in Philly. His parting of ways with Wally after they both got what they wanted.

Evan's brown face turned a shade of red, his anger rising. "My Miya gets gutted, her organs put in dry ice... and you keep this info from me?"

"I didn't know Wally was here. But if you think he is, the cops do, too. If he is here, they'll run down those rumors. You need to let them do their job..."

"Nobody's telling me shit, Philo!" His fist hit the table, food and empty beer bottles toppling, startling other patrons. He shoved himself upright from his seat. "I want that mother-fucker. If he's not responsible for that attack, he knows something—!"

Evan's phone went off, a shrill noise that caught them all off guard. He retrieved it. "Commander Malcolm here. What is it, damn it? Hello?"

It wasn't a call, it was a text. Evan pulled the text up, still agitated, and left the table to read it to himself. He keyed a response.

An auditory whirr that began in the background swelled in volume, soon overtook the white noise of the other picnic table chatter, then the crash of the waves on the beach. The low-decibel siren was unfamiliar to Philo, a warning or alert of some kind, a signal for the military.

Evan closed his eyes, composed himself, spilled. "What you're hearing is an early-warning crisis signal. An airspace security breach needs my attention. Someone will be here to pick me up in two minutes." He paced next to the table, still seething.

"I don't care how you manage it, Philo, but you need to find out where the hell Lanakai is. I want the cops on his ass right —the fuck—now."

13

"Only one of your facilities operates on Kauai. Am I correct, Wally?" she said.

Doctor Dolores Delphina, a chain smoker, blew the smoke away from Wally, a polite gesture that made no difference. The enclosed office was filled eye-high with a stale, swirling blue cloud of cigarette smoke. Polite was good, and Wally appreciated the effort, lame as hers was, but if she really cared she'd have aired the room out and not smoked while he was there. An impossibility for Doctor D.

He'd decided WTF, she was going to make him a lot of money. Magpie stayed in the hallway, not able to handle the smell or the dirty air.

Heavyset brunette in her mid-forties, Doctor D was a surgeon with a bad gambling habit to go with her cigarette addiction, clocking way too many hours on the offshore online casinos, an admission of hers. Years ago, it had been way too many hours at Wally's by-invitation-only poker nights in the islands. She'd paid down that debt, one that had been only a few short months in the making but was taking long years across thousands of miles, via Hawaii-to-Philly bank wire transfers, for its un-making. She was now within striking distance of being rid of all of it. Here was a chance for her to pay off the balance by performing only a few surgical procedures.

"*Two* facilities," Wally said.

"Oh. Right." Inhale cigarette smoke toxins, exhale less toxins, smile. "One here on Kauai, one on Oahu. What are you calling yourself, 'Livers 'R Us?'"

Haha, what the hell do your lungs look like, Wally mused, *at four, five packs a day?* She had to know how black they were, she was an organ transplant specialist. He had called her, said he had a business deal regarding her loans, found his way to her professional offices a day later, was here to make his pitch.

"I'm not forcing you, Doctor," he said. "But I'd really like to get rid of my... older loans. If you don't want to do this, I will, however, need to double the interest rate. Administrative costs are up. I'm sure you understand."

"But that would make the rate—"

"A hundred twenty percent," Wally said. "Yes, I know. Kind of prohibitive, right?"

"I feel good, Magpie, I really do. Doctor D rounds out our staff. Now make me feel better. Tell me you figured out who the hell 'Y' is."

The Escalade left the curb, Wally, Magpie, and a driver inside. Wally popped open a juice can.

"Still working it, boss. I have people on the streets around Kauai now. Spotters. Only thing they're seeing is the protection rackets. When we moved out, someone else moved in. Could be our guy."

"A name?"

"Checking, boss. Trying to do it without starting a war. We'll need to—"

"Wait." Wally stiffened, on alert. "You hear that? Power down the window."

With the window down, the siren became audible. Not loud, not gaining in strength, no Doppler effect, just a low, winding undertone not much more invasive than an earworm, hanging out there like an anemic bugle call.

"The Feds, boss," Magpie said. "Something's up with the military, or maybe it's a test of the early-warning system."

The siren wound down, faded, stopped, and was immediately replaced with a ringtone from inside the car. Wally's new phone. He looked at the number, didn't recognize it, let it go to voicemail. He listened to the message.

"*Hi, Wally. I have a lucrative, fun proposition that might interest you. It's from a friend of mine. Not leaving my name. Call me back at this number.*"

A female voice, a smile no doubt fronting a haughty, alluring, self-confident delivery meant to elicit a visceral male response. Except he already knew who it was. She answered after one ring when he called her back.

"Hello." Same soft, sexy voice.

"I see you've been working on your sex line voice, Shiko. Not bad. I have time to talk but it has to be right now. And I'm not interested in any cockfights. No bootleg saké either. What else you got, and who is this friend of yours?"

Shiko was Japanese, and during Wally's last go-round on the islands, she was a middleperson. She had access to, and existed mostly because of, men like Wally, who appreciated the finer female form matched with the finer aspects of pugilism in all its forms: chickens, dogs, vipers, hogs, men, women. Plucked from among the between-rounds ring walkers at legitimate boxing venues, Shiko was one of the hot chicks in the hot pants who held up the placards announcing the next round number—when she was younger. What Wally remembered of her twenty years later, from past encounters, was she could still fill out an outfit.

"No cocks, no dogs, no snakes, Wally. Straight bareknuckles, mano a mano. I'm right on your tail, so now's good, sweetie. Find a place to stop and I'll join you in your limo." She ended the call with a kissy noise.

Wally's driver found a restaurant parking lot. Shiko exited her car from the passenger side, slid into Wally's back seat. Heels, wide jeans to accommodate her significant hips, tight top that almost didn't accommodate her bosom. Shiny black hair in a bun. Intoxicating cherry blossom fragrance. Sakura, by Dior, Wally recalled.

"Nice Escalade, Wally dear. Good to see you." Her kissy lips brushed against Wally's right cheek. "My driver will follow us."

"I thought you were dead, Shiko," Wally said.

"Oh yeah? Why's that?" She smoothed out a crease in her buttoned-up, high-neck blouse.

"Because I thought I killed you."

"Oh. That. At that last cockfight. Yeah, that was brutal, wasn't it? No, my gamecock Orca died, so did my deadbeat ex-husband, but your bullets missed me. Then you went to prison. The Feds, right?"

"Right."

"Anyway, good to see you. So here's the deal..."

"No deal, because I have no interest, Shiko. Who's your friend?"

"'Course you will, Wally, after I give you the details..."

"And how did you find me?"

"And we're back to talking about 'my friend.'" She air-quoted. "It was him. *He* knows where and how to find you. But I can't tell you about 'my friend' because I don't actually know who he is. He pops up from time to time on my phone. Him and his money. Not even sure it's a guy. Anywho, he, they, whoever, has a fighter he's showcasing, is looking for some action. I'll get to meet him if I can get you interested. And since you're back in town..."

"Only temporarily." Wally reached over and grabbed her purse.

"Is that really necessary, Wally?"

He tossed the purse to Magpie. "Find her phone."

Magpie found a phone in the bag, started keying it. "Needs a password, boss."

"Shiko?" Wally said to her expectantly. "Give it up."

"Wasting your time, Wally, but sure. It's 'sayonara.' Back to the fight..."

Magpie nodded, the password was good, kept keying, searching.

"No fight, Shiko. If you're not willing to share any info with me, get out."

"Why not? Big money, and he'll make it a local venue. You could even take me. I could be your date. Like old times."

Wally eyed Magpie, looking for good news about the phone number search, friend search, email search, phone info dump, anything useful that Magpie might be able to glean from her contact info. "A new phone, boss. A burner. She chatted with Uber, that's all."

"Like I said," she said, "you're wasting your time. I don't have my personal phone with me. You're really being a dick here, Wally."

"Shut the fuck up. Here's what I'm gonna do. Magpie, give her the burner back. What's your phone number, Shiko?"

"Ha, sure, my personal phone number. Right."

"Never mind. I've got the number for the burner." Wally added it in his contact list.

"I'm sending you something, Shiko. A text with a photo and a name. There. If your friend can locate this woman for me—she could be anywhere—I'll think about participating in a fight he promotes. For the fight to be worth my while, the purse would need to be, let's say, three hundred thousand, nothing less. But I need a solid lead on this woman or no fucking deal. Got that?"

"Who is she to you again, Wally, this..." Shiko read the name from the text. "Kaipo Mawpaw? Your wife? A girlfriend? Who?"

"No more info, Shiko. Do as I say, maybe we can cut a deal. Now, back to my original request..." Wally reached across her lap, opened the door. "... that you get the fuck out. Get back to me if you learn something about this woman."

With their guest gone, the limo returned to the road. Magpie spoke up. "Boss, I think that was a bad move."

"What was a bad move?"

"Telling her your agenda, giving her that picture of Kaipo. Too much info. You don't need any more players. We've got a network. We'll find her."

"You're taking too long, Magpie. I... we need her back *now*. No one leaves Ka Hui unless I say so. No one."

"It gives someone else too much leverage, Wally. Who knows what they'll do if they find her first—"

Worse yet, Wally now opined, who knew what *he'd* do if he never found her.

He choked it all back, didn't, couldn't comment. His plans for her. His needs. What could have been, all of it going unrealized.

Scorched earth was where he was. All or nothing. If he couldn't have her...

No, he couldn't do that. He wouldn't let anyone do that. He loved her.

14

Kaipo was in mother-hen mode. An Uber picked her up at Vena's place early a.m., Vena hungover from switching to hard lemonade somewhere between seven and eight the prior p.m. With Vena sleeping in, Kaipo had some recon to do, meeting as many acquaintances who'd relocated to Kauai from homesteads on Miakamii as she could find, to spread the word. Destination number one, a suggestion from Vena, the Kauai Ultimate Off-Road Ranch Tour at the Kipu Ranch. Her recommended first contact was Toggle Monapalui, mid-twenties, younger brother to Troy Monapalui, a high-school friend of Kaipo and Vena until an on-the-job accident in the off-road tourism business took Troy's life.

She set aside three hours for this adventure-slash-counseling session. Helmet, safety goggles, seat belt, 4WD ATV, check. Unpaved trails that climbed eight hundred feet above sea level, and a decision made by Kaipo to remain a passenger and let Toggle drive, check. Rugged landscapes used in *Raiders of the Lost Ark, Jurassic Park,* and *The Descendants*, check. Been here, done this gig before, doing it all again to talk with Toggle, a transplanted native Miakamiian, check.

"So you get the picture then?" Kaipo shouted at Toggle to better the roar of the ATV, her hand on her helmet. "Too dangerous for you?"

Toggle's head was down, his chin tucked in. He was bracing for the next rise and fall in the trail. "If we don't hang on right—*here*," he shouted back, "none of that other dangerous shit will matter—"

Airborne for a full second, the ATV came down hard, tilted onto two wheels as they rounded a curve, dropped onto all fours, then jetted along the dirt route. "Having fun yet, Kaipo? Wooo-*hooo!*"

After another hundred yards through the tropical forest that covered most of the ranch, Toggle pulled the vehicle into a controlled fishtail, stopping the four-wheeler short.

"Whew. End of one line, the beginning of another." In front of them, a zipline ran between two embankments, one on either side of a river.

Kaipo dismounted the ATV, would have needed to check that her balls were still attached if she had any. Toggle was all smiles, all long hair, all thrill-seeker. But Kaipo knew the attitude was a placeholder—his on-the-job game face. He was vulnerable: he was young, he felt invincible, was dirt poor, and was Miakamiian. Fodder—prey—for snake oil salesmen like Wally Lanakai.

"Last leg, Kaipo. Ready?"

Toggle belted her into the zipline with canvas straps and clips, had her retighten her helmet and goggles, and pushed her off. She felt it—the adrenaline rush of ziplining thirty-five feet in the air at twenty miles per hour across a raging river, the coolness of the wind against her face, the spray of river rapids foam against her bare legs, the smell of fresh water. Toggle zipped across to join her on the other side of the river, where they could begin their trek back to the ranch's cabin entrance.

To her, he was a lamb of a young man, beautiful, fun-loving, naive. She had a closing argument queued up and at the ready. They removed their zipline gear, started walking and talking.

"It's a lot of money," Toggle said, pushing invasive foliage out of their way as they walked. "I could really use it to round out my finances for the next year. They'll even pay for six weeks post-op care in a medical spa while I recuperate. And the part of the liver removed rejuvenates, Kaipo. Kind of a win-win for the donor and the recipient, don'tcha think?"

The unadvertised offer of money for organs. Word of mouth had ferreted out the details, was making the rounds among the young and the restless and the underemployed.

"Toggle. Listen to me. There's a reason why it's illegal to sell your organs. Telling you it would be a risk would be an understatement. And how many too-good-to-be-true offers like this ever make any sense to you? Don't do it. These are unlicensed procedures, performed sometimes at locations no better than Third World MASH units."

"How do you know all this? You've seen them?"

She could not be totally truthful, otherwise he'd ignore the message and instead key on the messenger. "I know crime scene cleaners, even worked with them. I've cleaned up some nasty, nasty messes that needed remediation. Hacks posing as transplant specialists for black-market organs on the main-land. Big money, and most times no issues, but too many times... I refer you to my first statement: I know crime scene cleaners."

"Okay, I hear you. We're here." Helmet, goggles, and gloves found their way into bins on the cabin's back porch. They went inside, the café there with a menu geared to decompress adrenaline-fueled customers.

Kaipo eyed the offerings on a blackboard. "Sit with me a moment. I'm buying."

Two sarsaparilla bottles and bags of red-hot potato chips littered the table between them. Kaipo hadn't heard from him what she wanted to hear. "So? What do you think? Promise me you won't tempt fate?"

"I don't know," he said. "Maybe. Like I said, my cash flow—"

"One last time, Toggle: it's too risky, which is the reason for the high payoff. Promise me you won't go near these people. Please."

Another sip of soda for him; he was still on the fence. She had to go for the throat.

"Think of your parents. They've already lost your brother to one tragedy. Think of them, if you won't think about yourself."

Soda swirled in his mouth, his eyes down, unfocused; he slipped into a slouch in his chair. Kaipo figured he was visiting a place in his head that had something to do with his dead brother.

"Unfair, Kaipo. Okay. Fine. I promise."

Kaipo exhaled. "Super. Excellent. I'll call you later in the week just to see how you're doing. You're a good-looking Hawaiian guy. Maybe look for some modeling work, or do some temp office work..."

He smiled, embarrassed at the compliment, then perked up, suddenly aware of his sexuality, also suddenly more aware of Kaipo's, too. "I've had offers as a gigolo. I'm serious. Maybe, um, see, maybe you and I, we could, um—"

"I'm flattered, really I am, but no." She grabbed his hand, opened it, tucked a hundred bucks inside. "Your tip, Toggle.

My advice, stay away from the cougars and the bored mainlanders. No porn films, either. Too many diseases. I gotta go.
Thanks for a great morning."

––––––––

Her list was in her head. The people who had relocated, the
families who had stayed. Fewer and fewer had remained on
the island over the years, from what Kaipo recalled. The helicopter pilot, the research doctor, the street performer, all had
lived off-island, now all were gone, in gruesome, sensational
fashion. But the three hours she spent today with another
relocated Miakamiian had been worth it. Time to drop back in
at Vena's for a bio break, then she would get back at it.

The Uber idled in Vena's driveway. She took a long look up
and down the street before exiting. No lingering BMWs with
shady drivers. Kaipo got out, the Uber left. She entered the
open garage and knocked on the interior door. No answer. She
tried the doorknob; unlocked. She poked her head inside the
mudroom.

"Vena?" she called. "Get your lazy ass out of bed, you
queen, it's one o'clock. Vena...?"

The over-under washer-dryer unit was tilted, leaning on
two legs, a laundry sink propping it up at an awkward angle.
This lit up her senses; there'd been a struggle in here. Kaipo
reached behind her back, under her blouse, slipped her
handgun from its holster and listened, heard the fridge motor
kick in, nothing else. A two-handed pose with the gun led her
into the next room.

The kitchen. Drip coffee maker was off, the carafe half full,
the way Kaipo had left it. One bowl in the sink, a spoon in it,
the aftermath of Kaipo's breakfast Cheerios. No indication
Vena had made an appearance.

"Vena? Vena honey?"

Slow steps forward, Kaipo now almost out of the kitchen, except—

The backsplash. One cracked tile, ruining the bold orange look of the southwestern kitchen. Not cracked, it had a hole. Next to it, two holes in the drywall. If she dug inside all three holes, she knew she'd find bullets. Her eyes darted everywhere, her pulse quickening.

Fight or flight? The urges for both cartwheeled around her head. She had a reason to run, also had a larger reason in the person of her friend to stay. On instinct she eased forward, kept walking on quiet, steady feet, into the living room, resisting calling Vena's name again.

The deadbolt for the front door was engaged but the door chain hung loose. Had she been chased, with not enough time to open the door? The coffee table was pushed against the sofa, making a wider path. Blood droplets peppered the light-colored rug, continued onto the hardwood floor, into the hallway. No bullet holes visible anywhere in the living room, nothing obvious in the dining room either. Kaipo moved down the hall, past the empty bathroom, the door open. A cursory look inside, nothing of interest, the shower curtain pulled back from the tub. She reached Vena's bedroom. The door lay flat on the bedroom floor, the doorjamb around it splintered.

Where Vena had made her stand. Kaipo swallowed hard, stood evaluating the damage from the doorway. "Oh my, Vena. Sweetie. Please, please, please don't be in here..."

Her raised gun preceded her into the bedroom.

Pockmarks speckled the resting door's off-white panels, one, two... a total of five bullet entries and exits in the top half of the door, fired from inside the bedroom. She turned back to check the other side of the hallway, where the bullets would have entered the wall if they hadn't hit anything, found holes in the drywall. She counted only three.

Kaipo shuddered, but her heart also leaped with pride; she wanted to pull her friend in close to her right now, to hug her. The blood drips she'd seen in the kitchen and the living room —still viscous, maybe only an hour old—Kaipo was sure they were from bullets four and five, was sure they had found their way into Vena's assailant.

"Good for you, Vena," she said, a whimper. "So proud of you, baby..."

Inside the bedroom now, she treaded lightly. The dresser drawers were upended, flung into the corners. A crack in the wardrobe door. A shattered mirror, table lamps in pieces alongside their nightstands. An overturned mattress. A circular divot in the drywall, probably from the snow globe tossed with bad intentions, now on the carpeted floor. Kaipo's Christmas gift to her from the tropics-averse, wintry eastern coast of the mainland.

Two more bullet holes in the ceiling, directly above the bedframe. That brought the bullet count to ten, the Glock clip's official capacity. Vena had emptied her gun. "That's my girl..."

She slid a pillow out of the way with her foot to see the floor on the other side of the bed. Here was the Glock; Kaipo retrieved it. Still no Vena.

The master bathroom: the door creaked open when she entered. No signs of a struggle, the shower curtain closed, covering a tub/shower combo. The bathroom sink was discolored, hair dye trails left to dry. Vena had been coloring her hair when the attack went down.

Something chirped. Vena's cell phone, on the clothes hamper. A text had queued up. Kaipo read it.

It was from Kaipo. She'd sent it two hours ago, had only just arrived.

On my way back.

This did it. The text was what finally made Kaipo cry, a short burst of tears. She backed out of the bathroom, Vena's phone in her pocket.

She retraced her steps, came up empty searching the rest of the house. Vena had put up one helluva fight. Kaipo quickly realized she had to leave, like, right now, would need to do it by leaving behind no trace of herself. Not a problem for her to leave undiscovered, considering her after-hours work for Ka Hui, except... she had no supplies. Nothing other than whatever cleaning solutions Vena kept on hand.

She made do. Toilet cleanser, kitchen cleaning sprays, plastic gloves from an open hair dye package when she couldn't find any others. Fingerprints removed, glasses, bowls, utensils washed, DNA neutralized, hopefully. No attempt at remediating the bedroom crime scene; that was the assailant's problem. Kaipo gathered up her cleaning materials into a plastic bag that would leave with her.

Vena, gone. Why? Where to? Taken by whom?

The horrible thought, the one that nagged her as soon as she saw the first blood specks and bullet holes, was back: it was more likely that Kaipo was their target, not Vena.

She booked an Uber, stood inside Vena's garage wondering how the neighbors hadn't heard anything. Fucking suburbia.

Her own phone was a burner. She'd crush and lose it as soon as her Uber driver dropped her off, replace it with another. Vena's phone, in her pocket... she'd keep that one, look for any leads, lose it later today.

Wait. Vena's phone, Kaipo's delayed text to her... it had been a distraction. Had she missed something when inspecting the bathroom? Had she checked inside the tub...?

Back in Vena's master bath again. She pulled back the tub's shower curtain.

"No. My dear baby... Oh no. Vena—"

Tucked into the tub, her face and neck streaked from black hair dye, her torso splayed open bad as from a wild animal attack—her blood had pooled at the bottom of the tub, frozen there beneath the ice chunks surrounding it. Dry, not regular ice. So savage an evisceration... was it payback for harboring Kaipo? Had she been tortured? Why not wait for Kaipo to return?

She had to get out.

The Uber arrived and she climbed into the back seat with her backpack, her guns and phones tucked inside, plus a trash bag that included everything she used to clean up after herself. The car door closed. She reconfirmed with the driver a destination, held herself together until she no longer could.

The wave of guilt and remorse finally breached the levee, her eyes streaming tears from behind her sunglasses. She let them fall, unrestrained and with abandon, maintaining as best as she could a stoic appearance as her tears wet her fidgeting hands. Vena's house faded in the rear view.

"You okay, miss?" the driver said, focused on her in the mirror.

"Turn at this next corner, please. Stop the car and wait while I make a quick call."

Kaipo opened the door, stood outside for privacy, and made an anonymous 9-1-1 call to report finding Vena's body. Back inside the car—

"Let's go. A different address than what I gave you, please. It's not as far."

She wanted a drink, she wanted drugs, she needed to numb her conscience into the next millennium.

15

At Home with the Waumami Family. It would make a wonderful weekly radio program, Ella had often told Ben. She pulled apart more lobster meat, fed herself from the comfort of her canvas lounge chair. She and Ben were on the beach, a campfire between them. They'd scattered their rock lobster shells within tossing distance, which was also within picking-up distance, because that's what they would be doing after they finished their dinner. Always leave your environment cleaner than it was before you entered it. Another Logan family saying, and a good one. It kept Miakamii the paradise that it was.

"Just like that *Prairie Home Companion* on the radio, my love. I miss that program so much. Horseback riding, farming, picket fences, porches, bicycles. Our bees. The island's livestock. Our shell jewelry. Our church services."

"Indeed," Ben said. "People could learn how little they need to enjoy their lives."

They had radio feeds from the mainland, had an old Philco tabletop, a Cathedral model, with a battery backing up its solar-generated power; a few stations at least. They'd listened to Garrison Keillor religiously while he was still on the air. The Philco was good enough for their parents for entertainment, and their grandparents, so it was good enough for Ella and Ben.

The sun to their backs, low in the sky, reflected off the glistening swells of the Pacific rising and falling between their island and Kauai. A different reflection caught Ella's eye.

"Some late-day company," she said. The glint of binoculars from one location, a boat. Something they were accustomed to because of the scrutiny the island received. "More voyeurs, Ben."

"Interested in watching us eat our dinner. They're harmless. I saw them motor up then stall their engine."

Always under a microscope. Something the past and present Prohibited Island residents had to live with; decades and decades of busybodies. Distant envy at their little paradise.

Time to give these gawkers a little show, Ella thought. Let them see the Miakamii savages doing what savages do.

She removed her hunting knife from its hand-sewn leather sheath, all ten inches of shiny steel, and began picking her teeth with it. Ben used his own hunting knife to remove the meat from another spiny lobster shell. These were their standard responses to behavior that was so rude and presumptuous. After their displays, Ella retrieved her binoculars to give their observers a taste of what it felt like to be watched.

"Benign tourists, Ben honey," she said, lowering her spyglasses.

"Yes. But something has changed."

Ben reached for and found his wife's hand and gave it a loving squeeze, the two of them enjoying the last rays of sunlight slipping below the tree line behind them, illuminating the ocean, a sparkling, tropical postcard view.

"Ella dear, I must give you my regrets. It's been a wonderful dinner. I want to check on a few traps, maybe stop into the church before we retire. Would you mind—"

"I'll clean up and put out the fire, sweetie. I'm going to relax here a little longer."

Ella awakened with a minor start, the sea in front of her dark now below the stars, the lights of Kauai on the horizon. She'd drifted off to the rolling waves and a pleasant breeze, the tide on the rise but not a challenge to where they'd placed their chairs for their evening dinner. The noise of an airplane engine had jerked her awake, was gaining strength. Not a jet, but rather a piston-driven propeller aircraft. Ella concentrated on the sound.

"A Staggerwing," she said to herself, satisfied at having identified it by the engine noise. A Beechcraft product, a biplane revered for its beauty and performance and place in Americana, the model dating from the thirties and forties. She'd familiarized herself with many aircraft sounds after repeated visits to Hawaiian island hangars over the years. "How nostalgic," she said before settling back into the white noise of her dreamland's soundtrack.

The noisy engine sounds morphed. Ella's eyes opened again, were slits, her foggy brain analyzing brassy bursts of gunfire somewhere in her dream, layering them into hazy memories of childhood days at school and in church, and in the fields on the island. Oddly enough, they fit into all of it, much like the other white noise of the crashing waves, and the seagulls, and the foghorns, and the tinkling of an ammunition belt feeding an airplane gun, interrupting the baseline purr of the plane's engine.

Ella didn't try to wake up, this soundtrack lifelike, soothing, making her smile even in her dream. She'd cuddle with Ben soon, pull him into her after a few more minutes of peaceful sleep here, on the beach, in their paradise.

16

Police Chief Terry Koo sent Philo a text. *Mister Trout. I know this is highly irregular...*

It was nine p.m.-ish, and he and Patrick were beat, had each retired to their rooms at their cottage. Philo also suffered from the incredibly spicy Mexican food from their lunch at Da Crack. Chief Koo's text said to meet them at a crime scene that was "right up your alley," and gave them the address. The irregular part:

Scene's not cleared yet. You know your shit, Trout, so get over here now, please. Ask for me at the door.

Ten p.m. Philo and Patrick arrived at Pakala Village, a neighborhood on Kauai's southwestern shore. They negotiated its tidy, quiet streets, no house number needed, the police activity visible from half a block away. The front door to the address was open. A uniformed cop guarding the entry stepped up to stop them before Philo even had a chance to open his mouth.

"Sorry, sir, but it's not going to happen. Please leave the premises." Tall, gaunt, Caucasian, the officer and her bug eyes keyed on Philo and his cup of contraband Dunkin' in hand, no badge, no other proper law enforcement ID to give him rightful entry.

"Philo Trout and Patrick Stakes. I'll leave the cup outside. Chief Koo said to meet him here—"

"At an active crime scene? I don't think so, sir. Turn around and leave, please."

"But—"

"Get going, poser," she said, puffing up her upper torso, her nitrile-gloved hand now resting atop her sidearm.

Philo held back and chose not to argue regardless of how over the top her hard-ass attitude sounded. "Fine. Sure. Patrick, we need to back up, bud. Officer, please tell Chief Koo that Philo Trout and Patrick Stakes stopped by per his request—"

"Trout!" The shout came from inside, carried across the crowd of crime discovery personnel milling around the house's living room. "I'm in the hallway," Chief Koo called, then, to the officer, "Give them some supplies and let them through, Officer."

Wide-eyed from the caffeine, Philo navigated his way through the knots of gloved detectives and techs wandering the interior, Patrick right up his ass so the sea of people didn't need to part twice, the two of them gloved and masked, their footwear covered in elasticized pull-ons. Philo managed glances into the kitchen and the hall bath on the way past. They arrived at the bedroom. Chief Koo wiggled his upturned hand, had them enter.

"Some blood here, some in the kitchen," the chief said. "We're thinking none of it is from the victim, at least not in here, but we'll know later. Looks like it was one hell of a struggle, Trout."

Philo's eyes absorbed the room's chaos. A jumble of broken

furniture, lamps, mirrors, the tossed mattress, and the slug holes in the bedroom door. "How many people live here?"

"One, far as we know. Something the neighbors confirmed. Nobody says they heard anything, but we have more people to talk to. The vic is in the bathroom."

She sure was. What was left of her, her torso split open from neck to abdomen. Her rib cage was parted, and her internal organs had been ransacked, her spine visible because there wasn't much else inside getting in the way of it. Her head was bruised but otherwise intact, including what Philo noticed as newly colored black hair, with dark trails of dye framing her naturally tanned face, running down her neck and on the lip of the tub.

"She's a civilian worker at the military outpost in Howling Sands," Chief Koo said.

"You sure?"

"Her ID was in her bedroom, is in evidence now."

"Shit. That's not good. What's her name? You call the CO yet?"

"The ID said Vena Akina. Commander Malcolm? Didn't call him yet. We'll get to it."

"You'll get to it? Fuck that, I'm calling him now."

"Fine, I get it, he's your friend, but"—Koo grabbed Philo's forearm—"we have two crimes with similar circumstances involving people in the same circles. That includes Evan Malcolm. I'll let you call him in a minute. First, what do you see here, Trout? Anything stick out to you?"

"You're saying Evan's a suspect?"

"Person of interest." Chief Koo relaxed his shoulders and his grip on Philo, calmed himself, and gave a measured, more personal answer. "Officially he's a POI, but in my book, no, not really. I know him too well. It's just... procedure. Give me your feedback, then you and your associate can get a hold of him and get the hell out of here."

They walked back through all the other rooms, Philo and Patrick in the lead, eyeing the counters and other visible surfaces, touching some with their gloved hands, breathing in the stuffy air, opening and closing cabinets, doors, drawers, appliances, but generally not disturbing anything at the scene, just observing it.

Philo addressed Patrick. "What do you think, bud?"

"Someone else was here, sir," Patrick said, quick to respond. "Not just the killer or killers. Someone else. Someone who did some cleaning, sir."

"I agree with my associate, Chief."

"One other person at a minimum," Chief Koo said. "The person who found her and made the anonymous call to 9-1-1. A woman. No leads on her yet."

"So the victim gets surprised by an assailant," Philo said. "She puts up a fight. Those bullet holes... she was armed. She shoots an assailant, and the guy drips blood around the house."

"Why his blood? Why not hers?"

"Considering what they did to her when they finally cornered her, I'd say they didn't want to shoot her. So she went down with guns a-blazing. Your people find a gun in the house?"

"Not yet."

"Your caller shows up later, finds her. But before her call, someone, maybe the caller, cleans the place. Really, really cleans the place, hopes you guys find no trace of him, or her, being here. All these surfaces in these rooms, they were wiped clean. Not as clean now because your people are here, but the cleaning agents are still evident. The other bathroom is spotless, the mirror sprayed down. I smelled the bleach. In the kitchen I smelled the Lysol. Floor's been mopped, the mop in the closet is still wet. Problem is, why clean up everything and not clean up after the actual crime?"

"The person wasn't involved and didn't want to be blamed."

"Exactly. Plus something else. Did you search the house for the hair dye kit the victim used to color her hair? Looks like she was interrupted while she was coloring it."

"We did. Unopened dye kits are under the bathroom sink, but no used kits anywhere else, trash cans included."

"No stray splotches on the counter, or in the sink, no drips on the floor. Dye on her head, face, and neck, and on the tub porcelain, but nowhere else. And the hair dye kit is gone. Add to that, no gun. My take is the caller—maybe also the cleaner—gathered up evidence of his or her arrival and left with everything."

Soon as he finished his summary, a pang of awareness hit. "Whoa. The clear plastic gloves."

"From the hair dye kit?" Chief Koo said.

"Yes. My guess is the cleaner used the disposable gloves for the cleanup, didn't want to leave them behind."

Behind them a restless Patrick moved from foot to foot, his hand raised. It took Philo a minute to realize Patrick had been raising and lowering his hand the whole time Philo was in the zone, talking cleaning forensics. "Sorry, Patrick. What is it, you gotta use the john?"

"No, sir. I have a real good guess who it was, sir."

"The 9-1-1 caller? Go for it, bud."

"Could be that lady who disappeared from Philly, sir. The Hawaiian mob cleaner lady we met at your fight in the grain silo. Remember her, sir? She was really good..."

Philo's jaw unhinged and stayed that way as he remained

speechless, piecing it together, the Philly angle meaning nothing to the chief but meaning everything to Philo.

Her name was Kaipo, her last name escaping him. Wally's woman friend. Hawaiian. Very competent. Someone, maybe her, knew how to clean up after herself but had little on hand to do it with, MacGyvered her way into what was needed. Wanted no trace of her visit discovered. Didn't want to be found out. By anyone. Least of all by—

"Tell me what you know about Wally Lanakai and the mob here in Hawaii, Chief, and we'll tell you what we know about them in Philly."

17

Wally pointed at the empty curb, barked at his driver, today not Magpie. The spaces in the adjacent parking garage were too tight and not long enough. He wanted the Caddy limo parked on the street.

"These two spaces here. You know the drill."

The driver parallel parked across adjacent spaces, cut the engine. The other passenger objected. "Wally, this is police headquarters. Don't do anything to antagonize—"

"Shut it, Amos. You're my attorney, not my babysitter."

Defensive parking 101, to make sure the Escalade didn't mingle with the beater cars and the Maryjane-farming pickups and the Harleys that Kauai's police department head-quarters seemed to attract nowadays. Which meant two parking meters to contend with, which meant two fares. Which meant Wally was behaving as he should, would cover his ass and operate within all aspects of the law this time around, needing no reminders from his attorney.

Back in the day, he'd say fuck the Kauai parking authority, fuck the police, and fuck the local government, because he'd paid them all off. Then the Department of Justice swooped in, indicted the city government, indicted the police department hierarchy, and put Wally in prison on racketeering charges. Years after his release from the judicial system, he'd turned over a new leaf. He was still into questionably victimless services, was still in the rackets on the East Coast, in Philly. He'd embarked on a business play that at best pissed all over the medical industry's ethics. At worst it could do major harm, some patients lost during surgery and needing to be dealt with. On the radar in Philly, but nothing had ever been proven. Still, he'd remained below the radar in Hawaii this time around, yet the police asked him to stop in for a chat to talk about some of the most horrifying and sensational crimes in recent memory on Kauai.

"We will cooperate fully," he'd told a Detective Ujikawa on the phone, but where had this detective gotten his number, he asked.

"You don't need to know that, Mr. Lanakai."

Wally's best guess: Douglas Logan, who had a big reach across the islands. Would Wally be pissed at Logan for having given out his contact info, or gratified Logan had retained it? Either way, he'd need to be wary.

The driver loaded the meters with coins. Wally and his lawyer waited in the car, sipping guava juice, until the driver finished.

Inside headquarters they were led to a police interrogation room and made comfortable: coffee, bottled water, snacks. Two law enforcement types entered, both Hawaiian, one in rumpled plainclothes, one in a decorated uniform. A slight relief on Wally's part: his visit had at least merited the island's top cop. Smart on the police chief's part, too, to show some respect; props to their approach. The cops took seats across a table from them.

"I'm Kauai Police Chief Koo, this is Detective Ujikawa. I thank you and your attorney for coming in. Let's get started. Detective, you're up."

"Thanks, Chief. So why are you back in Hawaii, Mr. Lanakai?"

His felonies were well documented, but the men at the table shared no personal history. Clean slate for Wally, with time served. This was more than a getting-to-know-you question, it was a fishing expedition.

"Back in my home state? For business and for pleasure. I'm interested in purchasing a local cottage industry."

"Yes. The Miakamii shell lei business," the detective said. "Douglas Logan told us. But you want more than the business. You want the island."

Wally's attorney leaned forward to interrupt. "What does this line of questioning have to do—"

"It's okay, Amos. You're spot on, Detective. The island's stewardship has suffered of late. But Mr. Logan wants to sell none of it. Does not see the merit of returning the island to indigenous owners. Not the island or the business. With the right pricing, I hope I can change his mind."

"Or the right intimidation," the detective said. He shuffled through a pile of photos, set two aside, then slid them across the table in front of Wally. "Mr. Logan's helicopter, in pieces on the island. Here's Mr. Logan's pilot. His throat was cut."

"So everybody heard."

"Yes. Big news." Detective Ujikawa stood, arrived at Wally's side. "Like these other incidents were, too."

He placed a crime scene photo atop those of the helicopter carnage. In it a naked woman lay in a bathtub on a bed of dry ice, her chest flayed open, the dry ice surrounding her. The next photo showed the body of a Hawaiian man sliced open stem to stern who, according to bystanders, had been in a rolled-up blanket pushed out of a car onto the asphalt. What followed were more photos of the two respective crime scenes, horrific images with staying power, the detective dropping one after another onto the table, under Wally's nose.

"The woman was a middle-aged research doctor, lived near the Navy base. The man was a young street performer, his body left in front of a restaurant. All three murders are only days old. And now, a new one. A fresh female body in Pakala Village. From yesterday."

Another bathtub picture, the young woman gutted, more dry ice in the tub with her. Wally registered the appropriate amount of disgust as he viewed the photos. Honest reactions, maybe even a grimace, considering he'd never been anywhere near these victims or events.

"You seeing a trend here, Mr. Lanakai?"

"All the victims are Hawaiian. Excluding the pilot, some*one* or *thing* appears to have been interested in their internal organs. This is pure barbarism. Savage attacks…"

"*Planned* savage attacks. So here's what we're struggling with, and why we have you here. You want to buy Miakamii, take it off the Logan family's hands. The owner says he's not interested. Out of the blue, the owner's tourist copter pilot is murdered in flight, the copter crashes, his tourism business crippled."

"I had nothing to do with—"

"You return to the islands, and the bodies start piling up—"

"I'm not involved, Detective. Ex-cons might be first in line as suspects, but that's too convenient a circumstance, don't you think?"

"… and your borderline unethical business practices on

the mainland look like they've found their way here, Lanakai, along with you. You *know* something about all this, damn it!"

The detective's fist pound rattled the coffee cups and spilled an open water bottle. Wally didn't flinch; the water and coffee rivered together, running off the table edge.

"Are you finished here, Detective?" Wally said. "Because I am. Like I said, not me. If anything, I'm as interested in whoever is doing this as you are, bad as it's making me look. If this is all, I think I'll be going—"

The door to the interrogation room opened. A surprise guest.

Douglas Logan pushed through, a uniformed cop chattering at him from behind, about to try to wrestle him into cuffs for ignoring her.

"They said I could find you all here. I need to clear something up, Chief."

Chief Koo rose. "Officer." He eyed the cop. "The cuffs won't be necessary. Douglas, you can't be in here. Let's go, we can speak in my office."

"It will only take a second. It involves him." The river of spilled liquid drip-drip-dripped off the table. "Lanakai's not the problem. There's someone else."

Direct eye contact, Douglas Logan to Wally. Still no love lost on Douglas Logan's face, but there was also no contempt.

"Lord knows how I struggle reconciling his history, Terry, but he told me to my face that he wasn't involved in Chester's murder, and that he wants to help find out who was, and I believe him."

"I appreciate the feedback, Douglas," Chief Koo said. "Now give me a name. Who?"

"No one person. A group."

"And that would be...?"

"The Yakuza."

"Son of a bitch."

Wally could see the ticket tucked under the limo's wind-shield wiper as soon as he exited the police building and was now one pissed-off parallel parker. His attorney matched him stride for stride as they bore down on the car.

"Don't say a fucking word, Amos."

Wally was ready to strangle his driver for letting this happen, but the driver was MIA, only now approaching from a few storefronts away, a pack of cigarettes in his hand, exasperated and just as surprised. "Boss, sorry, thought I could step away—"

Wally snarled at him—"You had one fucking job, damn it"—and ripped the paper from under the wiper, was going to shred it. Except it wasn't a parking ticket, it was a typed note on a small piece of white paper, which he read, but not aloud:

Airport locker #46. Blood type A. You'll make it work. — Y.

Included were one- and two-digit numbers with dashes in between. The lock's combination.

Another gift, same anonymous benefactor. His first thought, *I'm gonna kill this smug bastard,* faded into his second, that the grotesque, savage photos he'd just seen during his precinct visit may well have been of the previous owner of the organs he expected to find in the locker.

He shoved the note into his lawyer's chest, yelled to his driver. "Get in. We're going to the airport."

Inside the limo Wally seethed while on the phone with Magpie. "Another gift arrived from my secret admirer. Drop what you're doing and get a hold of one of our surgeons to see if we can put it in play. Then here's what I want you to do. Go to our storage space..."

Wally had absorbed Douglas Logan's input at the police

station. That the Japanese Yakuza had not stayed in the lanes they'd established for themselves pre-WWII. Their activity had expanded beyond the Japanese-Hawaiian communities. Ruthless and barbaric in their dispensing of violence, they were bumping up against other neighborhoods, some of them where Logan's ranch employees lived.

And where, Wally speculated, they were rushing to fill the space that his Ka Hui family's exit years back had vacated. Were the trafficked organs appeasements to Ka Hui, the prior ruling class, or was the prior ruling class being ridiculed, or worse yet, framed?

"... and get me an inventory of what's in there, Magpie."

"Everything, boss?"

"Just the guns and ammo. Especially the military-grade shit."

18

"You sure of the address, ma'am?" the Uber driver asked.

The address was right, Kaipo's timing was wrong. Three years too late. Three years since her last visit here, which was during the time she was handling mob cleaning projects in Hawaii for Wally Lanakai. Which begot Wally's scorched-earth approach to keeping her sober when he realized she had an addiction problem. The Uber driver idled his vehicle in front of a sprawling ranch home on a small property in a residential neighborhood. The house was boarded up due to extensive fire damage. Halloween decorations were still on the lawn. Typical crystal meth house approach, the owners wanting to blend in, maintain a quiet coexistence, decorate for the holidays, keep the grass cut and the bushes trimmed, etc. Until, apparently, one end of the home burst into flames from a meth lab explosion in a bedroom. Amateur manufacturers, riding the wave. Meth production in Hawaii had reached pandemic proportions, proliferating in quiet neighborhoods as well as out-of-the-way barns on empty plantation farmland, operating below the radar. Everyone wanted some of the action because anyone could make the product. But not always safely.

Meth never interested her. Heroin and opium did, and the mom-and-pop business operating out of this address peddled whatever drugs could make them money. This one operation hadn't caught Wally Lanakai's attention. Which meant they'd sold to her back then because they hadn't known what Wally would do to them if he found out they had.

"Hold on," she said to the driver. Exasperated, she checked her phone, scrolled further down her contact list.

On her mind as she thumbed around her screen: Vena. Alive before Kaipo showed up on her doorstep, dead now. Too painful to accept. Kaipo needed to numb herself, right the hell now.

A few more texts to local Kauai contacts that were years old. Private phone numbers, not burners. She was using her alias. It got her only one response, and that was, *I don't know you. Not interested.*

No quick fix, damn it. She closed her eyes, searched deep for a reassessment of her short-term needs.

Inconsistencies. They impinged on her guilty conscience, questioning her grasp of the situation. Her close friend had been gutted, her organs taken. Wally was in the organ redistribution business, ergo, this was Wally's doing. But if Wally had tracked her to Vena's, he would have waited for Kaipo to return. She'd gotten in and out with no issue.

Something was off.

Maybe it wasn't Wally. Maybe there was a competitor. Someone a lot sloppier than him, the mess left behind on purpose to incriminate him. To expose Wally's new business model. To expose *him.*

A turf war. Which meant maybe Vena's grotesque murder wasn't Kaipo's fault.

But why Vena then?

"Miss, do you have another destination for me?"

More scrolling. "Yes. The Lihue landfill."

Trash trucks idled near the gated entrance, seagulls hovered overhead, swooping and diving and peeling off to follow the scent to the mother lode itself, the two-hundred-acre landfill, a cornucopia beyond the fence. Adjacent to the landfill, a maintenance yard anchored by an orange brick building the size of a supermarket absorbed a steady diet of street sweepers and trash trucks on their way inside a separate steel cyclone fence. It was quitting time for the first shift, the sweepers parking side by side in straight lines, fanning away from the building. Kaipo took a chance, had the Uber driver leave her near the employee parking lot where she knew she'd see the workers as they exited the building. She stood just outside the fence, her back against a mustard-yellow Plymouth Duster in the first row, her arms crossed. Her face widened into a toothy grin the size of a harmonica when she picked someone out of a crowd of tired street sweeper jockeys on their approach to their cars.

"If it isn't Birdy Tatoto," Kaipo said before Birdy noticed her.

"My God. Kaipo, is that you?" Her friend quickly closed the distance. Long face, dark complexion, thin, looking thrift-store chic with a loose checkered top and distressed jeans. A beak-like nose. So appropriate a nickname.

"Sure is, Birdy. You look great, hon. And"—she made a production out of sniffing her face and neck while holding her shoulders in her hands—"you *smell* good, too. What is that, Dove soap?"

Birdy pulled Kaipo in, spoke into her shoulder as they hugged. "The county finally gave us showers and a locker room. No more stinking like an outhouse when we leave here. You look really wonderful, Kaipo. I mean—really—you look fantastic. Are you, um, you know—"

"Sober? Yes." Her smile turned upside down, then it returned. "It's a struggle every day, Birdy. Two years, four months, twenty-eight days. Every day a new trigger. But you know that."

Trigger. Bad choice of words.

Birdy, unfazed, looked at her watch. "Three years, four months, four days, and... six hours."

Birdy was Kaipo's Narcotics Anonymous sponsor. Pinpointing her sobriety date was telling. It was etched in Kaipo's persona as the day Birdy had lost her boyfriend to a self-inflicted gunshot. The boyfriend's solution to his heroin addiction. Something she and Kaipo both shared, the loss of loved ones to drugged-out suicides, although Kaipo's lover had the decency not to do it in front of her.

Happier memories were needed. "Tell me, Birdy, I forget. How old is this car again?" The car was the reason Kaipo had found her so easily.

"A '72. I'm not doing the math. It was my boyfriend's. He used to race it on the street, and I used to watch. Now the closest I get to drag racing is watching my sanitation buddies race their street sweepers every once in a while. Kaipo, I gotta tell you"—Birdy's smile was genuine—"it's so good to see you. I never thought you'd come back from the mainland. At least not alive. How long are you in town?"

"Few days. Too long a story for here. First part of it is, you need to call me Aiata. Where can we talk?"

"We were a mess, weren't we?" Birdy said.

Birdy's place, a large camper, was twenty minutes from the landfill in an RV park on a steppe carved out of an inactive volcano's base. Their fold-down kitchen table talk had commenced over iced tea. A distant horizon that fell away from the volcano shimmered outside the kitchen window like a desert mirage on a hot day. Kaipo's name change and the reason for it came and went as a topic. Kaipo was now back at the beginning of their friendship.

"We were fresh off the island," Kaipo said, reminiscing. "Shitty jobs. No friends on Kauai yet. No money. But we always had enough money for drugs, didn't we? Which put us on our way to moving from one addiction statistic to another." Kaipo quit the romanticizing, lifted her backpack to her lap. "I need to give you something, Birdy, and you need to pay attention to me on this." She unzipped a side pocket. Some second-guessing crept in, suddenly freezing her hand inside the backpack.

"What is it?" Birdy asked. "What's wrong?"

Kaipo tucked away her doubt, exhaled, knew this was necessary. "I need you to take this. I need you to not argue."

She liberated the handgun. Same gun she'd handed Vena twenty-four hours ago, but hopefully this time it would result in a different outcome. A mini-pang of PTSD wrenched her stomach while she handled the semi-automatic. She placed it on the table between them, a bullet clip next to it.

"What the hell, Kaipo?"

Vena's words, too.

"Those recent killings," Kaipo said, struggling, "those mutilated bodies you've been hearing about—"

"Yeah. What about them?"

"Add to them one more gruesome murder yesterday, not in the news yet. Vena Akina, from the island."

"What? Vena? Oh, Kaipo—"

Kaipo took her friend's hands in hers, Birdy in tears, Kaipo fighting them. "The murders might have something to do with me, Birdy, but then again, they might not. I'm not sure yet. But what they do have in common is the victims are all from Miakamii. Islanders who moved to Kauai. So promise me this, Birdy. Promise me you'll keep this gun within reach for the foreseeable future, for protection, and—"

Kaipo's eyes and mouth moistened in anticipation of a good cry, with her nearly losing it relaying this information, this... admonition. *Vena, my poor Vena...*

"—confirm something for me, that you're not entertaining undergoing surgery to donate a part of your liver or any other organs for money."

"Wait, what? How did you know...?"

"Word of mouth, Birdy. Son of a bitch, I knew it. Listen carefully to me..."

Things were worse than she'd thought. Social media: the bane, or the salvation of this generation? Blessing or curse? Regardless, different platforms had picked up on this little get-flush-quick scheme that Ka Hui had going. Kaipo launched into her plea, told horrific tales of mutilated corpses and crime scenes she'd remediated with multiple dead organ donors.

She ended with, "... and selling any of your organs will bring you up close and personal with the people I used to work for. Organized crime, Birdy. Good money, yes, but from bad people. Too risky. If there are problems with the surgery, honey, you don't get patched up, you don't get to walk away."

Two more glasses of iced tea sealed it. Birdy accepted the gun, the bullet clip, and Kaipo's quick tutorial on how to load it, fire, and release the clip. Plus Kaipo's advice about not risking her life on the operating table for cash.

A worthwhile visit. It was now sometime after eight p.m. A good time for Kaipo to go.

"When can we expect Aiata to get back to Kauai from wherever she's been hanging out?" Birdy said from her front door. "So we can maybe have a medication-free girls' night out?"

"Not anytime soon, Birdy, sorry," Kaipo said. "And the less you know about my whereabouts, the better, hon. My ride's here. Always know that I love you, homie. Always."

Kaipo climbed into the back seat with her belongings, gave her Uber driver a different address than she'd arranged for the ride. "You okay with the change?" she asked him. It was a hotel and spa in Lihue.

"Yes, ma'am. Nice place, if I recall," the driver said.

"If I recall, too," she said under her breath. She watched Birdy through the rear window of the SUV, Birdy waving as they pulled away.

The visit to Birdy: overkill? Arming her, telling her what could be in store for her, talking her out of doing something as stupid as maybe walking into the lion's den for some short-term cash infusion... no, not overkill.

They arrived at the hotel, her Uber parking at the guest drop-off in front of the lobby entrance. The French provincial, with rooms in the main building and elsewhere on the property, housed a massive two-story lobby. Another sugar plantation conversion. She paid the driver in cash, climbed out, and was met by a hotel doorman.

"Take your bag and backpack inside, ma'am?"

"Bag yes, the backpack I'm keeping." She handed him a tip. "I'll be inside in a minute."

Her Uber left. Kaipo wandered to the end of the sidewalk, made a turn at the corner of the building, stopped. She eyed a separate building at the deepest end of the parking lot, one story, a bunkhouse in a former life. Guest VIP digs. She narrowed her eyes in the twilight. A large man sat on a deck chair out front in a tight suit, his phone monopolizing his interest.

A bodyguard.

The car in the space in front of the bunkhouse—an SUV limo, in gold—closed the deal for her. Wally Lanakai liked gold limos. In Wally Lanakai's past life, he also loved this hotel.

Tomorrow, if she still had the balls to do this, she'd march in to see him. Would have him call off whatever the hell he was doing related to these grotesque murders; possibly related to him looking for her.

One overkill aspect. If she was right about this, about approaching Wally, then Birdy and the other Miakamiians out there, wherever they were, would be safe, the Glock she gave Birdy not necessary. If she was wrong, and something else was going on, well, better safe than sorry. Either way she'd need to have a heart-to-heart with Wally regarding their future together, or lack thereof, and let whatever was going to happen between them happen.

Time to check into the hotel. Head down, she about-faced and thumbed her phone as she walked, caught herself in mid-stride just before plowing into a man in her path.

Japanese. Broad shoulders beneath a small smile. "Oh. Sorry, sir, I wasn't paying attention—"

The last thing she remembered after the pinprick to her shoulder was hearing someone speaking on a phone saying he got her bag from the lobby.

Kaipo felt the leather against her cheek, her head against the seat, her nose against the car door. Her mind was a wandering, unsettled mess.

What'd he give me, damn it...

"A derivative of the Michael Jackson drug."

Someone sitting next to her, a man... she'd asked the question aloud. Her fuzzy head processed the answer, translating it.

Propofol? The anesthetic?

Again what she thought was a mental response, wasn't.

"Propofol-lite. The real stuff could kill you. We'll be there in a minute. What a beautiful, starry night you will be missing."

Her mind latched onto something else. Getting injected with a propofol derivative meant she hadn't relapsed. A small comfort. The thought stayed a thought only, no comment from her kidnapper.

She struggled to sit up, her wrists and ankles wrapped in duct tape, her head burdened by a massive headache.

"We're here," he said. "Don't try to stand, I'll carry you."

Inside a motel room, he laid her on a twin bed. Three men, her guess Japanese, surrounded her, one at the foot of the bed, the others on each side. The one who carried her in pulled up a side chair, began speaking.

"Stay calm, do not scream, or we will tape your mouth shut. Not that anyone would hear you; we booked all the rooms in this wing of the motel. Oyabun will be here to see you momentarily."

They waited. Kaipo faded in and out, then was out for the count.

Her eyes opened, her body aching. The same man sat in the chair next to the bed, but behind him a slender man occupied a wing chair, his legs crossed, his hands folded in his lap.

Her face and body were softly lit by sunlight through a window. The man in the wing chair spoke, his voice calm and even. "Good morning, miss."

"What time is it?" Kaipo said through cotton-mouthed lips.

"Seven a.m. You slept through the night." He handed off what he was looking at. "Show her the photo."

The bedside associate thrust a photograph in her face. In it a woman sat ringside at what appeared to be a boxing ring at a casino. The man sitting next to her in the photo had his arm on the back of her chair, was smiling, but the woman had an I-can't-be-bothered look.

"You are this woman," the man in the wing chair said. "You are a part of Ka Hui. You are with Wally Lanakai. You are Kaipo Mawpaw, correct?"

"No. I'm... my name is Aiata Hauata. I'm visiting friends... I'm... please, let me go..."

"That is bullshit. You are Kaipo Mawpaw, and Wally Lanakai is desperately combing the islands for you. You mean something to him—a lot, I suspect. Except, I also suspect, he does not mean the same to you."

She got it now. They were watching Wally. Watching him, interested in him, probably not liking him. He'd spent a long time away from the islands—more than a decade. Time for other players, other organized crime factions, to materialize in Hawaii, to get a footing.

Like from Japan.

"I... Wally Lanakai and I were business associates," she said, "but not any longer. That's all. I needed to disappear. Be away from him. Not something that's easy to do. Why are you doing this? Why kidnap me?"

"Remove the tape," he barked to the bedside thug. Moments later, Kaipo's wrists and ankles were free. "Sit over here." He gestured at a wing chair on the other side of the floor lamp.

She sat as requested, rubbing her wrists, wary of her inquisitor.

"I will give you more information than you are entitled to, Ms. Mawpaw. Listen carefully and understand. I am Mr. Yabuki. I am oyabun of the Yamazuki clan. You might know us as the Yakuza. Your association with Ka Hui has put you in a bad position, and me in a rather good one. I want Ka Hui out of the islands, and you will help me accomplish this."

And suddenly she saw a way out of this. Yes. A very simple way out. "I'm more than a simple bargaining chip, Mr. Yabuki," she said. "I'm your solution."

"And the solution as you see it is what? Why you were there, at his hotel? To see him? To sacrifice yourself? That is your solution?"

Her confidence waned with his assessment, but she had to bite. "Yes. To plead with him to stop what he's doing. To stop exploiting people. To leave the islands again. With me, if that's what he wanted." The last statement she hadn't quite come to grips with, but there it was.

Mr. Yabuki sipped some bottled water, analyzing her. "Get her something to drink."

A bottle of water appeared. She sipped.

"I find this interesting," Mr. Yabuki said. "You are willing to sacrifice yourself. A very honorable gesture. Honor is a trademark of the Yakuza, as I'm sure you know. The days of the Samurai." Another sip of his water, then he put his bottle aside. He folded his hands between his knees and leaned forward, into her space.

"But *your* solution is not how this is going to go. You are naïve, Ms. Mawpaw. He won't leave the islands after he finds you. He's a businessman, like I am. He's just starting his operation again. Mr. Lanakai needs bigger incentives to leave. *Much* bigger incentives. Like threats of exposure about what he's doing, or what it *looks* like he's doing—"

She shuddered as an image hit her. The man taking pictures of Vena's place. Of Kaipo, arriving there. He was Japanese, not Hawaiian. Was Yakuza, was there framing Wally.

"—and the permanent loss of something he covets. You. He wants to find you, Ms. Mawpaw, and he will. In pieces, all over Kauai. Unless he agrees to leave the islands permanently."

She lost her composure, her temper boiling over. Her fingers tightened into a fist that delivered a short, sudden punch to Mr. Yabuki's pointy jaw, then she got up in his face. "You killed Vena... you *gutted* her...!"

The two thugs pounced, ripped a screaming Kaipo away from their boss, subdued her and duct-taped her again, this time her mouth included.

Mr. Yabuki wiped blood from his mouth with a handkerchief, stood over her on the floor while she mumbled and kicked and squirmed.

"That was a mistake, Kaipo Mawpaw-san."

An afternoon of sun and sand, beachside. Multiple bottles of beer were working their way out of Philo's system courtesy of a sunbathing sweat, a hard swim along the coastline, and trips to the head to relieve himself. Philo and Patrick had their lobster dinners delivered to their cabana, the Hawaiian sunset overwhelming while they noshed. Patrick, quite the lobster-eating machine much like he was quite the Philly cheesesteak-eating machine, pulled chunk after chunk of meat from monster lobster claws and dipped them into the butter. Philo, on the home stretch with his meal, began pontificating.

"We need a lot more of this, Patrick, and a lot less time doing..." Better to keep the gore of recent experiences out of the dinner conversation. "You know, the other stuff."

"Yes, Philo sir. More lobster, more sun, more beach and ocean, less dead bodies, sir."

"Not the way I would have put it, Patrick, but yes, that's what I meant."

And not the time for this incoming phone call from Evan. Good hearing from him, bad hearing what he had to say.

"Another one," Evan said.

The beach and the sun and the sea fell away, blanked out by horrific visions of more blood, more gore, and the despair he heard in Evan's voice. Beyond grief, beyond shock, Evan was experiencing an accumulation of tragic events, including news Philo had already had a hand in delivering, the first to tell him about the second home invasion, where one of Evan's female contractors at the Navy base had also been eviscerated.

"There are no words," Evan said, sounding spent. "You have to see this. I'll pick you up."

Philo and Patrick slid into a military Jeep, Evan driving. Evan's additional input: wear long pants, comfortable hiking shoes, long sleeves and hats, and soak yourselves in bug spray. He'd followed his own advice, his gear all Navy issue, including his sidearm.

"You carrying?" Evan said.

Philo rode shotgun, his bulky shirt resettled over the holstered handgun tucked under it, above his ass cheeks. Patrick was buckled up in the back seat. "You sounded serious," Philo said, "so yes."

"It's fucked up, Philo, it's all so seriously fucked up. I wouldn't tell you not to. We'll be there in twenty minutes. Then we walk."

Their destination: Kauai's Alakai Swamp. Evan steered onto a highway, began giving them a short verbal sketch of the terrain they would encounter.

"One of the wettest spots on the planet. Otherworldly. The world's highest rainforest and swampland. People hike two miles through an open valley on dirt trails to get to the swamp, where the terrain changes. We'll bypass the dirt, head directly to the boardwalk in the swamp itself. A few miles of skinny planks and terraced platforms and steps, and rocks. As the tourists say, 'fun.'"

It was on Philo's list of touristy spots for Patrick and him to experience. In Philo's way of thinking, terrific postcard-worthy scenery.

"We won't need to hike the entire trail," Evan said. "Part of what's out there is on the first half of the boards only."

"Part of it?" Philo asked. "It's spread out?"

"Across a few miles of it. What you'll see when we get there is an all-Navy response so far, no police."

"Why no cops?"

"No cops *yet*. That early-warning crisis event I had to attend to—what shorted out our taco lunches—we thought it was saber rattling by the North Koreans, showing off new missile capabilities. It wasn't. Took us a bit, but we figured it out. It was drones. A fucking squadron of them."

"Doing what?"

"Deliveries."

They reached the entrance to a state park. Evan idled the truck, showed his credentials to a saluting Navy seaman behind a wooden roadblock. They parked amid other military Jeeps and vans, got out. Evan snagged a small thermal-lined shoulder bag with bottled water and an ice pack in it, gave them each a flashlight. Still twilight for their walk on the way in, but it would be dark on the way out. "Let's hit the boards."

Cloud cover had moved in, was met at ground level by an enveloping mist. Evan's boots clip-clopped along the planks, Philo and Patrick in sneakers behind him. "Eyes open, gentlemen. Hoary bats in these parts. It's getting dark, so they'll be out. You won't miss them. Wingspans of a foot or more."

Philo knew about them from SEAL exercises throughout the islands, way back when.

"*Ōpe'ape'a*," Patrick said. "That's what they're called in the islands, Commander sir."

"Exactly," Evan said. "As long as there are enough insects, the bats won't be a bother. And God knows there are enough insects out here." He swatted at his face, leaned forward, squinted into the distance. "Up ahead is our first stop."

Two armed seamen stood side by side on the middle of three small, cantilevered wooden platforms. They snapped to attention when their CO got close. Between them, an electric lantern. Behind them, tangled in the overgrowth, head high, was a drone the size of a go-kart, with four black rotors outboard of a plastic body. Its payload was firmly in the grasp of its mechanical red claws, a Styrofoam cooler that had snapped apart at the bottom like it was a wafer cookie.

"At ease, sailors. Step aside, we need a closer look."

Evan marched Philo and Patrick to the edge of the platform, their flashlights blazing. Philo's jaw dropped. The cooler had birthed its contents onto the muddy floor of the swamp.

"That what I think it is?" Philo asked.

"If you're thinking it's a woman's severed head," Evan said, "then yes."

Dark skin, short black hair, open black eyes, swollen cheeks, unhinged jaw. Polynesian-Hawaiian. The decapitation appeared clean, a one-and-done blow across the neck as effective as a guillotining. Philo got into a crouch, focused his torch to examine it more closely.

"Jesus, Evan." Philo leaned left, tilted his head to see it at a different angle. Flies and other insects were starting to accumulate on the skin, wandering inside the nose. "When will the police be here?"

"Probably like right now. We held off calling it in long enough. Orders from my superiors, trying to gauge if there was a national security threat." Evan gestured at the planking laid out in front of them, leading north. "This was one delivery that didn't work. There were others that did. We need to keep moving."

"Is there? A national security issue?"

"Someone's screwing with the U.S. Navy, but we think no. Let's go."

Fifty yards into the next leg, Evan spoke freely, Philo shadowing him step by step. "We'll take the drone, let the police examine it at the base if they want to. We've already confirmed the protocol."

"I have to say, Evan," Philo said, "if someone is using drones like the one I just saw, this seems like a local breach."

"Right you are, Chief, one might think that. And the Navy thinks they know who it is, generally speaking. Me, I have my own theory. Here we are, the next platform."

Two more armed seamen, another lantern between them, more saluting. No drone, but another Styrofoam container, this one sitting uncovered and flat in the mud, abutting the platform, the lid missing. Three flashlights provided a look inside. A jumble of arm and leg parts, two of each, had been cut to fit the container.

"We're not done yet, men." Evan handed them each a bottle of cold water. "Hitch up your jockeys," he said, sipping, "our next stop is about a mile away."

Sparse chatting between the three of them, their flashlights swaying, their bug spray bath failing to keep away the insects they walked into. Evan gestured with his flashlight at a swarm of hovering bugs of unknown species. Within seconds a flurry of flapping wings announced their predators, swooping in for a nighttime meal.

"Hoary bats, two o'clock. Keep moving."

A flickering lantern beckoned them forward to the next stop. Same M.O., guards, guns, salutes, and an open Styrofoam container sitting on the ground within reach of another platform, and again, no drone.

"The final delivery, men."

They illuminated the inside of the white cooler with their flashlights. Buzzing flies feasted on their swampy picnic: a headless, armless, legless female torso. And on closer inspection—

"The internal organs are gone," Philo said.

"And this, my good Chief," Evan said, "is why I want Wally Lanakai's head on a silver platter."

Philo and Patrick leaned in, looked over the cooler's gory interior, the remainder of the woman unceremoniously dumped into the wild. This whole situation—someone had a flair for the dramatic, was Philo's assessment. The three containers spread out along this swamp trail—again, like with the other bodies, no one was trying to hide anything. On the contrary, someone was making a point.

"I don't think it's Lanakai, Evan. It might be someone trying to call attention to him, but it's not him."

"Not buying it, Philo. You yourself said he's into organ trafficking..."

"In Philly he cleaned up after himself. He had people to do that for him, to make crime scenes disappear, like what I do legally. This... this is nuts."

"Goddamn it, Philo." Evan paced the planks. "I am losing my mind over this—"

"Give me the other theory, bud."

"What other theory, damn it?"

"What does the Navy think is going on?"

Evan removed his naval cap, un-gritted his teeth. Exhausted, he surrendered to the question. "It could be the Yakuza. Or an offshoot of the Yakuza."

A blast from the past. A rumor as old as Philo's early SEAL

training days in Hawaii. A ruthless, dangerous cult, with origins among the Samurai, and organized to the hilt in Japan. But in Hawaii?

"In Kauai and around the other islands. They've terrorized the Japanese population here. Occasional beat-downs that make the news. They make examples of people, especially if someone helps the Navy in any way, for reasons unknown. I also heard that they're crazy brutal. A severe, more radical strain."

Which was what Philo also remembered hearing. "No ceremonial hara-kiri or seppuku, like in the old days," Philo added. "They behead people, even their own."

"Rumored, yes."

Flashlights approached from farther up the trail. "This will be the police," Evan said. "Our monopoly on the Alakai Swamp Trail is over, gentlemen. We're better off taking the trail forward and saying hello to them. I can get someone to pick us up at the end—"

Craaack-craaack-craaack went a handgun, piercing shots from behind them, deafening, echoing, causing Philo and Evan to draw their weapons. The flashlights in front of them on the trail started forward in a rush. Philo and Evan turned to see one of his seamen standing with his arms extended, his gun pointed at the ground, in the direction of the cooler.

"Sorry, Captain sir," the seaman said, "but the evidence was about to disappear into the swamp—"

The human torso had been dragged out of the cooler, onto the swampy mud. Three large, expired rats with bullet holes lay next to the torso.

"I hate those Pacific rat bastards, sir."

20

Sunrise on Mii Landing, the north shore of Miakamii Island. Ella grabbed her spot on the beach, the fourth chair of fifteen, each chair decades old, jutting from the sand like the statues of Easter Island and distant enough inland from the shore to avoid the tides. Carved out of large redwood trees from California that came ashore worn but well-preserved, from transpacific trips on ocean currents pushed by the winds, the natives planted them upright near where they beached, then hollowed them out. The shell lei makers, called stringers, brought their blankets and down-filled cushions to lessen the discomfort of the hundred-year-old hardwood seating. The fifteen seats were arranged in a semi-circle on the coastline close enough to each other for socializing. But this morning, as was the case for so many mornings of late, Ella would be the only craftsperson plying the trade at dawn on the beach. Today she'd finish her work on two shell leis, stringing them together, then knotting and tying off these wonderful, colorful jewels of the ocean, these *pupu O Miakamii*.

Ella placed her tools on a soft cloth she'd set on the sand. First was a handmade poker five inches in length with a cylindrical burnished-wood handle, the metal poking end used to make the tiniest holes in the tiniest of shells for the insertion of nylon thread. Next to the poker was a metal awl with a thin needle used to thread the nylon. Next to the tools, she set up bowls of shells of various sizes, colors, and shapes. With the softest of touches she went to work, removing every grain of sand from each shell, some of them no larger than a piece of rice. The art of collecting and sewing these rare shells into leis had been handed down generation to generation from her ancestral *kupuna*. Ella was a master craftsperson in a long line of master craftspeople.

She missed her friends, the women who occupied the other fourteen chairs when times were better and work was plentiful, and who had abandoned the shell trade in favor of other endeavors. Ella would complete two leis today, each about eighteen inches in length so they would sit properly on the neck. It had been weeks of tedious work per lei, but these two were already sold, for three thousand and thirty-five-hundred dollars respectively, one for a Hawaiian wedding, the other to celebrate the birth of a child. Mr. Logan brokered the work for them, no middleman fees involved, a complete pass-through to the artist, part of the pleasure he got from helping his islanders with their livelihood.

Ella began her workday as she did every day, with a prayer to Jesus Christ Her Savior, and she would end her work on the leis with a prayer to Him as well.

She closed out two hours of tedious poking and stringing and put her tools down for a break. Calling to her was the food satchel she'd brought with her, a bushel of mollusks in a burlap sack. At eight a.m. the smelly bushel became Ella's breakfast, some of the small shells viable for other types of leis after she consumed their contents. One shucking knife, one plate, one empty satchel awaiting shells that were too large for leis, and one hungry mouth awaiting the snail meat from the mollusks of all shapes and sizes. Ella shucked, pulled, sniffed, shuddered, slurped, and swallowed.

Ten minutes into her meal, Ella had surrounded herself with spent shells. She relaxed, releasing a hearty burp that brought with it a satisfied smile.

If a tree falls in a forest, and no one is around to hear it...

Behind her, an animal snorted from the scrub brush. The philosophical had begotten a material response.

A wild boar stepped onto the beach, wandered in close to her chair, its curved tusks ominous, its eyes shifty. Another snort followed another step, its boar nose inching closer to her pile of mollusk shells surrounding her in the sand. It nudged the shells, hesitated. Ella and the boar eyed each other in silence, a long moment that ended with Ella speaking.

"Go ahead, have some," she said.

The boar chomped into the pile, slurped at what remained of the mollusk meat, and crunched the shells with its powerful teeth. Seconds later it stopped, began gagging and sneezing and coughing. After a herky-jerky about-face it expelled the chewed bounty, squealed, and left the beach in a hefty trot.

"Ha!" she called after it. "Same as last week, and the week before. Serves you right, my lovely *puaa* friend. You know better. Stick with the oysters and the potatoes."

Snails from the waters surrounding the island became mollusk meat that was, at best, an acquired taste. It had taken centuries of digestive adaptation and intestinal fortitude by their harvesters to enjoy the delicacy without striking the entire Miakamii population dead from consuming it. The boar should have identified it from the pungent smell inside the shells, something that could take a person's breath away: hydrogen sulfide, the "rotten eggs" odor, boosted by gases from volcanic eruptions and hot springs emanating from deep within the earth. Eons upon eons where the earth's magma had coughed up its poisonous, dangerous content, with lava exploding into the atmosphere, lava colonizing the soil, and lava streaming into the ocean, all of it settling in the local ecosystem, in the flora and the fauna, and in the seafood.

Ella finished her parting words for the wild *puaa*'s retreat by chiding the boar for its short memory, thanking it for not partaking in her breakfast—"more for us Miakamiians, my lovely"—then adding her heartfelt condolences, with the Sign of the Cross, on the loss of its momma, one of the casualties of the helicopter crash.

21

They were met at the pasture gate for Mr. Logan's Kapilimao Valley ranch by two *paniolo* on horses, the island's version of cowboys, if Philo's memory served, clearly with a strong Mexican influence. The horse and cowboy escorts accompanied their SUV slowly up the trail, dust scattering amid their slow trot.

"Mr. Logan can help, Patrick. He says he's got tons of records. Maybe he can trace things back."

"Maybe, sir. Those hats, sir. The *paniolo* hats?"

"The sombreros? What about them?"

"I just remembered something, sir. Where they keep their guns. Small holsters inside their hats, sir."

One couldn't miss their bandoliers, each cowboy's chest crisscrossed with multiple bullet clips, but the corresponding guns weren't visible on the cowboys' persons. Handguns in hats was an affectation Philo always thought silly from his earlier days in training on the islands.

"Yes. One under their shirt, one inside their boot, one inside their sombrero, bud." The SUV rolled along, Philo pressing only slightly on the gas pedal. Funeral dirge speed. "Silly, right?"

"Nope. Lightweight Sigs. Plenty effective."

Philo waited for Patrick to finish his statement, to close it off with a "sir" or a "Philo sir." When it didn't come—

"Tell me why, Patrick. What do you remember?"

"About what, sir?"

And they were back.

"Why guns inside a hat would be effective."

"Head-to-toe firepower, sir. Waist, foot, head. I... I saw it work, sir."

"When?"

A flustered Patrick picked at the hem of his shorts. "Collection day. When I was a kid. They... someone pulled the driver out of the car I was in."

"They pulled out your dad?"

"Maybe. I was nine. No, ten. Someone dragged him out, took the laundry bag with the money, put a gun to his head. On Nawiliwili Road. He had, umm, just come out of the gym. We were stopped at a vegetable stand, and... and..."

"What, Patrick?"

"This guy... this guy holding a sombrero to his chest, talking with the vegetable farmer's daughter, he... he dropped the hat, showed two guns in his hands, then shot the guy robbing the driver. Sir."

Robbing your bagman dad, Philo thought, but he didn't say it.

"He saved his life, sir."

They pulled into Douglas Logan's ranch home driveway. "We're here."

Douglas Logan spoke from behind his desk, small towers of file folders piled left and right of him, one folder open in the middle. Philo and Patrick occupied the chairs fronting the desk.

"Here are the results of the 2000 and 2010 censuses for Miakamii." Mr. Logan removed paper from the folder, placed it in front of Patrick. "Take a look at it, Mr. Stakes, so we can get our bearings."

Philo and Patrick leaned in.

Total Miakamii population had declined between the censuses by thirty people, from 160 to 130. The names and genders of all the inhabitants for both censuses were on the spreadsheet. Five had died. Which meant twenty-five had moved off the island. There had been no births.

"I knew all the people on the island, but I can't say I could have matched every face to every name. I can say that I don't remember you as any of these people, Mr. Stakes, in either census, but I'm getting old, and my memory is suspect nowadays. You can keep that. There's also this."

He moved another folder front and center to him on the desk, opened it, scanned the first page. "The Island of Kauai censuses for the same years. Here are some comparisons where we can see the names of every person in each census for Kauai who listed Miakamii as their birthplace. Some of the twenty-five people who left Miakamii aren't on the Kauai census because they moved elsewhere, or they died. Again, if you or your family were among the people who moved from Miakamii to Kauai, I can't validate that. I'm sorry."

Patrick's eyes had glazed over, but Philo understood the net of it. These lists weren't definitive enough in divining Patrick's parents without having census data on all fronts for each year, for Miakamii, the other Hawaiian Islands, and the mainland, where Patrick ended up.

He patted Patrick on the shoulder. "We'll have to wait, bud, for the Ancestry results to come in. Might still happen while we're here. Grace and Hank will let us know."

"But Philo sir. Look at this list," Patrick said.

Philo looked over his shoulder. "What about it?"

"These people, sir. Her, her, him, and him. We know their names, sir."

"He's right, Trout. The four murders—my friend Chester, Captain Malcolm's fiancée Miya, the Navy contractor Vena Akina, and Ichigoo the street performer—they were all transplants from Miakamii."

A concern hit Philo dead nuts: Logan didn't recognize Patrick as a Miakamii transplant, but he couldn't be sure that he wasn't one, either, and Miakamiians were dropping like flies.

"You need a gun, Patrick," Philo said.

"Sir, I can't—they won't sell one to me—"

"I'll take care of it. There's a fifth death, Mr. Logan. The cops and the Navy are looking into it." Philo perused the list further, wondering if the fifth murder victim, another gutted woman, her name unknown, was on it. "Her body parts were dropped by drones all over the Alakai Swamp. The Navy found them two nights ago, next to the trail. The cops, they're trying to ID her—"

Philo arrived at the last name on the list. His face blanched.

"Holy fuck..."

"Trout, that language is not acceptable around here. I ask that you please refrain..."

Philo held the list up to Patrick and pointed.

"Holy fuck," Patrick said.

"Gentlemen, language, please!"

"Sorry, Mr. Logan, but you need to tell us more about this woman, the last person on this list. Kaipo Mawpaw. Do you know her?"

22

Fresh from his surgical chop shop, where his doctors found a home for a partial liver with an opera star from the sixties and seventies, Wally had Magpie drive them back to the hotel. He was exhausted, having held the woman's hand all through surgery prep, then for an hour after she woke up. Eight p.m.-ish on a warm night, Magpie made the turn into the hotel parking lot, coasted down an incline in the direction of their VIP luxury accommodations. A few limo lengths forward he had to jam the breaks, jolting Wally.

"Magpie, I told you, screw those crazy chickens, damn it—"

In the limo's headlights a drone hovered, white lights trimming its arms, red lights blinking underneath, the white rectangular package held in its claws mesmerizing them. Then Wally came to his senses.

"Shoot it down."

Magpie drew his weapon, couldn't get out of the car fast enough. The package dropped onto the asphalt, the drone humming skyward, into the darkening night.

Another white cooler. Wally threw open his door, drew his

own semiauto handgun, and took aim, shooting wildly at the drone as it gained altitude, his gunfire too passionate for accuracy. He stood there breathing hard, cursing loudly. He climbed back inside the car. His phone rang.

"What?" he screamed into the receiver.

Not just an audio call, but rather a video connection, and he found himself staring at a Japanese man with a thin, disinterested face that seemed the antithesis of excitable.

"My, my," the man said, "aren't we a bit testy."

"Who the hell are you, asshole?"

"Someone you would like to talk to. I am Yabuki, oyabun of a Yamazuki clan."

"*Who*?"

"You know me as 'Y.' Head of a Yakuza family. I left you another offering. I believe it was just delivered."

"You Yakuza sonovabitch!" Wally yelled, expelling spit. "You're setting me up! I don't want your fucking body parts. When I get a hold of you—"

"You must calm down, Lanakai-san. I have the greatest respect for you and your work here in the islands, past and present. I have a friendly proposition arising from this respect, in addition to the couple of million dollars or so that I've already handed you in human livers. What I have in mind is an event that will celebrate the passing of the scepter from one ruling family to another, yours to mine. A competition. It will involve a wager in a sport I know interests you greatly. Would you care to join me in promoting a bareknuckle boxing match?"

Wally's anger had him hurling obscenities at the screen; the fucking nerve of this guy, this spindly-looking Japanese fuck whose head Wally knew he could pinch off at the neck with one hand.

"Fuck off, Yabuki! I'm not interested! And quit making me

look like a ruthless prick, murdering people from Miakamii. Stop this shit—"

"I can tell from your fervor that you would like to meet me, correct? A bareknuckle fight will accomplish this. So, why don't we—"

"Lose my fucking number," Wally said, and hung up, winging his phone onto the floor. "Goddamn it…"

The phone rang again, another video chat request from the same caller. Wally let it ring, Magpie saying nothing from the front seat. Ring, ring, ring…

Wally picked up the phone. "Listen, you Yakuza prick—"

Yabuki said nothing, his grim face visible for only a moment on the screen, repositioning the phone to replace his image with a photograph he held in his hand. It was the picture of Kaipo Mawpaw that Wally had given cockfight promoter Shiko, asking for her help in finding her.

Wally started forward, gasped. "What the hell…"

"So. Now that I have your attention," Yabuki said, "the bareknuckle fight was only part of the reason I called. It gives us a reason to meet. The good news, Lanakai, is that we found your former associate, Ms. Mawpaw, and we intend to return her to you. The bad news is it will be in pieces, so you will at least make some money off her organs while we continue to frame you for these murders…"

"Yabuki, you motherfucking piece of shit—!"

"… unless you leave the islands for good. The hell with you and your Ka Hui crime family. Hawaii is mine. Oh. Here. This is also for your viewing pleasure."

The next photo Yabuki held up took Wally's breath away. Kaipo was doubled over at the waist and on her knees on a bed, the side of her head flat against a mattress, her grimacing face visible. A leather strap encircled her neck, with more leather straps connecting her wrists to the headboard, her arms fully extended. She was naked from the waist down, a side shot of one butt cheek. What made Wally nearly choke on his tongue: a Japanese man knelt behind her on the bed, his pants off, ready to mount her from behind, his face looking into the camera, smiling and giving a thumbs-up.

"Tell me what you want," Wally said, seething.

"I already have what I want. Your bitch. This photo is only a few minutes old, Lanakai. I will stop this... situation—there are more men in line, out of the picture—if you agree to the bareknuckle fight. My man against whoever you put up. So here are the terms. If you don't take the fight, you get her back in pieces, and we throw you out of Hawaii by any means or condition necessary. If you do take the fight, and you lose, you will still get her back in pieces, and you agree to leave Hawaii and stay out. If you take the fight and win, she gets returned to you whole, but you still need to leave. Capisce?"

Wally pursed his lips and scowled into the camera. "Deal, motherfucker." He gritted his teeth; he had more to say. "And when I do win, before I leave the islands, I will have you bound up in leather just the way Ms. Mawpaw is here, and then I will force your men to mount you, and I will listen to you squeal and cry like a baby when they insert their micro dicks into your ass. Or I'll just kill you myself."

The call ended, no other terms of the fight discussed. Magpie was quick to comment, leaning his bulk over the front seat.

"Boss, I am at your service. I volunteer for the fight. I fear no man. I will crush whoever his fighter is. You know I'm good for it."

Wally stared out the window, analyzing what had just happened, taking shallow breaths, trying to calm himself. "We need to get this organized fast. Bring that cooler inside the car and let's get back."

"Boss—"

"They are going to kill her, Magpie."

Wally contemplated what would need to happen next, what his new priority was, and how he would prepare to handle it.

"I do not doubt that you would lay down your life for Ka Hui, and for me, Magpie. You are a good man. But I have someone else in mind."

23

Philo recognized drunk texts when he saw them, sometimes simply by their timing. Anything after midnight would always be suspect. He'd received them from women he'd dated long-term, from women who'd been one-night stands, and occasionally from wingmen he'd frequented the bars with over the years. He'd authored enough of them himself, after nights of debauchery celebrating bareknuckle fights where he'd earned large purses, or after SEAL missions he could never tell anyone about, having drunk himself into oblivion to ease the physical beating he'd taken to earn those purses, or complete those missions. But this one, this text arriving 11:37 p.m. from one former wingman in particular, was heartbreaking.

I am in pain, Evan's text said.

He had Evan's home address, near Poipu Beach in Koloa, a gated condo community a half block from the ocean. Its hip-roofed building housed single-floor residences with gorgeous tropical architecture in soft greens and blues, and bright white wood framing that gleamed in the moonlight.

Another late night for Philo, which was becoming routine in its exclusion of the kind of company, female, that he was hankering for when he'd booked this Hawaiian junket. To his knowledge, Patrick had no experience in talking people off precipices, so Philo would have him sit this excursion out.

Evan opened the door to his condo, stood at the threshold in gray boxer jockeys and a Gold's Gym beater tee in yellow. He leaned severely starboard, the doorjamb keeping him upright.

"C'mon in, you SOB," he said fondly. "Beer's in the fridge."

Beer was not what Evan was drinking. A fifth of tequila was nearly empty on the coffee table, a couple shots of the crystal-white liquid in Evan's tumbler, then in Evan's mouth. The TV was off, no music on the stereo. His only company, the only diversion of consequence, was his unholstered sidearm next to the tequila. Even in its silence, the handgun had the loudest speaking part in the scene. Philo popped open a bottle of beer, tossed the cap into the sink, and sat across from his intoxicated friend in a tufted chair.

"I'd ask you to talk to me, Evan, but I don't want you to feel any more pain than what you're feeling already. How can I help?"

"Less pain since I sent you that text. That bottle's been a help." He drained his glass, poured the equivalent of another few shots into the tumbler. "Sumpin to show you. Came tonight, special delivery."

"Where's your holster?"

"The study."

"That's where your sidearm belongs. I'm taking your gun. Be back in a minute."

Philo walked one way with the gun, Evan wobbled another. When Philo returned, Evan was shoving papers out of the way to close an inch-thick binder on the dining room table, many pages dog-eared. He stumbled back into the living room with the binder and dropped it into Philo's lap. "Start reading."

"What am I looking at?"

"Miya and her team's research. A draft version. I'll wait."

"Evan, give me a hint. What am I looking for?"

"She had the goods. She validated the rumors. She and her research team had the proof. The solution."

"The solution to what?"

"Alzheimer's. Read."

Philo started paging through the binder, deciphering what he could. The clinical trials. The subjects, from Miakamii, from Kauai, from the other islands, and from the mainland. The blood work. The health records. The lab test results. Medical data going back fifty-plus years. The chemical analyses. The brain scans. Philo took only cursory glances at each sheet, not understanding much. An impatient Evan tried standing up from the couch, fell onto his knees, pulled himself into a crawl, and closed the short distance between them.

"You're taking too long, damn it." He dragged the binder off Philo's lap, slobbered on his fingers to moisten them, then turned page after page from the seat of his pants while squinting at the print. He stopped to jab a finger at the paper in front of him. "Here, goddamn it. Right—the hell—here."

Findings, the heading said. Next heading, *Recommendations*. Next heading, *Impacts*.

"They can cure it, Philo. But there'll be some unintentional —*(burp)* unintended—consequences."

Philo reviewed the summary info and charts, all too technical for him, but he got the gist.

Dr. Miya Ainaloli and her team had unlocked the genetic coding, had isolated the part of the DNA string that kept Miakamiians from getting sick from the disease. And they showed proof that the amazing chemical factory nature of the Miakamii human liver originated from the ingestion of the "meat of the momi," the small snails who created the beautiful "pearls of the Pacific" molluscan shells. It was not the handling of the shells that provided the immunity; it was generation after generation of eating the detestable mollusk meat. Specifically, Miakamiian mollusk meat, whose high hydrogen sulfide content from eons of volcanic activity worked to reduce the oxidative stress on the human cells of the people who ate them. It helped their cells stay stronger, last longer, not break down, yet it did break down the amyloid plaques that were said to accumulate on the brain caused by advanced age, thereby reducing neurodegeneration. The stronger the snail's hydrogen sulfide content, the better the protection and the more effective the plaque removal, the research proved. It appeared that all Miakamiians had this protection.

The research team's recommendations: harvest the snail meat, break it down, atomize its hydrogen sulfide content, inject the little plaque scrubbers into the bloodstream, and watch 'em go.

Impacts, intermediate: potential depletion of natural resources in/around Miakamii; worse yet, potential depletion of Miakamii natives if nefarious types decided to go directly to the source. Impact, longer term, with smart administration: disease immunities spanning wider populations; a disease cure.

"You ever eat Miakamii snail meat, Philo? Miya fed the mollusks to me one time as a joke. Made me *(burp)* sick for days. 'Scuse me."

Evan pushed himself upright, stumble-rushed to his powder room, and lost his stomach contents to the porcelain. Philo found the overnight pouch that had delivered the clinical papers, found and read the typed note that accompanied the package addressed to Commander Evan Malcolm, who continued his heaving in the background.

Joke of the Day: Female Miakamii dog makes unanticipated personal organ donations to her own study; American mobster Lanakai transplants them; the U.S. Navy mourns. One slaughter, three bucket-list groups embarrassed: Miakamii Island, Ka Hui, and the U.S. military. What do you call this? A good start.

There couldn't have been enough alcohol in the house to numb the PTSD or blunt the anger that had arrived on Evan's doorstep with this package. Philo lifted his head in the direction of the powder room and listened; he heard snoring.

The key words from the note, Philo decided, were actually among the first few: *Miakamii dog.* Sending the scientific study to Evan... Philo felt it was an afterthought, the research findings a tangent. Of primary importance was the note-writer's opinion of Miakamii natives, calling them "dogs." Three more of these "dogs" had faced similar horrific treatment.

A second late-night text beeped on his phone. What other drunk was contacting him at two a.m.?

How would you like to make $100K, Philo?

The origin phone number meant nothing to him, but including his nickname in the text forced him to read it, not delete it outright like other spam. Additional texts followed the first, legitimizing his interest.

First class airfare to Hawaii. I'll cover your expenses.

Two weeks in the islands.

You need to come now.

This anonymous asshole now had Philo's attention. Philo texted back, *Who the hell is this?*

His phone chirped with a new text.

Wally Lanakai.

Chunky crime boss, murdering loudmouth. Crooked businessman. Grandiose gambler. Felon. Dangerous. Philo's eyes narrowed at the phone screen, his thumbs hovering, his blood pressure rising. Did he want to get into a conversation with this... criminal?

He would bite. The hell with texting. Philo called him.

"I thought you were back to jail, Lanakai. Where are you, and what do you want?"

"I'm in Hawaii. If you're smart, you'll hear me out, so don't hang up. It's worth a lot of money to you. I need you to fight someone, Trout. Bareknuckles. As a favor to me, but it will be for big money."

The balls on this guy. Philo shook his head, unimpressed. "You fucking kidding me? You're doing the same illegal transplant shit in Hawaii that you were doing in Philly. You ruined the life of one of my closest friends with your criminal organ trafficking. Lose my number, Lanakai, I'm not interested. By the way, I'm letting the cops know you contacted me."

"I wouldn't do that, Trout. I'll make it up to you and your friend, damn it. You have my word—"

"My friend's fiancée is *fucking dead*! An anonymous tip he just got says you're the reason."

"'Just got' means what? When did he get it?" Lanakai said.

"Today." Philo didn't mention the research docs that came with it.

"On my honor, I didn't kill any of those people, Trout."

"Someone out there is saying you did. You see the news? Three of them, all gutted like field-dressed deer, all on Kauai. My friend's fiancée was a research scientist..."

Philo detailed the horrific murders with the precision of a crime scene cleaner. "Now there's been a fourth. Her body parts were dropped around the Alakai Swamp after her evisceration. Too huge a coincidence that you're back in Hawaii and all these people are getting gutted and hacked up..."

"Trout, listen to me. I swear on my island ancestors that I did not kill those people. Someone is framing Ka Hui. They do the deed, then they deliver their organs to me..."

"Framing Ka Hui? A crime family you told me no longer exists? What do you do with the organs? I'm thinking they find their way into someone else's body for big payoffs—"

"That's not the point. The point is I'm not killing people and taking their organs..."

"I guess I don't really give a shit, Lanakai. The cops are onto Ka Hui, and I'm fine with letting that run its course."

"It's not me, Trout, goddamn it! It's the fucking Yakuza!"

Invoking that name low-bridged Philo, forced him to hit the reset button on the conversation. He knew the Yakuza, knew about them way back when he was a new Navy SEAL twenty years ago. You couldn't go out at night in the islands without seeing one or more of their head-case warriors terrorizing the nightclub owners. He'd found the Yakuza stereotyping to be true: slicked hair, sharp dressers, and full-body tattoos, genitalia included, something he'd personally validated in one barroom brawl involving saving a damsel in distress from a rape. Feared and revered, they were a menace to the Japanese-Hawaiian community, yet they occasionally acted as a benefactor. Classic mob family behavior. Steal you blind but hand out paper towels and water when your community gets hit with a hurricane.

And then there was the Yakuza affectation for severed pinkies: *yubitsume*, or "finger-shortening." An odd punishment for one indiscretion or another, removing the tip of the pinky finger on the left hand, penalizing Yakuza swordsmen from centuries past. A generations-old practice. Misplaced machismo. Idiots. Add to this their newfound fascination with the U.S. Navy per Evan...

"You tell me it's the Yakuza, and that's supposed to make

me enlist? You want to put me between *you* and *them*? I'd get killed in the crossfire. No thanks."

"Philo. Please." Lanakai's tone changed. Philo sensed the desperation, could almost see his pleading face. "They've got one of my associates. If I don't cooperate, she ends up like the others."

She, Lanakai said. A female prisoner held by a crime cult that prided itself in barbaric loyalty to its male-dominated organization. Things would not bode well for this "she," before, during, and after her death.

Philo's mind continued rebooting, recalculating. He needed more info, and Lanakai kept talking.

"You might remember her. She was with me the night of the Philly fight. She's a cleaner like you, except she works for me. Or she did."

She'd told Philo her name, then told him to forget it. Told him to forget her avocation, and to forget who she did it for. Knowing who she was, she'd said, would be too dangerous.

But Philo hadn't forgotten her; no way could he forget so kindred a soul. To not betray what he felt for her—it wasn't covetous or flirtatious, it was an affinity, an appreciation, an *understanding*—to not give Wally any sort of upper hand about her, he'd need to short circuit the rest of this discussion.

"I don't want a name. The less I know about her, the better. So here's the deal. It's your lucky day, Lanakai. I'm already in the islands on vacation. I will help you—"

He needed to keep Lanakai off balance. Needed to keep him from sensing any of Philo's personal connection to her. Better for him to come across like an opportunistic bastard.

"—for two hundred grand. Take it or leave it."

24

A handcuffed Kaipo paced in her room in the one-story wing of a shitty pay-by-the-hour Kauai motel. One double bed. Cable TV with every other channel pay-per-view porn. A bathroom with a painted cement floor that extended into the shower, the shower floor flush with the rest of the bathroom. Easy to clean with a hose, like at a gym or the penguin exhibit at the zoo.

Her use to the Yakuza so far had been a posed soft-core porn photo taken on a cell phone. A degrading picture, but no other harm done. A marketing photo meant for one customer only, as bait: Wally Lanakai.

A fist pounded on her door. "Step back," a man's voice said. "We're coming in."

With breakfast, she hoped. She did as she was told, moved away from the door. Two Japanese men entered, well-groomed in their dark suits and shined shoes. Conspicuous in one man's hands were leg irons and chains. The other man was the letch they'd posed her with in the racy photo, a big guy whose smile said he would totally enjoy seeing her in these chains.

"What, no breakfast?" she said.

"You will eat breakfast with the oyabun," the man with the leg irons said, "but you will need to wear these."

Mr. Yabuki's motel room was next to hers. They walked her in, her chains dragging. Better accommodations than hers, but not by much. The table had been set for two: flowers, napkins, Chinet dishware and utensils. The bags the food came in said Uber Eats, their contents filled with local mom-and-pop restaurant containers. A deadpan Mr. Yabuki, seated and already eating, gestured at his men with his fork to deposit her in the seat across from him. The cuffs and the leg irons came off, but the handguns came out, all trained on her.

"American comfort food plus some fruit and vegetables and some sushi," Mr. Yabuki said. "Eat."

She raised a fork; the guns followed its path. She put the fork down, pissed. Mr. Yabuki grunted in Japanese. The weapons returned to the holsters under their jackets.

"Let me begin. We are not animals, Ms. Mawpaw. We are businessmen. I brought you in here with me this morning to A, feed you some breakfast, B, update you that Wally Lanakai has been properly incented and is now mulling over a proposition I made that concerns you. He is still, by the way, quite attached to you. And C, you are here to understand what is happening. It is something much larger than me ridding the islands of Ka Hui." He glanced at her plate. "You are not eating. You need to eat."

She eyed the food, chose to address her host. "Wally will not stay in the islands. He's here to make a quick buck and to get leads on me, then leave. Law enforcement's been through this with him one time already, will never let him stay. Once he leaves"—she raised her fork, took a small bite—"the police will become more interested in *you*."

"Ms. Mawpaw." Mr. Yabuki continued to eat, chewing through his words. "That does not worry me. Our organization is bigger, older, smarter, and more venerable than anything Ka Hui ever was. We are flourishing."

"In Japan," she said. "Here in the islands, you're viewed as interlopers who should stay in their own lanes. Only the *nikkejin* revere you, afraid their Japanese-American heritage could betray them again. The rest of the islanders find you a pesky nuisance. A bug that needs to be squashed. The Feds eliminated Ka Hui first, with good reason. The *big* dogs. The cops will get around to you soon enough. They haven't yet because you never mattered."

Mr. Yabuki slowed his chewing, stayed interested in his plate, snubbed her rudeness, his deadpan face returning. His non-reaction was chilling, something Kaipo felt from across the table.

He put down his fork, used his napkin on his mouth, and moved his plate out of the way. He folded his hands on the table and finally gave her his full attention, evaluating her more closely. He cleared his throat.

"You were going to return to Wally Lanakai when we picked you up, correct?" he said.

"I need to talk him out of his organ trafficking efforts here in the islands."

"Ah, yes. Sure. It would more likely have turned into you becoming his whore in return for him rethinking his transplant business. '*I will let you fuck me if you stop exploiting the people here.*' Noble, but nothing more involved than that. You would satisfy his carnal needs, like a good whore does, with the whore hoping she might 'change him.'" He air-quoted.

She stayed silent, didn't snap at the chum Yabuki had tossed in the water.

"You are wasting your time, Ms. Mawpaw. Lanakai-san has had a taste of the biggest paydays his black-market organs could ever demand. Any acquiescence to you would be temporary. Once he gets in your pants with regularity, he will go back to exploiting Miakamiians. Your people. The immune ones. My approach is smarter. It saves Ka Hui and the Yakuza a lot of trouble. Here it is: if I eliminate the predator's food source, I eliminate the predator."

Killing native Miakamiians. The raw materials for Wally's scheme.

"The first was the helicopter pilot. Dramatic, and it cripples the tourism for that disgusting blemish of an island and the man who owns it. I plan to keep going until all the islanders are dead. And eliminating the food source gets Lanakai out of Hawaii for the long haul. That makes your approach moot."

And would make *her* moot, too, in relation to Mr. Yabuki. He knew her origin, her ethnicity. It could have come from a good guess on his part, or it could have been from real research, but regardless, he knew.

"So you intend to kill me."

"It could have gone that way, yes. But lucky for you, Lanakai is making it interesting. We have a wager. If he wins, I promised him he would get you back in one piece. If he loses, he won't. You have five minutes to finish what's left on your plate, Ms. Mawpaw."

"You are wrong, Mr. Yabuki."

"And how is that?"

"You—the Yakuza—*are* animals. To kill innocent people, just to eliminate a competitor, is barbaric. But you can't pull it off. You don't know who or where they are."

Kaipo was fishing. The more she could learn about his agenda...

Mr. Yabuki spoke in Japanese to an attending Yakuza who responded by removing his breakfast dishes from the table and replacing them with a folder. Mr. Yabuki pulled out some papers and put on a pair of glasses.

"If you live on Miakamii, or anywhere else in the islands"—he shuffled the paper pile—"I know where each of you calls home as of the last two U.S. censuses. All one hundred sixty of you. A matter of public record, as are the number of occupied households on your island. But the names and home addresses of all who migrated from the island are not. The census databases are, however, eminently hackable. Plus the genealogy services are wonderful tools. We connected the dots. The ones who died, the ones who stayed, the ones who moved elsewhere in the islands, and—"

Kaipo had moved to the U.S.

"And by process of elimination, the ones, if any, who have left Hawaii entirely. Lanakai is complaining, but we are giving him exactly what he wants, Miakamii livers, just accelerating the process a bit. As an aside, there was only one Miakamii native who left Hawaii. That, of course, is you. And, as quite the convenient circumstance for us, here you are in person."

Mr. Yabuki barked an order and the chains and cuffs reappeared. Kaipo was brought to her feet and shackled again. What served as breakfast time was over.

"Get your rest, Ms. Mawpaw. I'm busy making arrangements with Lanakai regarding our bet. He doesn't have a chance at winning you back, but I'll keep you in good condition, and safe, so he thinks he does. Until your fate can be determined."

25

"I can handle it, Philo sir. I need to see it."

A drive to the Kauai police station in mid-afternoon. They hoofed it to the front entrance from the parking lot, Patrick still defending his decision to see a certain video after Philo had confirmed his eagerness.

"It's why we're here in the islands, sir. Vacation and discovery, sir."

"Exactly, Patrick."

"Mr. Logan said it could be him, sir."

"That's what he said on the phone, bud."

"I can do this."

"I think you're good for it, Patrick."

Philo's opinion of Douglas Logan had changed. He knew him only as an ornery old bastard, but he was one helluva protective ornery old bastard when it came to that small speck of an island, him advocating for every islander that Miakamii had ever produced during his reign as its steward. He'd gone out of his way to engage the police chief regarding a fifteen-plus-year-old crime involving the homicide of a transplanted Miakamiian who was, quite possibly, Patrick's father.

The police had footage from the shop's security cameras. A street-corner grocery store. All the players in the video had been identified at the time of the crime. The shop owner was killed by one of his customers. It turned into an involuntary manslaughter conviction, the bullet meant for another customer. Logan recalled the circumstances and had the police find the evidence video. He then called Philo to relate what the video showed: "*The shooting was witnessed by the store owner's young son... pre-teen... both father and son were from Miakamii. It was an argument between two customers...*"

Douglas Logan arrived after them, grunted an acknowledgment to the cop on duty at the front desk, and thumbed the waiting Philo and Patrick through the doors to the detectives' bullpen. "Chief Koo will meet us in an interrogation room with the detective. Follow me."

No half-measures when it came to Douglas Logan, everything at full speed including his stride, plus Logan had been through this already. They marched up an aisle and followed Logan into a hallway. Detective Ujikawa ushered them all into a side room.

"Sit here, gentlemen," the detective said, directing them to the seats turned around to face front and center for the best view of an overhead flat screen. "Before we roll the footage, Chief Koo would like to say a few words."

"Mr. Stakes." The police chief's crusty, pragmatic disposition rivaled Douglas Logan's. Philo could see him alongside Logan on the beach in ten years, the two of them surfcasting while still sniping at each other. Also like Logan, underneath the chief's hardened crust, his compassion showed.

"This is gruesome footage. There is no audio. The film is spliced together from three cameras, and is the film used during the original trial. It shows a homicide. The perpetrator was caught, convicted, and he went to prison. Justice was served, but for grieving families there is only nominal satisfaction from seeing someone go to jail. Detective, go ahead, please."

The black-and-white film footage started, was shadowy but cleared up quickly, from an outside camera above the store's front door. Parked cars lined the street, at least one with its flashers on. A Japanese man entered the store, was casually dressed, his collar open, showing gold neck bling, a bare chest under it, his long pants sharply creased. The second camera, trained on the first fifteen or so feet of the store's interior, picked him up as he selected a few packs of chewing gum, then grabbed a single red rose in a tube.

"It was Valentine's Day," Chief Koo offered.

The customer moved out of the frame and passed a young man, more like a kid, who was stocking shelves.

"Pause the video," Koo said. He waited for a reaction from Patrick. "Anything familiar here, Mr. Stakes?"

"No, sir."

The spliced footage continued, moving onto a third over-head camera, this one trained on the cashier, a Hawaiian man, the camera above and behind him, hanging from the ceiling. The man with the gum packs and the single red rose approached the counter. The camera showed the aisle that ran the entire length of the store from the cashier counter to the entrance door, a north-south view from on high.

Chief Koo spoke. "Pay attention to what goes on behind this customer."

A second customer entered the screen from the right, a man, this one Hawaiian, someone who was already in the store. He stood behind the first customer in line, looked past him, over the man's shoulder, to make eye contact with the cashier.

"Stop the film, Detective," Koo said. "Here is the tell that made all the difference in the world to the cashier, who was the store owner."

The cashier's nod was almost imperceptible, directed at the second customer in line. The detective re-ran it in slow motion a few times to prove what was there: the nod was a signal. The film started up again.

The second customer started an argument, words only, no threatening gestures, until the Japanese customer puffed up his chest and got nose to nose with him. The cashier could be seen leaving the counter and reentering the camera footage in the rear, behind the arguing men, who now circled each other. The cashier grabbed his son's shoulders and shoved him out of the aisle, off camera.

In full view from behind, the Hawaiian man punched the other customer to the floor, ripped the rose tube out of his hand, and pushed the thorny rose into the Japanese customer's mouth, cramming it down the man's throat with both hands until he drew his gun and put it under the Japanese man's chin.

Over the next three seconds the struggle moved the gun from the throat of one man to the cheek of the other before it went off. Neither customer was hit, but the cashier, still in the aisle, took a bullet to the mouth and was killed instantly. When the gun fired, it was in the Hawaiian man's hand.

Chief Koo glanced at Mr. Logan. His cue. "Douglas?"

"The store owner," Douglas said in a grim tone, "was one of my ranch hands before we moved our cattle operation from Miakamii to Kauai. I helped him get that store. He was a good man, Mr. Stakes. He left behind a wife and the pre-teen son you see here on the film, both of whom I lost sight of years later, the two having left Kauai. Was that pre-teen boy you? Was this your father's murder?"

Patrick sat quiet, blinking hard, didn't answer, seemed nearly catatonic until a tear rolled down his cheek.

"Patrick, I know that was tough to watch," Philo said. "What do you think?" Still nothing from Patrick. Philo turned to the chief. "You have names for them? The father and the son?"

"Yes, of course. Detective, would you—"

"No!" Patrick said, his chest heaving. "He wasn't my father. That wasn't him. No. And that's not me in the store."

Philo looked to prod him more on this, thinking he hadn't given it enough consideration. "Maybe if we have more info on the people. You know, bud, some names, the storeowner, the boy—"

"Know why I know it's not me, Philo? You really wanna know why?"

Patrick was suddenly enraged, his tan Hawaiian face reddening, with no "sir" suffixes on the horizon. "You see that car outside the front door? The one with the flashers on? I'm in that car, in the back seat, playing Nintendo. That's the bagman's car. The guy I rode with while he shook down people for money—the man with the gun in the video, the shooter—*he's* my father. The mob bagman was my father, damn it..."

All the air left the room. The chief, the detective, Douglas Logan, and Philo—they all retreated for a moment, assessing Patrick's realization. Patrick leaned onto his knees and buried his tearful face in his hands.

"Detective," Chief Koo said. "What other info do you have?"

The detective flipped through some pages. "The shooter was Denholm 'Ōpūnui. Awarded nine years. Involuntary manslaughter. Served the entire sentence because, you know, he was Ka Hui. When he was paroled he left the radar because he moved to the mainland, apparently buried his Ka Hui roots. The fight was over 'Ōpūnui's wife. The Japanese customer had been stalking her."

"Do you have her name, Detective?" the chief asked.

"Haneen 'Ōpūnui. It says here she's Japanese-American. Went by Jenny."

"Kids?"

"One. Interesting." Detective Ujikawa paused, a sympathetic smile crossing his face. "A boy. His name was Patrick."

Patrick stood. "Get me out of here."

26

Patrick's world had changed in one afternoon, his identity solved, something that had confounded him for five, six, seven years or more. An elusive success, but at what cost?

At a minimum, his dignity.

"I wanna get drunk, Philo. Sir."

They'd left the police station with plenty of answers and one full-blown coincidence: his name was actually Patrick. But the answers left him with no direction, no compass, and no good feelings about himself. In Navy terms, completely rudderless.

"We'll not be doing that, Patrick. Drinking solves nothing. Do your best to wrap your head around this, and realize that it changes nothing about you or your moral core. You are a kind and decent person. I wouldn't be hanging with you if you weren't."

Philo drove west, heading back to their vacation cottage. An early supper would precede them heading out to see Wally Lanakai in the evening, or Philo would go it alone if Patrick couldn't stomach it. They were waiting on the meeting location.

"We'll have a lot more to talk about with him now, won't we? About Ka Hui. About your parents, what happened to them..."

The rush of info on his parents bordered on overwhelming, coming from an iPhone internet search for Denholm and Haneen ʻŌpūnui as soon as they got to the car. A brutal attack in Philly took their lives one winter, during a cold snap that nearly killed their son Patrick after he'd been severely beaten and left for dead, perpetrators unknown. Until now, the crimes hadn't been connected.

"I will need to tell Grace and Hank."

"Of course you will. Grace and Hank love you, bud, you and all the baggage that came with you. There's no shame here, Patrick. None. You're a good person."

"But my father wasn't."

No way to spin that cloud into a silver lining. Philo let that one sit out there with no comment.

"We'll order in tonight, Patrick. I'm thinking Chinese."

———

"You can bring him to meet with me if you want, Trout, but you need to assure me there will be no drama. It would not end well for him."

"No drama, Wally. But should there be, I can assure you that it won't end well for anyone in attendance. Are we on the same page?"

The "him" Wally Lanakai referred to was Evan Malcolm. Lanakai knew the risk arising from the Navy commander's volatility, Evan having lost someone to so gruesome a circumstance, and having attributed the loss to Ka Hui.

"Seven p.m., Hiilani Spa at Kuluiula on the south shore," Lanakai said. "I have a steam room reserved. You and your guests will be issued bathrobes and towels. Clothing not allowed. I'll send a car to your cottage to pick up the three of you."

Lanakai had looked for reassurances regarding Evan only. He hadn't flinched on his FaceTime call with Philo when he mentioned Patrick attending. So be it. Let the discussion about Patrick be a surprise.

Kuluiula as a destination boasted more than three hundred days of sunshine annually, making most of its evenings comfortable as well. Arriving curbside for the wellness complex, they were ushered through meditation gardens into dressing cubicles with lava rock walls. The bathrobes came with welcome packs of tear-off oils and tonics and fresh-pressed juices in sippy pouches tucked into each robe's kangaroo pockets. At the entrance to the steam room, Philo, Evan, and Patrick hung up their robes, and before towels replaced them, they needed to showcase their respective naked Caucasian, black, and Polynesian asses so Lanakai's bodyguards could perform a visual body search. The mist-filled room was expansive, with natural lava rock ornamenting its rear wall, the wall's black, pocked honeycombs shrouded by the steam.

Wally Lanakai didn't stand to greet them. He instead left two towel-clad men to meet them inside the heavy door. The larger of the two, six-six, six-seven maybe, dark-skinned, and bulky top to bottom, gestured at a long wooden bench across from Lanakai. "Sit there." They complied. "Are you comfortable, or should we lower the steam?" he asked.

"Fine for the moment," Philo said. With all of them now seated, the six men faced each other.

"Good to see you, Trout," Wally Lanakai said. "You look like you're still in excellent condition. I'm happy to see that."

"Still working out, still go a few rounds on occasion, in gear, not bareknuckle."

"And still undefeated, I hear. What is it, sixty-five and oh?"

"I'm touched you remember. Look, I'm retired, but you want me, so you got me, one time only. For the price I said. With a deposit. When and where, Wally?"

"In a minute. Some introductions are needed. One of my associates wanted to meet you. Magpie"—Wally gestured at the larger and blacker of his two men—"this is Mr. Tristan Trout, Philo to his bareknuckle followers. Philo, this is Magpie Papahani."

"The pleasure is mine, Trout."

"Likewise," Philo said.

"Magpie volunteered for this fight, Philo. I have the utmost faith in him, and I'm sure he'd give a great account of himself, for obvious reasons. But I wanted you as my champion, as freakishly talented as you are in this sport, considering what's on the line."

Philo's attributes: large, heavy hands and wrists, leveraged punching power, a one-punch knockout artist, military conditioning, and a granite chin.

"And now that I've floated your name to my opponent," Lanakai said, "he's happier than a hard-on that you're taking this bout as well. He's got some whiz-bang ex-mixed-martial arts champ in his camp. You might have heard of him. Jerry Mifumo?"

Sure had. All boxers paid attention to the mixed martial arts circuit. They didn't much like it because it drained money from the boxing game. Pure savagery, drawing from the worst aspects of gladiator warfare coupled with a Roman coliseum atmosphere, minus the cat-o'-nine-tails and axes and other barbaric weapons from that age. A no-holds-barred spectacle where combatants could be subdued just short of their expiration. If Philo's memory served, Jerry Mifumo was—

"A doper. Fought as a light heavyweight. A Japanese Olympian. Boxing banned him."

"And the Ultimate Fighting Circuit banned him, too, Trout. After three strikes for testing positive for steroids with the UFC, he moved back to Japan."

"So he's Yakuza."

"He's Yabuki's boy, so yes. I should say Yabuki's man. He's now a full heavyweight. From what Magpie tells me, he killed the last guy he fought. Some kind of Yakuza death match."

Magpie nodded in agreement.

"It was bareknuckles," Lanakai said, "until it wasn't. The loser was beheaded. I just learned this. Beheading's a Yakuza thing, with this crime family at least. I've been given assurances the bout will stay bareknuckles only."

"Great," Philo said. "You've been given assurances. Wonderful."

"Which is why I'm doubling your purse, Trout. Consider it combat pay. And because of the nature of our... rivalry with the Yakuza, chances are the only two people who will not be carrying weapons during the match will be you and Mifumo."

"It just gets better and better."

"I will be forever in your debt, Trout."

"Let's talk about that right now. You said on the phone you have something you want to tell my friend Mr. Malcolm here."

His name dropped, Evan's dark, grim face stayed laser-focused on Lanakai, waiting. Philo sensed in Evan a great need to pummel someone or something, or he would explode. Whatever the crime boss had to say, it would need to be extraordinary.

Wally stood and crossed the small room. When he arrived at their bench, he took a seat next to Evan.

"Mr. Malcolm. I know you've suffered a great loss. It was the Yakuza who murdered your fiancée, not me or any of my associates. What they took from her person, her core organs, her very inner being, they sent to me, although I didn't know at the time who sent them, or whose organs they were. They were being cute and mysterious, and were looking to frame me for her murder, plus other similar murders they're committing. I can share with you one more thing. If you would like to know, I will tell you who received her organs."

He produced an envelope. "In here are the names of three people. You will recognize them instantly. If I give you these names, you must promise to never approach any of them about this, and to keep their names a secret, even from your friends here. Deal?"

Evan nodded, then accepted the envelope. The apology, the offer of the information, the information itself, it had an impact. Evan's seething disposition dissipated, especially when hearing that all three recipients needed the organs to reverse deadly illnesses. Philo wouldn't have put it past Lanakai to lie about the recipients or the circumstances, but Lanakai was smooth and convincing in delivering the info, which made it easy to believe him, plus it was probably true.

A shocking, classy move, something Philo didn't think was possible from this man. A home run. Philo nodded his appreciation, but there was more to discuss. "You got anything else to share, Wally, since you're in so benevolent a mood?"

Lanakai returned to his seat across the room. "Yes. Of course. The location of the fight. The Yakuza want to hold it—"

"Hold that thought. We also need your help with something else." Philo leaned out, looked past Evan to Patrick, who thrust out his chin a bit. "What can you tell us about my other associate?"

"Mr. Stakes? What about him? I don't follow, Trout."

"Try following a little harder. Think ten-year-old kid, helping his Ka Hui bagman father collect protection money. Think Kauai corner store shakedowns. Ring any bells?"

Lanakai's body language showed no tell, no indications. He remained stiff, his eyesight hardening on Philo. Philo would need to forget being coy, would need to cold-cock him with a name.

"Time's up. Denholm ʻŌpūnui. What does that name mean to you?"

Lanakai didn't move. No facial twitch, no blink, no resettling of his fat ass on the hard bench, no nothing. The only tell came from Magpie, who turned to face the crime family patriarch. "Boss—"

His boss dropped his hand hard onto Magpie's leg, gripped it. "No, Magpie. Just… don't."

Lanakai's lips tightened their hold on each other, seemed determined not to part, determined to stifle any emotion, him willing something away, willing something distasteful into non-existence, until—

His eyes moistened; he blinked out a tear. Lanakai spoke to Philo, part question, part shame-filled declaration. "He knows?"

Patrick answered for himself. "Yes, I know."

Patrick stood, which made everyone else stand, the drama so thick it could be cut with a machete.

The last one on his feet was Wally Lanakai. "Patrick. I made a promise to your father—"

The promise, on the occasion of Denholm quitting their criminal enterprise and leaving all his Ka Hui manpower and properties to Wally, Lanakai related, was to never recruit Patrick into the business. And the only way to keep that promise, after the tragic beating Patrick had taken during the Philly attack that claimed his parents' lives and left him brain-damaged, was to let his amnesia stand even after Ka Hui learned where he'd ended up.

"I left you alone. So you wouldn't know. So you wouldn't be tempted. So *we* wouldn't be tempted. I—"

"I ate from garbage cans," Patrick said. "I hid in dumpsters behind restaurants, waiting for food. I couldn't speak. My head. Look at my head!" He jabbed at himself, at the slight dent in his forehead that had come from the beating.

"We didn't know," Lanakai said. "You disappeared. When you turned up—when we learned the Blessids had found you, took you in, put you to work—your father was my best friend. He would have been so proud of you, son..."

Patrick was having none of it, snarling through his anger. "There's so much missing up here, in my head!" He paced, his eyes down, his hands fisted, making Lanakai's nervous body-guards stand. "So much I don't understand. My father, my mother... they were my family! I had no family, and now I do, but they were criminals..."

"Calm down, bud," Philo said. "More is coming, Patrick. The ancestry info, any day now the Blessids will have it—"

"It'll be wrong, Philo! Tell me, whose scorecard had me having a Japanese mother? Whose, damn it? I need some air!" He pulled open the heavy door, retreated outside the steam room where he began pacing again.

A side of Patrick that Philo had never seen. More coherent, and with smarts behind the sarcasm. Less childlike.

"Wally, this has been interesting, but we gotta go," Philo said. "Telling him, not telling him... I can't say what you did was right or wrong. All I can say is this is going to leave another mark. Tell me where to meet for this fight and when. I've got some work to do to get ready."

"Give Patrick my respects again, Philo, please. Make him understand. Magpie, fill Mr. Trout in."

"We agreed on the old Malinas Chicken Farm property, inside the Kalaheo borough," Magpie said. "An abandoned chicken ranch. This Saturday, two p.m."

Three days. Not much time.

But it would need to be time enough, if Philo didn't want to die out there.

27

"I have your breakfast," called the male voice from the portico. "Step away from the door."

The motel door opened, creaking out of the way. A fast food bag and two jumbo cups of coffee entered her room, held as a peace offering by a large Japanese man. Kaipo backed up, stood at the foot of her unmade bed in loose gym pants, gym shoes, and a form-fitting workout top over a sports bra. Stark still, her arms at her sides, she watched the Yakuza thug enter, her face bright, her smile small; she was going for Hannibal Lecter intensity. The creepiness stopped her guest momentarily, then he started forward again.

"Your cornrows are beautiful," he said. "I didn't get a good look at them before, when, you know, we were together."

He was the bastard behind her in the staged porn shot. "Fuck off, asshole. Leave the food and get out."

"Sorry, but no, I need to stay and watch you eat. Oyabun's orders." His snide snicker made him out to be one oh-so-clever soldier. "Besides, I like to watch." He grabbed a desk chair and pulled it closer to the other end of the long dresser where he'd left the food. He dropped his ample ass into it, crossed his legs, and reached for his takeout coffee. His sip said it was still too hot, so he returned it to the dresser.

Kaipo was hungry. She ate the egg and muffin sandwich sitting at the other end of the dresser, then a second, then the hash browns, then gulped her OJ down. Her first sip of coffee made her grimace; still too hot. After she wiped her mouth, she eyed the oaf sitting comfortably at the other end of the dresser.

"I've finished my breakfast. Go."

He didn't, instead got chatty.

"You don't have a chance of surviving this, miss. Zero. You will end up in pieces in a trunk, delivered to your *koibito*." Her slouched admirer uncrossed his legs, then resettled his dark tie to let it dangle over his crotch area, where he rubbed it. "I would think you might rather close out your last few days with your legs spread, screaming in ecstasy. I can help with that."

"I don't think so, sport. Long tie, short dick, right? That's been my experience. And Wally Lanakai's not my lover. Leave now, before you hurt yourself."

He glowered but he was otherwise undeterred. "And usually, after I watch"—he raised his girth from the chair, removed his suit jacket, and hung it over the chair back—"I like to participate. Let's make this happen. Take off your clothes."

She was out of her chair now, made no attempt to comply, instead backed up a single step and squared her feet. He undid his shirt and tie and removed his trousers, laid it all across the chair, then spoke calmly. "No reason to soil my suit. You really should take off your pants and panties, miss. Your top, too. If I have to do it, it will all end up in shreds."

White cotton undershirt and briefs under his dark business suit. Heavily tattooed. A fleeting thought had her wondering how so boring a Yakuza-mandated uniform could cover such imaginative body ink. His first steps at her were casual, plodding.

She had little room to maneuver in the tiny space, so she did not give any ground. Once within arm's reach he surprised her with his quickness, his hand snapping up to grab her throat. He squeezed, his other hand tugging at the waist of her gym pants, sliding one side down, past her hip, with her trying to push herself away.

The push didn't work, but both her hands were still free, a mistake on his part. She grabbed the hot jumbo coffee from the dresser and shoved it down the front of his skivvies. He backed up, shrieking. Her other hand grabbed the second takeout coffee from the dresser, the cup still hot to the touch, and threw its contents in his face.

"Oh, I'm sorry, was that coffee too hot?" she screamed at him. "Sue me—"

Fists pounded the front door, with two men shouting in Japanese and English to open it. Kaipo was busy, pummeling her attacker with hands and feet while he was on his knees, her final blow an upward palm thrust underneath his nose, blood from his nostrils and mouth splattering the dresser. She was ready to stomp his head in when the two men who'd pushed into the room subdued her against a wall, one with a handgun against her cheek, the other with yet another hand around her throat, and no more hot coffee within her reach.

"Calm down, miss. *Calm. Down.* The oyabun will deal with him—"

Motel housekeeping wouldn't know what to do with her room, the blood, the coffee, the feces—he'd actually shit himself. She knew how it would need to be cleaned, but she wasn't about to tell them. Maybe her host would move her to the room adjacent to his on the other side, to keep his hostage close.

Somehow, she'd figured early on, raping her was not part of the Yakuza plan. This assertion was being validated at that very moment. Still in her room, seated facing a shared wall, she listened as Yabuki scolded her attacker in Japanese and English. The dressing down was severe, addressing his insubordination, his wayward libido, and his incompetence at being bested by a woman.

Then she heard what she didn't want to hear.

"You know the *bushido*! The way of the warriors! You understand the honors bestowed on all Yakuza who take the oath and follow the code. You are Samurai. You have brought shame to yourself, and to me. Death... is now your duty. Here is your tantō. You must use it."

Tantō. A Japanese word she knew. A small ceremonial sword used as a knife... for disembowelment.

The adjacent room went silent. Footsteps were followed by the rearranging of furniture, followed by the distinctive sound of steel scraping steel, a long blade or saber being removed from a metal sheath. This was not the tantō. Silence resumed, no voices, raised or otherwise, no speaking, only whimpering, then soft crying, then silence again, until—

"I am sorry, Oyabun, for my weakness then, and for my weakness now." Her assailant's voice. "Please forgive me, O Master. Please, let me live..."

"Begging... does not become a Samurai," Mr. Yabuki grunted.

"But I will do better—"

One angry yell from Yabuki in Japanese ended it. A thump on the floor. To Kaipo, the thud revealed an unconscionable outcome. Not hara-kiri; a beheading.

She'd now changed her mind. It had been a huge mistake to think she could ever be satisfied returning to mob life by hooking up with Wally again in any form, even temporarily. She needed to get off these islands immediately. Chances of that outcome were looking slim.

Within the hour, she was moved to a different room farther down the motel wing. An hour after that, Mr. Yabuki moved into the room next to hers.

28

Wally and Magpie walked past the storefront's security detail in the lobby and approached the nurses' station.

"Surgery starts soon, Mr. Lanakai," Nancy said. She giggled, covered her mouth. "Sorry, sir. Our new patient, I love her, she's always made me laugh *so* hard..."

A loud voice carried from down the hallway. Distinctively raspy, the African-American female comic was no stranger to foul language on stage and off. Repeated F-bombs and *cocksuckers* took up three quarters of the joke she was trying to tell.

Wally Lanakai's diminutive Hawaiian nurse administrator was in stitches, their two patients, prospective donor and recipient, in various stages of surgery preparedness. Nancy lifted copies of paperwork off her desk and handed them to Wally. NDAs that he'd seen already, all signed by each doctor, nurse, patient, donor, and Wally. It wasn't like a court of law would ever see these documents if a participant breached the NDA, knowing this business operated below the radar and bordered on unethical, but the prospect of retaliation put more teeth into Wally's verbal threats of "you'll be sorry" if any of the participants blew the whistle.

Suddenly the echoing guffaws from the hallway shut off, the joke cut short just before the punchline. Wally recognized the territory. The plaque in the woman's brain had choked her off mid-sentence, leaving the speaker bewildered, confused. Nancy made busy work for herself at the desk, did not comment, the territory familiar to her as well. Dementia took no prisoners, could silence the best and the most gifted in all walks of life, and it did so without notice, without discrimination.

Two surgeries were scheduled back-to-back, surgery number one, removing a living-donor partial liver from a Miakamiian man. Surgery number two, grafting the partial liver from surgery number one onto the liver of a beloved comedienne from the smoky clubs of the seventies and eighties and the late-night talk shows of the nineties. Wally and Magpie passed Nancy's station, entered the main hallway.

The banter started up again as abruptly as it had stopped, good-natured ribbing that the female comic had for her doctors and her donor. As they approached the operating theater, a large man—untucked tropical shirt with red parrots, shorts, silver swag around his neck, and a Rolex—appeared at the end of the hall and trudged toward them. The comic's son. A masked nurse in full surgical gear exited the surgical theater, was on her way into the windowed anteroom to secure the doors. She switched on the overhead "IN USE" sign for the hallway.

"What the hell, Lanakai, what took you so long?" the hustling man called. They met midway, outside the operating room. "I've been waiting for you. I do *not* want you to start the surgery..."

Wally reacted, pointed at the nurse through the window, pounded it, then raised one wait-a-moment finger when he had her attention, signifying the surgery shouldn't start yet.

"What's the problem?" Wally said.

"I just read what my mother signed. She's getting only part of a liver? I don't think so."

The problem for Wally and Magpie was this man was a cop—retired SWAT—and not all that clean. He was someone who could make things difficult for them going forward, if not right now, the testosterone levels in the hallway rising.

"That's the way live donor transplants work," Wally said. "It has to be that way. Partial livers for both parties. She'll be back to her pre-dementia self in no time. You'll just need to be patient with her."

"Transplant the whole liver," he said.

"I can't do that," Wally said. "You know why."

"Yes, you can. I already checked out the donor. This guy's a drug user with a record. Shit happens."

"Shoplifting and receiving stolen goods. Hardly a record. And he's in recovery. Four years. I don't take active drug users as donors. If they lie to me about it, trust me, that's when the shit happens. The answer's no."

"She'll pay double. She'll double your fee, Lanakai—"

"A million and a half? That's... No. She doesn't *need* the whole liver—"

"Make it happen or my mother and I leave now. I know people. Do it, or I shut this operation down."

The discussion now had a large audience: doctors, nurses, the lobby bodyguards, and tiny Nancy. Magpie interceded, a hand on Wally's chest, pushing him out of the way. Magpie got in the ex-cop's face. "Back off, asshole..."

"Enough," Wally shouted. He pushed past Magpie.

He eyed his audience with a sweeping look into the operating room, then down the hallway, returning his gaze to confront this pain-in-the-ass, uninformed, dirty-cop loudmouth with an iconic and beloved comic as his mother.

Wally's scrutiny went from the donor to the potential recipient, then wound up back on the donor again, where it lingered.

The donor's family. Wally lamented about what he might need to do for them after this.

29

Philo piloted the SUV through a small business park, was nearing their destination, what was once a chicken farm on the *mauka* or "toward the mountain" side of the Kaumualii Highway in Kalaheo. Twenty-five-plus acres of prime Hawaiian real estate, the property was protected by a preservation society long working to have it recognized as an historical landmark. Today Philo and company would get a closer look at it during an impromptu sparring session arranged for his benefit by Wally Lanakai.

"The Yakuza want the fight here," Philo said to passengers Evan and Patrick, "and I understand why. If I know the history, they for sure know it, too."

Soon after the Pearl Harbor attack, the Kalaheo Stockade, a wartime detention center for Japanese and Japanese-Americans, rose from among the farm's chicken coops and egg hatcheries, or this was the believed history at least. Elderly detainees with personal recollections of the internment camp had fingered the farm property as the most likely location, but their eighty-year-old memories were inexact. The inability to pinpoint the locations of their extinct barracks and cottages had hindered the historical designation process.

The SUV emerged from the commercial park and idled at a stop sign across the street from the farm.

"Far as I can tell from the car's navigation, we've reconned the entire perimeter," Philo said. "The old chicken farm, the business park, the residential neighborhood. This is it, gentlemen, this open space in front of us. Here we go."

Philo goosed the engine, then immediately hit the brakes. A passing street sweeper bettered the forty-miles-per-hour speed limit as it ran the stop sign at the intersection and continued hauling ass, its large circular brushes raised. "One of these days I'm gonna call that 'safety is our goal' phone number..."

The first road into the farm was paved, the blacktop pockmarked and patched, with dips in places that made them hold onto their seats as they negotiated them. A bumpy ride, but not as bumpy as the dirt road Philo turned onto next, headed for a barn on the horizon. Make that two barns, side by side, as they drew closer.

"You really want to do this, Chief?" Evan said. "I've seen the YouTube videos of you out there. You're good, but a lot of those guys you fought looked pathetic."

"Checking up on me? Sure, there were a few tomato cans in there, but only a handful of my fights were filmed. Smartphones weren't popular back then. Many of the guys I knocked out were monsters. 'Course, some of the bigger ones weren't used to having smaller guys punch back."

"A whole side of you I never knew about, Philo. But seriously, today you're gonna fight some former pro?"

"Not today. Saturday. Today I'm doing some sparring."

"Right. With that goon who watches Lanakai's back, his

bodyguard, Magpie whatshisname. What's he weigh, three hundred, three fifty?"

"I have no idea. Him, plus Lanakai's got another one lined up, a different body type, just to give me something to hit."

"They're bodyguards for a crime boss, Philo. You think they're not gonna hit back?"

"You're not helping my head here, Evan."

Evan turned around in the front seat. "You have an opinion on this, Patrick?"

"'Float like a butterfly, sting like a bee.'"

Evan snorted. "You're no help. All I can say is the chief here better have a white towel in that bag of his so you can throw it in when it gets rough in there, today and Saturday both."

"Much appreciate the vote of confidence," Philo said.

"Fine. How's this, then. At least you kept yourself in shape. Still not an ounce of fat on you. Does that do it for you, stud?"

"Stamina makes little difference in these things. They're usually over in five, ten minutes tops. But I do appreciate the man-crush. You made it move a little for me."

The comment should have brought at least a chuckle, but Evan stayed somber, peering out the window, his look distant. "All these assholes will be carrying weapons, Philo. Way too risky..." Evan's voice quivered; he couldn't finish the thought.

"Look, Evan—you should sit this thing out. It could get ugly."

Evan swept a tear away from his cheek. "No fucking way. I'm counting on it getting ugly. I wasn't there to make a difference before, for a person I loved. This time I will be."

Weathered gray, tan, and white, the barns had wooden frame windows that were missing glass panes, and a few of the planks serving as vertical siding had curled and shrunk. Both barns were still underroof, their overhead corrugated metal rusty but appearing intact. Philo stopped the car next to the one other vehicle parked already, Wally Lanakai's gold Escalade limo. This was the fight venue, free and clear of Yakuza for today, that was the deal, so Lanakai and his fighter could scope it out. Philo pointed beyond the limo. "That building out there, three hundred yards at one o'clock," he asked Evan, "is that a military bunker?"

"It's a slaughterhouse. One of three on the property. They all date back to WW2. They were in use until the farmer went out of business. Empty for decades, far as I know."

Now that the guest of honor had arrived, the limo's occupants exited. Wally Lanakai was in a suit, his driver Magpie and one other man in gym clothing. Philo slipped his lanky frame out from behind the wheel, exited the SUV, stretched his back and neck muscles. He heard mumbling in Hawaiian coming from the limo audience, specifically the anonymous man, who was on the chunky side. He was sizing Philo up, a snicker or two mixed into his exchange with Magpie.

Philo had seen and heard this welcome before. No respect, his opponents oftentimes in designer nylon outfits with nicknames stitched across the backs of their shiny silk jackets, just like in pro boxing, their trash-talking mouths big but without the skills, or the balls, to back them up. Philo was in jeans and sneakers, and under his light jacket, a sleeveless tee. Under the jeans, a steel cup inside a jock inside his boxer briefs, for protecting the jewels.

"*The clothing what brought you here.*" Something his deceased sexagenarian boxing buddy Hump Fargas had routinely called Philo's outfit. "*No shame in going old school. Whatever makes you comfortable.*"

Oh, how he missed Hump.

He ignored the rude comments, tossed his gun, wallet, and phone back into the car. Magpie had not, however, ignored the rudeness, was instead teed off, chastising the other boxer in Hawaiian for his disrespect, backing him up against a car, a finger in the guy's chest. Philo clearly heard the words "sixty-five and oh" in English before Magpie reined in his temper and quieted himself.

Respect. Good show, Magpie, who then invited Philo and his posse to enter the barn first.

Inside was what Philo expected: a barn, nothing more, or maybe something less after its many decades of non-use and decay. Two stories, a dirt floor, small pens for small animals left and right of an open center area, a second level of planked flooring that ran around the perimeter, for storing hay bales. The exterior vertical wood siding hung precariously loose from the framing lumber in spots, was knot-holed, letting in sunlight that dotted the barn's interior. No different from barns on the mainland, except for what Philo now noticed was on the dirt floor: spray-painted white lines in the center. A square, replicating a boxing ring, but larger. The large size interested him.

Wally spoke up while wandering the perimeter of the "ring" area, Philo walking it as well. "As I understand it, Trout, your opponent likes having room to move."

This sent chills down Philo's spine. For the first time in maybe twenty fights, he felt apprehensive about an opponent. Room to maneuver was Philo's game. Most of his bareknuckle challengers over the years were larger than him, their size and girth the source of their bravado. That always gave him an advantage, his ability to stick and move and stay away. This much space was a surprise.

"I heard Mifumo's a brawler, not a boxer, and big," Philo said.

"Still big, Trout, maybe even too big, but now he's fast," Lanakai said.

"Huh." Philo pondered this, a question hitting him dead center: *What the hell did I get myself into?* "Big *and* fast? How'd he manage that? Let me take a wild guess."

"Yes. Steroids," Lanakai said. "Word is he's still using. Strength and speed both. So to answer the question you're asking yourself right about now, yes, this guy is capable of really hurting you."

"Huh," Philo said, this time with less ponder, more God-fearing resignation, but soon chased by Navy booyah enthusiasm.

Though I walk through the valley of the shadow of death—

"Let's get started." Lanakai wiggled his fingers at his bodyguard.

—I will fear no evil—

"Magpie will take you through the paces."

—for I am the meanest son of a bitch in the valley.

Magpie ushered them into the center of the barn floor, Philo's only protection a mouthpiece and a steel cup. If Philo had to guess, his sparring partner outweighed him by thirty pounds, plus there was the flak jacket protecting his ribs and the padded gear on his head.

"Mr. Trout, meet Suki-san," Magpie said. "You'll go two minutes with him, take a break, do two more minutes, take another break, then a final two minutes. Then you'll work with me. Consider him your heavy bag for today, Mr. Trout. He's good for it, but he will hit back. However"—Magpie looked Suki-san in the eye—"nobody throws anything overly hard at the head. Not one punch. Stomach, ribs, arms, make it hurt a little if you'd like, but no headhunting. Got it?"

Philo stuck and ran, stuck and ran, then stuck, ripping off shots up and down Suki's body, some heavy hands making his sparring partner wince when they caught him in the stomach and ribs, even with the padding. Philo's approach: leverage, and the snap of his large wrists and hands. Suki retaliated with punches to Philo's solar plexus that were hard enough to back him up and get an admiring nod from Philo before he waded back in. Intermission, then another two minutes of Philo throwing speed punches at Suki's padded face, and light head shots designed to help with Philo's timing, not bombs that could take the man out. Except one did. Suki landed face first in the dirt, shaking out the cotton candy between his ears when he raised himself to his knees.

"Shit. Sorry, man, so sorry. Magpie, I got a lot more in the tank. I thought I was being polite."

"All well and good, Mr. Trout. Not to worry. He'll be fine. You can stand down, Suki-san."

Magpie removed his jacket, limbered his neck. He waved Philo into the center of the square, spoke in a low tone while eyeing his boss Wally, who was preoccupied with his phone.

"So here's the deal, Trout. Don't hold back with me. I wanna feel it. I want the boss to see what he's hitched his wagon to. Because I'm not going to hold back with you. I want your best two minutes, and you'll get mine. You get the better of me, you're ready. I get the better of you, the boss maybe hitches himself to me instead. Just so you know, and as a frame of reference, my allegiance to Ka Hui means I will kill for that man. I already have."

"Look, Magpie, I have no beef with you. C'mon, be reasonable, we can't be trying to cancel each other ou—"

Magpie's left hook glanced off Philo's forehead, but the blow put Philo on notice, like a sledgehammer that had come dangerously close to shattering the bones around his eye socket. Magpie got back into a boxer's stance as a right-hander and stepped in closer to Philo, about to engage again.

The punch to his forehead had come from the man's left hand. Philo could ill afford to see the damage the right could do. He backed up a few steps and evaluated a smiling Magpie, who was relishing the respect and admiration that Philo no doubt had to have for the punch he'd just thrown.

That wasn't quite where Philo was. A calming, inspiring—head-clearing—thought occupied his mind: *this guy stands between me and four hundred thousand dollars.*

Philo moved back inside, his head tucked between his fists, bobbed, weaved, then delivered an uppercut to Magpie's double chin that lifted the big man off his feet. It wasn't the gravity-defying aspect of a punch that raised three hundred plus pounds an inch or so off the dirt, it was the snapping back of the man's head that did it. Magpie landed on his back outside the square, his wits scrambled, with Philo's prospect of earning the large purse still intact.

"Was that necessary?" Lanakai said. "Seriously, Trout. This was supposed to be a sparring session. What the fuck?"

Magpie got no further than a sitting position, Suki now attending to him.

Philo looked Magpie's way. "Sorry, guy, I got carried away."

Magpie met his gaze, wiggled his jaw to make sure it wasn't broken. He raised himself and managed a smile at the smaller man who'd just made a believer out of him. "I'll live, Mr. Trout. Apology accepted."

"That's it, gentlemen. Let's call it a day," Lanakai said. "Trout. I trust you found this workout useful, maybe removed some of the cobwebs?"

"Sure. It reminded me I don't miss this sport one bit. Tell me something, Wally: are you in the right ballpark with this fighter?"

"Your opponent? We shall see. Bigger than Suki-san, smaller than Magpie. But more of a killer than both these men combined. That's the word. I have no choice. If you're worried about your purse, I promise to pay you win or lose. Or your estate." He paused. "That was a joke, Trout."

"Yeah. Funny. But what about Yabuki? Will he honor the outcome after I, you know, KO his guy?"

All eyes were on Lanakai. Tough-guy crime boss, here and on the U.S. mainland. He couldn't entertain the prospect of an unsatisfactory outcome of the fight. Philo could tell this from the man's expression, puffy with emotion; could tell that this was serious business, and it was taking a toll.

Lanakai swallowed hard, blinked himself whole again, rallied. His grim, murderous bastard face returned. "You need to win, Philo. It will all be moot if you don't."

30

They rousted Kaipo at five a.m. She'd slept in her stretch workout clothes like she did the prior night. No knocking, no request for her to move away from the door. The entry was quick, efficient, and commando-like. Three men; Yabuki's Yakuza thugs. Two dragged her out of bed, put her in cuffs, and chained her up in leg irons again. "You are moving," the third Yakuza thug said, his gun drawn. "We have reached the home stretch. Today you learn your *unmei*."

"My what?"

"Your fate."

A push at her shoulder forced her to stutter-step toward the door. "I need to get my things..."

"No you don't. All you will need is this..."

A cloth hood went over her head, making her gasp for air. She doubled over, put her head into her cuffed hands, tried to pull it up and over her head again, couldn't get the leverage—

"Stop, you'll smother yourself. This is not to suffocate you, it's for travel. Stop fighting it—"

The man's grip on her head through the cloth bag made her straighten up and quit the thrashing. She calmed herself with deep breaths, then thrashed violently while the men guided her out of the motel room, into the back seat of a car. Someone belted her into the center seat and tugged on the belt to make sure the shoulder harness was secure.

The car moved slowly through the parking lot, then slowly while on the local streets, then accelerated, had to be a highway, but the car was still in no hurry. *Respecting the traffic laws*, she told herself. To not draw attention. Dawn broke, the car driving into it, the sun lighting up the windshield and brightening the thin opaqueness of her black hood. She was between two men in the back seat, shoulder to shoulder, one taller than her on her right, the other shorter, based on where her shoulders touched his. No one spoke, five minutes, ten minutes, longer. She decided to change that, spoke through the hood.

"Where are we going?"

"Shut up," the man on her right said.

"Why so nasty and mysterious?"

"Because you won't like where we're going. Shut up."

"The chickens for sure didn't like it," the smaller man said, snickering.

The larger thug scolded his associate in Japanese. One word she recognized to mean "idiot."

"Why are you treating me like shit? Your oyabun—"

"Quiet! We lost a good man because of you," the larger guy said. "Oyabun... he is old-school Yakuza and Samurai, and does not tolerate people who do not follow orders. This relocation needs to be without incident. Which means you shut up, or we *make* you shut up..."

Ten, fifteen minutes passed this way, none of them speaking. The car suddenly left the blacktop and turned onto a dirt road, the potholes deep, the car rocking in and out and side to side, the seat belts doing their job. She wondered just how bad the terrain had to be off-road for on-road to be the better choice, the car moving ten miles per hour at best. Five minutes of this and then the road settled down again, the car accelerating briefly, then an abrupt stop. The four doors opened and they dragged her out, two sets of hands under the arms, hustling her up and over what felt like a grassy knoll, her feet barely touching the ground. She listened to the surroundings to pick up on any sounds, heard little: no barking dogs, no traffic, no horses or sheep or cows, and no chickens, only wild crows cawing overhead. If they were on a farm, it was considerably underutilized.

Her captors pushed her through what sounded like a small gate with a spring, the gate snapping shut behind them. Still no clucking or other animal noises, only wings flapping and leaves rustling as birds took flight from nearby trees.

"Sorry, boys, but I'm not hearing any chickens," Kaipo said, her breath short. She was now doing more walking but still being pulled forward. Some hutzpah with sarcasm, meant to hide her fear while eliciting information.

"You won't. Shut up."

They stopped. Someone searched through keys on a chain, and a minute later she went from overhead daylight to darkness, the air in the space a lot cooler.

Inside a building. A door opened, metal. No, not a door, another gate, this one sounding like chain link fencing. Once inside, the space they'd entered felt large, open. "Hello?" she called, a test, her voice raised. It came back in a short echo, but she did hear it, followed by a cawing crow. Her intuition was right, it was a large, open space, with a ceiling tall enough for birds to gain entrance and find interesting, but with abysmal acoustics.

"Quiet. Let's go."

A second entry opened, not a gate, a door, and after they

pulled her through, this was where her journey ended. They sat her in a creaky chair with wobbly legs in a room of unknown size with a smell she couldn't put her finger on, but it was penetrating, pervasive, and gag-inducing.

Then she had it: the stink of death. Her days as a cleaner-fixer for Ka Hui had given her the nose for recognizing it. Rooms large and small, living quarters, kitchens, basements, hot tubs, commercial and industrial buildings, garages, any number of closed spaces where someone or something had died or been murdered and she'd been tasked with cleaning up after the mess. But a very large number of somethings had died in this space, her intuition said, here and throughout the building.

"Hold still, I'll undo your hood," the larger thug said, reaching under her chin. "It will feel like it's just in time, because I'm sure you'll be losing your stomach momentarily. There's a bucket in here. Use it when you puke. The restraints will come off later. Don't get too comfortable." Her light-deprived eyes adjusted to the change, his sarcastic smile greeting them. "You won't be here long."

With the hood off she could see her surroundings. The two unremarkable men in suits who brought her in; a long room, concrete blocks for walls; a smooth cement floor. A three-story ceiling crisscrossed by metal air ducts and the vestiges of electrical lighting, the low-hanging light bulbs on. This was the front end of an assembly line, with sinks, heavy tables, and a rubber conveyor belt. The floor was filthy, splotched black in spots and caked with small, scattered piles of unidentified hardened content that ruined its otherwise smooth surface.

She felt a slight rush of air against her ankles from under the door they'd used, which was heavy, industrial, and metal. The draft entered when another door in the building had opened and closed, stimulating the airflow and providing momentary relief from the accumulated stench. It also lifted dust and detritus off the floor, making it temporarily airborne.

Mixed in with the detritus, feathers. A closer look at the corners of the room, the rafters, the ductwork: more feathers. She was in an abandoned chicken slaughterhouse. How long abandoned? Long enough for desiccated chicken organs and parts to outlast maggots and other insects staining the floor, the piles of detritus way past hardening, on their way to fossilization. But where were they on Kauai? Not a clue.

And the moment that her one abductor had said would come, did: she needed the bucket for two jolting releases of her stomach contents. She'd seen and smelled much worse, knew much worse, some that had come by her own hand. But here, it was less the stench, more her nerves. She was finally getting the picture. The true embodiment of bait for Wally: the potential execution of a promise to gut her, maybe hang her body on a hook somewhere inside this slaughterhouse.

The door to her prison opened. One, two, three, four men entered, filling up the space on both sides of the entry, then a fifth. Mr. Yabuki.

"Ms. Mawpaw," he said. "I trust your accommodations are quite... discomforting. Such is the nature of things. This is what you should expect going forward. But do not despair. You'll be here only through the evening hours, until a certain contest is decided. Would you like some breakfast?"

"I want these chains off. I want to know where I am."

"Nothing to eat, then?"

"Look at this place. You think I'd keep anything else down?"

"Gentlemen." He was addressing his men but stayed focused on her. "Bring her some jug water. For drinking and washing. Bring two more empty buckets so she can wash and toilet herself. You will be hungry, Ms. Mawpaw. They will bring you something to eat later. Fruits and vegetables, something your stomach should be able to handle. Regarding where you are..."

Yabuki maintained his tunnel vision, which was still directed at Kaipo.

"I can't bring myself to look at this place. This... prison. It is unholy. A grotesque affront to the Japanese people by your wartime United States of America. *That* is where you are. Gentlemen, remove her leg irons but keep her handcuffed, and keep her confined to this room. Ms. Mawpaw, I bid you sayonara until this evening."

31

"Snacks. Where's the cooler and the bag of snacks, sir?" Patrick said.

"The kitchenette," Philo said.

The afternoon of the fight. After sixty-five bareknuckle bouts in venues around the country ranging from abandoned grain elevators to parking garages to school basements to closed malls, Philo knew to travel light. He'd arrive in his fighting clothes—jeans, cutoff tee, sneakers; steel cup; multiple mouthguards. Bottles of water for the cooler, plus Gatorade, oranges, bars of chocolate, Advil. His holstered Sig Sauer 9mm handgun, with an extra clip. Patrick found the cooler with the food in the cottage's kitchenette, Philo's gym bag next to it. Philo was in the bathroom, the door closed, talking on the phone.

Everything Philo had rattled off was in the cooler or the bag. With him busy toileting, and Patrick's ear to the bathroom door making sure Philo actually was busy on the phone while toileting, Patrick picked up a nearby kitchen towel and considered it carefully. It wasn't white, but it was close enough to be symbolic of it. When he checked Philo again he was still on the phone, he and Commander Malcolm synching their timetables. He unzipped a side pocket on the gym bag, folded the hand towel flat, and tucked it in. He whispered a preemptive apology. "I believe in you, Philo sir, but... forgive me. I don't want you to die."

Philo emerged from emptying his bladder and completing his phone conversation. "You check us down, Patrick? We have everything?"

"I did, sir. Yes."

"Great."

"But I'm confused, sir."

"About?"

"Commander Malcolm. What you just told him on the phone, sir. A later start time for the fight, and he should go there by himself?"

"Yeah, about that. He's too close to this bareknuckle clusterfuck, Patrick. He'll lose his shit all over the Yakuza if he's part of the fight. These pricks killed his fiancée; Evan won't abide by any Japanese honor code. If he gets a chance he'll come out blasting, go right at them. That wouldn't end well for any of us. So now he's going to get there too late; it'll be after everyone's gone. It has to be this way, bud. Too much of a risk otherwise."

"I dunno, sir. Maybe he won't believe you. Maybe he shows up on time anyway."

"It's covered, Patrick. It'll be fine." A look through rustling curtains out the cottage window. Lanakai's gold limo had arrived. "Our Ka Hui escort is here. Let's go."

Arriving at the farm, they passed the barn they'd used for the sparring session yesterday and headed into a jungle of trees where Philo's SUV rental found tire ruts in the dirt. They were one of two SUVS and an RV that followed Wally Lanakai's limo, the four vehicles bouncing through muddy pocks in the terrain. Philo didn't have to ask who or what was in the other vehicles behind them. Insurance was the best answer, by way of men with guns. Their mood was somber, reflective, the silence a veil that was on them as soon as they'd reentered the farm property.

"You okay with all this, Patrick?" Philo said.

"I'm okay, sir."

But Philo knew this barrage of new info that Patrick had learned about his identity had slammed his damaged employee with insights that even a person of average intelligence might struggle with.

"I'm here to help you sort this all out, bud. Mission accomplished, right? At least now you know your origin."

"Mission accomplished, Philo sir." After a beat, "I texted Grace about it, sir. She wants me to come home ASAP."

"I heard from her, too. We'll head home soon as we see this thing through. Either tomorrow or the next day."

"You need to come back with me, sir."

"I will, Patrick."

"Alive."

"Patrick—"

"Promise me you won't do anything stupid, sir."

A little bit strange hearing Patrick's plea. *You mean beyond what I'm already doing?* But the concern was genuine, and it hit Philo in the feels. "Copy that, Patrick. Promise."

They bounced into a clearing that fronted an unpainted cinderblock building, three stories and long, like multiple military barracks end to end. Other vehicles, Philo counted six, were already there and empty of their occupants. Two Japanese men with long rifles stood guard. Beyond the cars was a dual loading dock with overhead doors, cement steps leading up to them.

Lanakai, Mr. Suki, Magpie, and eight other mob guys exited their cars. Lanakai spoke, his people assembled behind him. "I see you were able to ditch your Navy CO friend."

It had been a ruse he'd felt uncomfortable executing, making Evan think the barn they'd sparred in was the real deal, complete with the spray paint on the dirt floor. Evan would show up late for the party, and at the wrong place, after all this was over.

"Not one of my better moments. He will never forgive me."

They'd parked in an open area in front of the building. The jungle had crept against the building on two sides, growing up and onto the metal roof, the rear not visible.

"Evan said there are three of these slaughterhouses out here," Philo said. "So they all look like this, all overgrown?"

"I have no idea, Trout," Wally said. "I heard the same thing. If the other two are on the farm property somewhere, the jungle's done a good job of reclaiming them. Let's head inside. We're already late."

One overhead door was open floor to ceiling. Once inside, they realized the door wasn't open, it was missing, the interior walls overgrown with creeping vines. The jungle's assault on the interior continued through glassless loading dock windows, the leafy green vines creeping up and over the sills. Philo started paying attention to the floor, to make sure nothing was moving on it, except things were. Magpie drew his handgun; his men drew theirs.

"Pacific rats," Magpie said. "With the sugarcane gone from the islands, they've gotten bold. Watch your step."

They reached a set of metal doors abutting each other, rubber-tipped, on swivel hinges. Magpie pushed through, held one side open. Inside was the front end of a chicken farm slaughterhouse, a large space illuminated with natural light coming from second-story windows. The cement floor was outlined in white paint with no vegetation on it: the boxing ring, this one also larger than regulation. Beyond the center space was the room's shadowy edges where silhouettes had gathered. The shadows emerged en masse following a dark-suited Japanese male, his charges well-dressed Japanese men also, their suits looking identical. All had raised weapons in their hands, matching Lanakai's men.

"Good afternoon, gentlemen. I am Yabuki. Now that we're all on record as being armed, we can all put our weapons away. Does that work for you, Lanakai-san?"

Wally nodded.

"I will count us down. Men, re-holster your weapons in three, two, one... Thank you, everyone. Please, Lanakai-san, do not be emboldened by my decision to bring less than the number of men we agreed on. My other men are close by but are otherwise engaged." He nodded at a person to his left. "I trust you know Shiko-san."

Philo saw a rather curvy Japanese woman in crotch-hugging gym pants, a top too small for her, and heels, with a martini glass in her hand.

"Hello, Shiko," Wally said. "From the looks of things, Yabuki, someone's getting laid tonight. Enjoy yourself. She's fun."

Shiko gave Wally a single finger salute.

"Now, if you don't mind," Yabuki said, "I wonder if you and I might chat a moment." Yabuki stepped forward, alone, toward the center of the boxing ring.

Lanakai took a step before a concerned Magpie grabbed

his arm. He shook loose to meet Yabuki halfway and spoke loud enough for all to hear.

"Let Kaipo Mawpaw go, Yabuki, or this will not end well. Let's make this between you and me, and not involve an innocent woman."

Yabuki's measured look at Lanakai was quizzical. "A perfect segue. I couldn't have asked for a better introduction to what I have to tell you..."

Philo remained interested in their exchange but stayed busy scrutinizing Yabuki's men, looking for one person: his opponent. He'd seen Jerry Mifumo before, a tall, light heavyweight who was visible as a boxer for exactly those reasons, as the only Japanese fighter to ever compete successfully in the heavier weight divisions. Mifumo wasn't among Yabuki's posse at the moment.

"First, she's alive and in good condition," Yabuki said. "Second, I'm afraid you, Lanakai-san, are only partly consequential to these recent... events. You left Hawaii, I took your turf, and I'm not giving it back, case closed. Third, every organ donor during this recent spree is from Miakamii. They are making you rich."

"Donor? You mean every victim," Wally Lanakai said while he began to circle Yabuki. "You need to stop that shit. Keep your stolen organs to yourself."

Yabuki reciprocated, followed Lanakai's footsteps, their circle tight. "Do you know how we know who these people are, and why we're able to find them?"

Around and around and around they went...

"Tell me."

"Because we developed a hitlist from hacked census records and genealogy services. Names, addresses. Complete as of the last census."

"Almost ten years old, then."

... and around...

"Yes, but it's one hell of a start, wouldn't you say? And it keeps you in body parts. Win-win."

"Not seeing it, Yabuki. A hell of a start at what? How is this a win for you?"

Yabuki stopped walking, turned to ready himself for the inevitable, an in-your-face close-up. "Because I get to exterminate an entire island population, and you get framed for it."

Philo felt the heat index in the room increase ten-fold.

"Kaipo Mawpaw is Miakamiian..." Lanakai said, his eyes narrowing.

"She is at that. Relax, she's still alive. That tells you she'll stay that way until we handle this little contest of ours. And by the way, your boy is a six-point underdog at the Yakuza betting parlors."

Lanakai snapped his hands up, grabbed Yabuki by his lapels, pulled him into his face, screamed at him. "I pay people for their donations! Why are you killing them for their organs?"

Fifteen, maybe twenty guns reappeared from inside the suits of every observer, Philo and Patrick excluded. Lanakai and Yabuki stayed nose to nose, weaponizing their scowls, until Yabuki pried Lanakai's fingers from his lapel, Lanakai still seething.

Yabuki spoke, remaining calm. "You are being rude." Then, speaking in a remorseful tone, "He would have come back a living hero," he said, his comment sincere.

"*What?*"

"My *ojiisan*. Grandfather. My *jiji*. A proud Samurai. Your spear-chucking Hawaiian rodents killed him when his plane crashed on Miakamii. Not killed in battle; murdered when he tried to leave. Twenty-two years old. He left one child behind: my father. This month we celebrate my jiji's hundredth birthday. I choose to honor him," Yabuki said proudly, "by avenging his death. Mark my words, Lanakai"— he gritted his teeth, then scowled while he spat out his intentions—"I plan to eliminate every fucking Miakamiian descendant I can get my hands on. That includes Ms. Mawpaw, because I do not expect my man to lose this match. We're not sure how many Miakamii rodents are left on the island itself, but whatever the number is, it's too many."

Lanakai pushed his forehead into Yabuki's, drilling a stare. "Your jiji deserved it, you cold-blooded asshole."

The blades came out, Yabuki's tantō, Lanakai's small machete, each man backing up to take measure of the other. Their hands went in motion, feinting, sweeping, jabbing. On the outside of the boxing ring, raised hands with guns jerked side to side, repositioning themselves, selecting their targets across the room from each other.

From behind Yabuki's posse came a single shout from a booming voice: "Oyabun-san!" It sliced through the tension, forcing everyone to listen.

The crowd parted, and a large Japanese man emerged, stepping across the spray-painted line on the cement, halting the knife play. He presented himself to Yabuki in the center of the ring with a bow. "I am at your service, Oyabun-san," he said.

"Mifumo," Philo whispered to Patrick.

"Yeah," Patrick said, "sure is, sir."

Ass- and leg-hugging black spandex, a second-skin short-sleeve stretch tee in a burgundy red that revealed massive biceps, toned pecs, and mountainous trapezii. First impression, a superhero in costume; second impression, steroids gone wild. His height, the same as Philo's, far as he could tell. Mifumo followed his bow to Yabuki with a bow to Lanakai.

"Yoshio Mifumo, Lanakai-san," he said, introducing

himself. "I am known as Jerry Mifumo in the United States. My pleasure to entertain you."

Lanakai's heaving chest deflated. He lowered his weapon; Yabuki mirrored him. The blades returned to their sheaths, the guns returned to their holsters. Yabuki spoke.

"Yoshio is not only Yakuza, he is Samurai, with genealogy tracing back to the Shogun clans. I am honored that he represents me. Thank you, Yoshio-san," he said, and the two traded short bows.

Philo removed his jacket, handed Patrick his holstered Sig, and walked his lanky underdressed frame—jeans, white sleeveless tee, sneakers—into the middle of the room.

"So you are Lanakai's fighter," Yabuki said to Philo. "Interesting. I have to say I'm a bit underwhelmed, Mr. Trout. You look undersized, and old." He smiled at Lanakai, then Mifumo. "This shouldn't take long."

"Yeah, I'm his fighter," Philo said, "for today at least. That was good, Yabuki, that comment. Smart. It's in my head now. It took me off my game a second, made me want to cut your balls off with your little dagger, so it worked. But here's what it also did. Your fighter—Jerry here—he's thinking about it too, feels a little pressure now, can't lose to an older, smaller guy, and he needs it to be over quickly, to satisfy your expectations..."

Philo stared down his bareknuckle opponent. "By the way, Jerry, this old guy is undefeated in sixty-five fights, and I hear you're not."

Philo called to Lanakai. "If anyone is gonna referee this thing, get his ass out here now. I'm ready to go. And Yabuki, here's the thing, you old Yakuza fuck—

"My father was a Navy pilot during WWII. He lost friends because of your jiji. We all have heroes we avenge. My father is mine."

The metal door to the chicken farm's death room burst open, two men quickly invading Kaipo's space to grab her by her handcuffed arms. They slammed her onto her back on the flat conveyor belt and held her down. Swinging arms, fingernails, sharp elbows, and sharp teeth—all of her defenses went into motion, bloodying one man's nose and gouging the other man's eyes. She struggled, grabbing hair, ears, and genitals, but after another two men arrived she was no match for the four of them. They pulled her wrists forward, had her momentarily subdued. One of them produced a key for her handcuffs.

Excellent, she told herself, her adrenaline off the chart. *With my hands free, now they're gonna see some shit.*

The man held up the key in one hand to taunt her with it, smiling knowingly, then unholstered his handgun with his other hand. His smile turned into a grim dash before he raised the gun's butt end above her head.

Lights out, Kaipo.

She awoke on her back, head throbbing, wrists by her sides, attached with plastic cable ties to the conveyor belt rails. Her ankles were restrained the same way, all zip ties tight and unforgiving. The men were gone, the door was closed, daylight showing through a window. The stink of dead chickens made her stomach rise again; she vomited off the side of the conveyor belt. Exhausted, she fell asleep, dreamt horrifying scenes of death and dismemberment, the PTSD from her cleaner-fixer work for Ka Hui kicking in.

The door swung open, jolting her awake. A gasoline generator on squeaky wheels entered, a man pushing it. He set it up in a corner, left the room without even a nod in her direction. The door swung open again, the same greasy-haired Japanese man entering, this time pulling a large piece of travel luggage, more like a trunk on wheels. He found a spot he liked for the suitcase and tipped it over to lay it flat on the floor, then went for the heavy-duty zipper that kept its payload in place, unzipping the top and finding other zippers for other compartments. The first item out was a folded plastic mat in blue, heavy, with the consistency of a boat cover; he laid it flat. Then came the suitcase's contents item by item, with him placing each on the mat.

All this activity, the generator, the luggage piece, what was in the luggage... all was familiar to her. The same M.O. for when she worked for Ka Hui.

On the mat were vise grips, knives, needles, a bone saw, a sternum saw, an electric circular saw, scalpels. To the side, multiple Styrofoam coolers, their lids off. The only thing missing was the lye. It wouldn't be needed if the body parts were meant for delivery somewhere.

He stepped into a one-piece hazmat coverall, found the rickety chair in the corner, and sat. He retrieved his phone, spoke one brief phrase into it in Japanese. When the call ended, he slipped a headpiece with a plastic face shield over his greasy-haired head, then worked his hands into a pair of nitrile gloves. Hazmatted head to toe, he placed his hands on his knees, which allowed for perfect posture while he waited. He was now looking at her from across the room, an eerie visage, although she couldn't see his eyes, a human form inhabiting a space-age protective suit, about to do an inhuman thing. A déjà vu experience for her, the vantage points reversed.

She didn't understand what he'd said on his call, but she was sure she knew what it meant: *I am ready*.

Kaipo knew now she was going to die. Her only unknown was how much torture would be involved.

32

They met in the middle of the slaughterhouse floor. Magpie, the largest of all the men present, accompanied Philo. Mifumo's cornerman oozed pure ancestral Samurai in a leather chest piece and arm coverings, leather headpiece, and colorful robes underneath, and two sheathed swords by his sides. Mifumo's entire body dripped sweat, his shirt and tights and exposed skin glistening as though he'd been spritzed for a TV workout commercial, including his bare feet. Philo had worked up his sweat by pacing, shadowboxing, and, what he didn't want to admit to himself, fretting.

The referee, one of Yabuki's men, looked the part with a white shirt and black trousers, and wasn't nearly large enough to separate the two men if they didn't want him to. He searched each of their faces before speaking. The man's hand squeezed Philo's shoulder in a few places, then left his bicep to grip his forearm, then traveled from his forearm to his wrist. Philo had the distinct feeling he was calibrating his physique to decide how much of a bet to place on Mifumo.

"Last time I saw you fight on UFC," Philo said, glancing at Mifumo's hard stomach under his tight top, "I had you and your fat ass on the way to going full sumo. Look at you now. Thank God for steroids, right? Don't forget your shoes..."

"When we're done here, Trout," Mifumo growled, "I am going to eat you."

The referee pushed both fighters back a step so he could insert himself between them. He spoke in Japanese-accented English, Philo still mumbling about Mifumo needing shoes.

"Only instruction is to Mr. Mifumo. Mifumo-san, please do not kill this man." Then came the bluster appropriate enough for the bareknuckle fight parlance each boxer knew was coming, the referee puffing out his chest to deliver it.

"Mifumo-san! Trout-san! Bring your toes to the line!"

No touch of each other's fists for good sportsmanship, no head nods in deference to each man's stellar pugilistic resume, just death stares, something Philo never knew he had in him, yet always had to muster. But still on Philo's mind...

"What about your shoes, Jerry—"

Mifumo flexed his upper torso, bounced from bare foot to bare foot. He barked a Japanese slur at Philo, then followed it up with, "Your promoter insulted the oyabun! Prepare to get the beating of your life."

"But your shoes..."

Mifumo inserted his mouth guard, Philo mirrored him.

"And... fight!" the ref said.

Philo knew what no shoes meant—mixed martial arts, not a bareknuckles bout—knew he'd need to adjust, but didn't expect it to be this soon. Open hand deflections met thrown fists as each fighter felt the other out, speed, power, reflexes, and their ability to parry, until a spinning leg kick whizzed into Philo's jaw, knocking him sideways into a stutter step before he regained his balance. Heel to mouth, one of the hardest blows he'd ever received in a fight, bareknuckles or otherwise, and a near knockout so soon after the referee's opening break. He wiggled his jaw to check it. It had been broken before; not this time. But damn, this guy's legs and feet were just as juiced as the rest of his body...

Lanakai bolted forward, Magpie restraining him, an arm across his chest, Wally barking through Magpie's hold.

"What the hell is this, Yabuki! We agreed no MMA! Bareknuckle boxing! No martial arts...!"

"You insulted me," Yabuki yelled, "which means you insulted Yakuza, which means you insulted the Samurai. You shouldn't have done that."

Now on notice, Philo stayed in retreat mode, readying his head for a different kind of fight. Sixty-five wins, no losses in bareknuckle boxing; 0-0 in mixed martial arts. Philo's heavy hands were devastating, his best physical trait, so many men KO'd by punches that were crisp and with pin-point accuracy, but in MMA, fists were only part of the required weaponry.

Mifumo waded in, cutting off the ring. Kicks went to Philo's calves and thighs, meant to sweep his legs out or cripple him, which they didn't, but they redirected Philo's retreat each time they connected. *Thwap, thwap, thwap...*

Philo's jeans took some of the brunt and canceled the sting he would have otherwise gotten from bone-to-bone contact. Plus Philo was now gauging the timing, the repetition of the leg kicks, their order, left-left-right, right-right-left, then left-left-right again. On the third sequence Philo snapped an open-fisted grab at the right leg, snagging an ankle in his large hand, raising and twisting it until Mifumo lost his balance and left his feet. Philo was on him, a knee to Mifumo's chest, fists a-blazing to the man's head until Mifumo could only defend himself by a tuck inside his arms and a roll, stumbling into a crouch on a single knee, now out of breath. Rather than attack, Philo used the breather to kick off his sneakers and socks. His corner erupted, screaming at him to screw removing his shoes, just go for the kill. Mifumo regained his footing, was steadying himself but remained dazed. The spectators exploded, the noise now at a fever pitch, one side imploring their fighter to engage, the other imploring their fighter to avoid engagement.

Philo's assessment: Mifumo should be unconscious with the punches he'd delivered to his temples, chin, and cheeks, but he wasn't. More of the same might not be enough.

While Mifumo shook out the cobwebs, Philo loosened his belt and stepped out of his jeans.

"Philo! Get on him!" Lanakai screamed, Magpie and Patrick pleading as well. "Don't lose him..."

Philo instead kicked his jeans in Patrick's direction, talking to himself. His muscular thighs and calves, now exposed from the bottom of his black boxer briefs to his ankles, bore tattoos in brilliant colors—some reds, blues, greens, yellows, but predominately black. Beautiful artwork showcasing symbolism that Patrick was the first to appreciate.

"Whoa," Patrick said, awestruck.

On Philo's right calf in black, the *kouf-mem* open circle for the Hebrew letters *kouf* and *mem*, logo for the elite Israel Defense Forces' self-defense system known as Krav Maga. On the left calf, the Navy SEAL trident logo. His calves and thighs had enough definition to make the tats really pop. Philo stripped off his sleeveless tee, showing a buff upper torso. Tattooed in black around his waist, including a 3D image of the cloth knot, was a martial arts black belt.

Philo would now fight shirtless and in his underpants, his only real protection the steel cup inside his jock.

Mifumo, pacing, his wits returned, took notice. "The honors that your ink showcases... they pale in comparison, Trout," he said, panting, "to jiu-jitsu. Jiu-jitsu will always reign supreme..."

"A lot to be said for that, Jerry. A lot to be said for this, too—"

He marched across the floor, fists raised, bobbed left then right, then came up underneath Mifumo's forearms with an uppercutting fist to his chin with more bad intention than the one he'd thrown at Magpie during their sparring session. It connected, snapping Mifumo's head back, but the man stayed on his feet.

Well that's not good, Philo told himself.

Mifumo was on him, arms around Philo's waist, bearhugging him, lifting him, slamming him onto the cement floor, onto his shoulder, where he heard and felt a pop.

That's not good either, damn it...

Mifumo heard it too, plus Philo's pained grunt, and the close-in grappling began, Mifumo swiveling around Philo, lifting him by the waist from behind, off his feet...

A shoulder separation meant the match was over, or could be over, if his opponent saw it the same way. Philo was left to count on Mifumo's killer instinct, that he would instead go for the pain, not the win. Mifumo twisted Philo's torso while raising him up and overhead, would go for a throw-down against the shoulder, maybe snap a clavicle...

Pain rather than win. A bad choice, and the opening Philo needed.

He twisted in midair and jackknifed a leg around Mifumo's neck, an acrobatic move that snagged his opponent's raised arm while overwhelming his head. A tuck of Philo's foot behind his knee locked his leg around Mifumo's arm and neck together. When they slammed into the floor, Mifumo's face took the brunt, not Philo's shoulder, with Philo maintaining a submission chokehold. Mifumo shook, rolled, twisted, pinched, punched, and scratched, wiggling on the floor like a flounder, but like a hooked fish on a boat deck, he was unable to breathe with Philo's locked leg around his neck, applying pressure. Mifumo was losing consciousness. His hand went out, clawed at the cement floor, then he pounded it, signifying his submission... the fight was over...

Philo ignored the signal, tightened the leg lock on his neck and arm, couldn't be sure this wasn't a trick. "I hate this fucking blood sport!" he shouted at the fading Mifumo, "but I'm told... I'd be good at it..."

Yabuki's men screamed, pushed forward from behind their leader, intending to rush Philo, to make him unclench, but Yabuki's arm went up as a stop sign to keep them from interfering. He shouted at them in Japanese until they all quieted and retreated. Stone-faced, he watched Philo as he squeezed the life out of a subdued man, Yabuki's black, dead eyes telling him to finish the job...

...which made Philo unclench his opponent's neck. Mifumo remained on his back, unconscious but alive. Philo rose to his feet in torn briefs, panting, one shoulder drooping, the shoulder separation real and painful as hell.

Yabuki waded in, stood over Mifumo, spoke to Philo. "You chose to spare him." He eyed the defeated fighter at his feet. "But I will not. Get my fighter out of here," he shouted at his men.

Mifumo coughed and sputtered groggy apologies as two Yakuza dragged him off, exiting the room.

"About our agreement, Lanakai—" Yabuki said, his bodyguards with their hands inside their jackets.

Wally's own muscle surrounded him, all of them already on the move, arriving center ring, Magpie on the periphery, a phone to his ear while he eyed Wally. He nodded at his boss and Wally nodded back.

"Where the hell is she?" Wally grunted at Yabuki.

Philo joined Patrick in the back of the room. "Get all our stuff *now*, bud... we can't be in here..."

Yabuki inserted his fist between his and Lanakai's middle-aged, angry faces, and turned his thumb down, the gesture slow, dramatic. "I never had any intention of releasing her. She and her body parts will now sleep... with the chickens. Similar to everyone left on that island..."

He barked an order in Japanese. His men showed their guns. Lanakai's men reciprocated.

"Go, Patrick, we need to get out..."

Gunfire erupted, Philo and Patrick making themselves smaller, less of a target in their retreat, and not looking back. They reached the loading dock, peeked out a door, scanned the parking lot. The two Yakuza protecting the vehicles were now rushing the steps keen to the gunfire, to enter the building through a different door.

"Go! You drive!" Philo said, pushing Patrick.

"What about Kaipo, sir?"

"I know. Just get in the car..."

"He said she'll now sleep with the chickens, sir...!"

"I heard, Patrick! Close the goddamn door!"

Patrick backed the SUV up, slapped the transmission into drive, spinning the tires in the dirt until they caught traction, the vehicle rocketing into the tire ruts as it headed back into the jungle.

The SUV idled in a clearing. Philo pointed. "This one. Go up here."

They were running out of farm property to investigate. Fifteen minutes post-fight, he was sure they were near the property line, could hear street traffic. He had his jeans back on, his socks, and his footwear, was now negotiating his shirt around a throbbing shoulder that needed medical attention.

"Seat belt back on now, sir," Patrick said, turning where Philo pointed. "This trail looks really bouncy…"

It was one of a few offshoot tributaries they'd passed on their way to the chicken slaughterhouse that had been the fight venue. The vegetation grabbed at the SUV's raised undercarriage and the side mirrors, stalky, heavy, with scraping noises against the car's frame and the side panels, but a little less of it because they were inside tire ruts. Choking, enveloping vegetation that smelled like what it was, photosynthesis at work, leafy, dusty, sneezy, and chlorophyll-laden. Philo hit his head on the roof with the vehicle dipping into and out of the ruts—"owww!"—until he'd finally harnessed himself into the seat.

"There, up ahead, Patrick. What is that?"

"Dunno, sir."

It sank into the hill, a landslide against one side of it. Another long building, this one spreading out left of where they sat. The landslide had reached the metal roof and nearly devoured it, the building underneath. This could not have been the main entrance, yet they couldn't see the other end, the building disappearing into the jungle, although this jungle shrubbery seemed to border the developed parts of Kauai. The door leading inside the building was gripped by aggressive, advancing vegetation, was open, but barely. Could they even fit through...?

"We'll check here, Patrick," Philo said, exiting the vehicle. "You need to take this." He stuffed a gun into Patrick's hand, one of his Sigs, then stuffed his own Sig behind his back, under his untucked shirt. "Point and shoot, bud, if you feel the need."

"Point and shoot, Philo sir."

Patrick gripped the edge of the building's exterior door, moved it enough to shoulder it open, bettering the vines that held it in place. They both slipped inside.

Sunlight through a skylight, then additional sunlight through the side windows of each room they investigated. No evidence of recent human activity here, a room with desks that looked like an abandoned office, dusty, drafty, but with left-over human detritus: shelving, an old icebox, shoes, dressers, and slatted bunkbeds.

"Philo sir."

"Yeah?"

"In the corners, sir. Nests."

"Yeah."

Along the edges of the room and in the corners, loose twigs, branches, and wispy things that floated as their shuffling feet kicked up the dust. Whatever animals had found homes in here—mice, rats, stray dogs, cats—they hadn't had far to look to make their digs comfy. The wispy things were feathers, the room lined with them.

Patrick stopped in his tracks.

"What is it, bud?"

"My mother."

"*What?*"

"She was Japanese. She said *her* mother lived with the chickens..."

Patrick was recovering a memory, Philo realized. His eyes bulged, a PTSD moment hitting him, unexpected, showing him no mercy. "Here. In Hawaii, in... in the..."

Internment camps, Philo finished for himself.

"What if she was here—"

"Patrick. We can't do this now, we need to check the rest of this place out, see if Kaipo is here, get her out..."

The farther they moved inside, room by room, the more artifacts they found on the floors and the shelves. Bowls, dishes, Japanese dolls, "geisha" hair pins and other hair ornaments, bolts of cloth, chopsticks. And a sampler, on a shelf: an embroidered American flag, a heavy layer of dust covering it. Philo kept walking. Patrick picked up the sampler in his wake, blew off the dust, held it up close to his face.

"Patrick. C'mon, bud, move it—"

Patrick put it down. "Sir, forty-eight stars, sir. I counted them."

"Fine, keep it, put it in the bag, but let's go!"

The artifacts trail ended at one large, vault-like door, ajar. They squeezed through sideways, Philo's shoulder protesting, him grunting under his breath.

On the other side, a voice beyond a wall. Male. They halted, held their breaths to listen. It was a one-sided conversation in Japanese. When the voice stopped talking, no other noise filled the void.

Until something mechanical started up.

A generator, Philo mouthed silently to a nodding Patrick. Philo retrieved his gun. Confrontation time. He poked his head out far enough for one eye to see around the corner.

One man, hazmatted, his headgear in place, his tools and other paraphernalia scattered about him, needles, clothing, saws, tarps; a scalpel in his hand. A cell phone sat on a separate table, a handgun next to it. Plugged into the generator was a circular saw. Beyond him, a woman lay strapped onto a conveyor belt.

Kaipo Mawpaw.

Sunlight showed her face, her head, her hair. Cornrows. Not how he remembered her, but it was her. She did not seem awake, her eyes closed, yet she wasn't attached to anything. Then he saw the blood. It dripped from an open wound in her abdomen, onto the conveyor belt, then onto the floor. A bloodied Sleeping Beauty, maybe already dead...

Patrick sidled up next to him to spy on their target.

Philo whispered, "See anyone else in here, bud?"

A headshake.

"On three, then."

They rushed their man after the countdown, Patrick taking him out like a linebacker does a defenseless quarterback, putting him on his back. Philo arrived, leaned in, ripped off the guy's headgear, stuck his Sig in his face. "If she's dead," he groused, *"you're* dead."

Their prey stayed mute with no attempt to retaliate, instead glanced past Philo's drooped shoulder at additional company now in the room.

"Put your gun on the floor," came the order.

Behind them, three Japanese men leveled multiple guns

on the two undesirables who had crashed their torture party. Philo placed his weapon on the floor.

"Raise your hands."

Their hands went up, three hands at least, Philo having trouble raising the fourth.

"All the way up!" the Yakuza said, but Philo couldn't comply, groaning in his attempt. "No? Then I will do it for you—"

"Stop!" a loud voice boomed. From the rear, a recovered Jerry Mifumo powered past Yabuki's guards to move front and center in confronting Philo and Patrick. Loose workout pants, a comfy sweatshirt, and a duffle bag across his shoulder hid the man's magnificent physique and, Philo supposed, his shame.

"I separated this man's shoulder," he said, addressing his associates, but his interest lay solely in Philo and Patrick, "before this man separated me... from my dignity. Three raised hands will have to do." He looked skyward and spoke a quick Shinto prayer in Japanese, ending it in English. "I have been given the chance to remedy this. Thank you, ancestral warriors..."

A closer look at Mifumo's duffle. It resembled what baseball players carried to their games, with long side pockets for baseball bats. In use was one side pocket only, a black bat handle exposed. Mifumo gripped it and slid it out. Not a bat. A Samurai katana sword.

An exaggerated, noisy, metal-against-metal release separated sword from sheath. The Yakuza cavalry mumbled among themselves. Then came the nodding and the smiling.

"Quiet, please! You are all dismissed. I will take it from here. You, doctor-san"—he addressed the hazmatted man standing like a statue in a corner—"you should stay."

The soldiers snickered, their arm gestures mimicking

chopping, endorsing this as an outcome, then they filed out of the room.

Mifumo dropped the sheath, circled behind Kaipo, who was still horizontal and still not moving. Seeing the exposed blade, Philo started forward.

"Oh, you fear for her," Mifumo said. "I wouldn't, Trout. All that blood, she looks dead already. And this isn't for her. Please keep your distance."

"Where's Yabuki, Jerry?" Philo said, refocusing him, advancing a step.

"The oyabun? He's arranging a... surprise." On stealthy feet, Mifumo neared the door the men had used to exit the room. He gently closed it, placed a chair under its handle, then faced Philo again. "Just like I have a surprise for you."

Philo, Patrick, the Japanese doctor-slash-executioner, and Mifumo were left to assess each other, Kaipo Mawpaw in repose.

Mifumo raised his sword with a flourish, brought it near to his face to admire it. "There are notches on this handle," he said. "This katana is generations old. Hundreds, and hundreds, and hundreds of years old, handed down from Samurai to Samurai. How many have been beheaded by it, I'm not really sure, but I suppose the notches would tell the story if we cared to count them, there are so many. And now—"

His examination of the handle ended. He bowed dramatically toward Philo. He presented the sword to him, handle first. "You must do me this honor, Philo Trout-san. The victor... must vanquish the defeated."

"I'm not doing that, Jerry."

Rebuffed, Mifumo laid the sword on the floor. He began disrobing. Shoes, socks, shirt, pants, leaving himself in his gym trunks only. He dropped to one knee, leaned forward, and bowed to expose the back of his neck.

"Pick it up, Philo-san. I would rather you, my conqueror, restore my honor than suffer more scorn at the hand of the oyabun. Please. Do this for me. A warrior like you. Pick it up... use it..."

Philo eyed the sword, then eyed the gun he'd discarded, then came back to the sword. Patrick and the doctor didn't move.

"Jerry, no."

"So be it." Mifumo reached into his bag and found his small tantō knife. "Philo Trout, I bid you good-bye... as a true Samurai."

The tantō blade entered Mifumo's abdomen with a hard, two-handed push and a soft "unhhh," the Samurai warrior muting his scream, his eyes widening while he rotated it internally to do maximum damage. As his insides spilled onto the floor, he fell forward onto them and the tantō, pushing it deeper, apologizing through the pain to his ancestors in Japanese.

A distraught Patrick moved to Kaipo, hovered over her body, assessing the damage from a scalpel to her midsection. The Yakuza doctor rushed to Mifumo, a helpless, bloody mess.

Philo pocketed his gun and reached for Mifumo's sword, one-handing it off the floor, its heft considerable. "Hey, Doc," Philo said to the Yakuza doctor, the sword by Philo's side. "C'mere..."

A new plan. The room was about to get a lot messier.

34

The door kicked open and the Yakuza soldiers streamed into the room with the chicken slaughterhouse conveyor. A man speaking on a phone trailed them, walking swiftly to make his entrance behind a bevy of drawn handguns. A collective gasp plus groaning and gagging rose up from the room's newest occupants.

The man spat on the floor, trying to rid his mouth of the taste of death, then spoke into the phone again. "We are, um, here, Oyabun..."

A voice blasted through the phone's speaker. "Is the doctor finished?"

Yabuki's man surveyed the room. "Are you?" he said to the room's only occupant, their grim-reaper executioner contractor who was hazmatted head to toe, and who answered with a muffled "yes" and a thumbs-up.

"We are checking, Oyabun," the soldier said into the phone to Yabuki.

Blood had splattered the floor, the ceiling, the conveyor belt, the executioner's hazmat suit dripping with it, from headgear to shoes. No body, just squishy mush underfoot and multiple white Styrofoam coolers lined up along a back wall, a cloudy mist above them from dry ice, their lids ajar, bloody handprints on them.

He elbowed the doctor-cleaner out of the way, began pulling open cooler after cooler, finding splayed arms, hacked feet, minced buttocks, strips of muscle and bone, a gloppy mixture of internal organs, grimacing at the sight inside each cooler, having to quit after only a few, unable to stomach the search. He yelled at the doctor. "The head? Where is the head?"

Their grim reaper located a certain cooler, lifted off the lid, reached inside with both gloved hands. He gripped the head in front and in back, lifted it, a profile reveal only: black, blood-soaked hair, blood-smeared face, neck as far south as the shoulder line.

Yabuki's voice came screaming through the phone's speaker. "Did you forget about me? Answer me! Is it done?"

"Yes, Oyabun, it is done."

"Excellent. Now bring all of her to me. I will give that Yankee dog Lanakai what he wants. Next, listen carefully. Have the men take my yacht and motor over to that unholy island. It's time for us to tidy it up a bit."

Each man's ticket out of the bloodbath of a room was to carry a cooler full of body parts slop. With the bucket brigade of coolers winding down, only a few left, Yabuki's man texted his oyabun: *What do I do with the exterminator?*

He waited for a response, did a slow turn to see where their hazmatted contractor was. Not here. Not in the next room. Not in the next. Gone. He retraced his footsteps. Nowhere to be found. He went to a window.

A steep drop started a few feet beyond the ledge, leading away from the abandoned building camouflaged by heavy vegetation, hiding in virtual plain sight. Seventy-eighty yards away at the bottom of the hill sat a quiet business park and a neighborhood, all connected by paved streets, the only vehicle on the road an idling street sweeper.

The return text from Yabuki: *Eliminate him.*

He swore in Japanese, stopped cursing only when he saw a blur of blue hazmat on the bottom half of the hill, scrambling to stay upright, then finally sliding the last few yards onto the curb. Tucked under the man's arm was one of the white Styrofoam coolers. More cursing, which was interrupted by a drawn pistol that sprayed semiauto gunshots down the hill, zipping through the tree canopy, the bullet spray reaching the street sweeper, pinging the metal. The blue target got to his feet and scuttled to the protection of the other side of the truck, climbing into the driver's side door.

The Yakuza man's screams echoed his carelessness, him now needing to scramble around this horrific blood-filled room, flipping lids off the remaining coolers, their dry ice mist escaping. He pulled the top off the last cooler...

Finally he exhaled, said *hai* to himself, Japanese for yes. The severed head was still there. He grabbed the hair in one hand, lifted the head out to see the victim for himself, again, to get the full impact, to appreciate the spoils. Still salvageable as a completed task for the oyabun; all was not lost. Another prayerful Shinto thanks was in order. He lowered the head, then stopped short when he saw the Adam's apple.

Philo pulled at the tarp with one arm, two edges gathered together in his hand, Kaipo inside it. He slid her along the jungle floor amid wild tropical overgrowth and over bumps of twisted tree roots and patches of volcanic ash hardened into rock. The blue tarp was good for it, was heavy and durable, and it helped that she was still unconscious, much like the exterminator doctor they'd spared after they had him cut up Mifumo's body at gunpoint, rendering him a genderless, unidentifiable mess. The executioner now rested outside the slaughterhouse window, beneath the sill, unconscious and underdressed.

Kaipo mumbled, then came an agonizing groan, then came more mumbling, then an *ouch*.

"Sorry, didn't see that rock. Hang in there, Kaipo, we're almost down the hill..."

Kaipo mumbled more, spoke words this time, kept speaking until she was almost fully lucid. "I... I can smell you..."

Philo eyed her face, her closed eyes while he grunted through his steps, saw her REM-ing through her dream state that now mostly wasn't. "You... you *what*?"

"Smell you, in your SEAL hidey-hole... Miakamii..."

Their conversation continued a few yards more, their re-introduction including complete sentences that sealed their shared history from Philly and Miakamii both, dating back to her time on the island as a teenager and his time as a SEAL. Philo was now running out of gas, his inflamed shoulder in torture overdrive. He couldn't go on like this much longer—

He lost his footing and fell on his ass, slid feet-first down the hill, grimacing from the pain in his shoulder, the vegetation slapping his face yard after yard until he hit bottom, spilling onto a curb. Kaipo, still in her tarp, bumped against him a second later. He took some deep breaths, grabbed the edges of the tarp again, ready to move. Ten yards to their left, a behemoth of a truck moved in their direction. He squinted to better the glare from the sun on its windshield, to get a look at the driver, was greeted with a smiling Patrick in hazmat.

"Guess our ride is here, Kaipo," he said, breathing hard.

With Kaipo jammed behind the front seat and cocooned in the tarp, Philo hauled himself onto a running board, the sweeper on the move again, Philo holding onto the window ledge, a tight live-or-die grip with one hand only. The brown-faced guy riding shotgun greeted him with a nervous smile and big, wide eyes that said he was scared shitless, focusing on the gun tucked into Philo's pants.

"This is Marty the sweeper driver, sir," Patrick said.

"Hi, Marty," Philo said, shouting to better the road whine. "Relax, you can go with us or you can leave, your choice. If you haven't figured this out, we're in deep shit, but trust me, we mean well. I'm really hoping you stay behind, Marty, 'cause I've got a big favor to ask…"

———

"Good decision, Marty," Philo said to himself. He checked the sideview mirror from the safety of the passenger seat, watched the uniformed sanitation worker at curbside stare at the departing street sweeper, a smallish white Styrofoam cooler at Marty's feet. Marty stayed focused on his stolen truck while he made a phone call as it drove away.

Shit… he's dialing 9-1-1. Cops, damn it…

Do me that favor, Marty, please. Follow through, bud…

"Philo sir?"

"Yeah, Patrick?"

"You think Mr. Lanakai survived that gunfight?"

"He owes me a lot of money, so yeah, I'm counting on it."

Philo refocused the mirror to see many blocks behind them, into the distance. A car bolted onto the rear horizon, a silhouette against the setting sun, came down hard on its shocks, sparks scattering.

Company that wasn't cops. *Shit-shit-shit…*

"How fast does this thing go, Patrick?"

"No idea, sir!"

"Pick a left turn and make it, into a neighborhood, anywhere, we need streets with corners..."

A sharp left and then more gas pedal, the sweeper approaching a stop sign, no cross traffic, a hard right onto another street. Philo dialed 9-1-1.

"*What's your emergency?*"

"See, we're in a street sweeper on Kela Drive, in a residential neighborhood, being chased by pissed-off Yakuza mobsters... No, I'm not drunk... Philo Trout, retired SEAL. I know Chief Koo. Turn here, Patrick...!"

"*You sure you didn't carjack that sweeper, Mr. Trout?*"

"Yeah, ah, no, well, maybe, but we're not the bad guys here. These mobsters... we sprang their hostage..."

At the next hard turn the phone jumped out of his hand, landed somewhere on the truck floor, out of reach. In the middle of the street, kids on skateboards. Patrick jumped the curb, started across the lawns, a bad move that would not end well for pedestrians. They needed to get out of the neighborhoods and stay out of them, find a stretch where they could accelerate, take their chances—

"Turn here!"

They turned onto a four-lane highway with a long straightaway, the first road sign, *HOWLING SANDS – 4 MILES*.

"The Naval base, bud," Philo said aloud. "Really goose this thing, Patrick—"

"Yessir, Philo sir, fifty-five, fifty-seven—"

Philo watched the sideview mirror a full thirty seconds, no activity behind them, hoped their pursuers hadn't taken out any kids; he'd have so much PTSD trouble with that. They passed a Lamborghini, a convertible in neon blue on a lazy early evening drive along the coast. Philo touched the Sig to

266CHRIS BAUER

his forehead in a friendly salute before realizing how bad a look that was. The sports car driver slammed the breaks and let their truck have both lanes of the highway as a right of way.

"Something I said?" Philo said, checking the sideview mirror, frowning.

"I'd say it was the gun, Philo sir," Patrick said.

"I'd say so too, Patrick..."

Another look in the sideview mirror. A sedan careened left out of the neighborhood and onto the highway behind them, now less than a quarter mile away. Philo needed his phone, it was on the floor somewhere, couldn't find it. Patrick handed him his. He punched in some numbers.

"Commander Malcolm here."

"Evan!" Philo shouted.

"Yeah," an annoyed response, "who's this?"

"Hey! We're in a real fix now, bud, really need your help—"

"Philo? You fucked me over about that bareknuckle fight, goddamn it. I'm with Lanakai's people right now. They feel my pain, Philo. I want a piece of that prick Yabuki..."

"I know, I'm sorry, Evan. Look, we're on Kela Drive near Howling Sands Airport..."

"Near the base?"

"Yeah! Yabuki's men, they're right behind us. They catch us, they kill us, Evan. We're in a fluorescent-green street sweeper..."

"Sorry, bad connection, I thought you said a street sweeper."

"You heard right, damn it, which should make you realize we're pretty much SOL. I need some support at the end of the line, bud..."

He leaned out the window, looked behind them, was fired on. The gunshots dinged the side mirror, then more shots blasted most of the mirror into pieces, a large chunk knocking the phone out of his hand, the black plastic handheld disappearing behind them on the asphalt.

Fucking damn it... Fuuuck...!

The sedan was now only ten, eleven lengths back. Ahead of them—

Howling Sands - 1 mile.

"Patrick, lower your head, bud, get down in the seat, watch the road from inside the steering wheel..."

Philo leaned over, checked the dashboard in front of Patrick. "What's that button say?"

"'Engage brooms,'" Patrick shouted.

"Brooms?"

"The cleaning brushes, sir. The big brushes under the sweeper..."

"Press the button!"

All four circular brushes emerged from the underside on metal skeletons, two each side, on robotic arms that lowered them toward the asphalt while increasing the sweeper's wingspan.

"That red button there, Patrick, what's it say?"

"'Eject brooms—'"

"Do it!"

Four heavy-duty brushes two feet in diameter with thick bristles embedded in circular wooden frames bounced off the road and away from the sweeper, then went airborne in their wake. Philo positioned a remaining sliver of side mirror to see two of them impact the car behind them, one a direct hit through the windshield. The car careened left, then right, then ran into the shoulder, skidding back out onto the highway where it flipped onto its side. Smoke and fire rose up, blurring the blacktop behind it.

Philo howled in ecstasy, pounded the dash with his good

hand. Patrick howled louder than Philo, adding, "I think I peed my pants, Philo sir!"

Philo leaned over to squint at the red buttons on the dash to read the caution language next to them: *Do not eject brooms while truck is in motion*—a design flaw if he ever saw one...

They heard a rumble behind them. Philo again glanced at the sliver of mirror still in place. Another sedan emerged from the smoke like a black bat out of hell, swerving around the crippled car, then accelerating.

"Shit."

The Yakuza car roared alongside the truck, the men firing semiauto long rifles at will, taking out the side window glass, the bullets lodging in the padded interior ceiling, additional shots piercing the heavy-duty passenger door. Nearly flat in his seat, Philo saw the door's interior metal stop the slugs just short of breaking through. The car inched ahead of them, the men now firing into the engine compartment, shots pinging wildly off the fenders and the hood, the engine beginning to smoke. Their final maneuver was to pass them and move into their lane, in front of the sweeper, maintaining their distance at nearly sixty miles per hour. The long guns came out again, this time from both sides of the sedan, the semiautos aimed at the windshield. The rata-tat-tat noise was deafening, obliterating the windshield and punching through the grill, glass flying around the cabin like they were in a tornado, more bullets and glass ripping the padded ceiling and pinging out through the broken side windows with Philo and Patrick crouched below the dashboard, showered by the debris. Their street sweeper now whined and wheezed and coughed up steam. It slowed, was rolling to a stop...

Two handguns were in the truck, Philo's and the one he gave Patrick. Impossible odds, facing off against multiple long rifles. Philo hazarded a peek over the dashboard, saw four

Yakuza exit the sedan ten yards away, their AR-15s in play, leaning into a crouch, approaching the truck like commandos. He ducked back down, awaiting the inevitable, listening to sand and stone crunch under their approaching feet.

"Patrick, bud, they're either gonna kill us or capture us..."

"I know, sir. Love you, Philo sir."

"Love you back, son."

The crunching sand and stone noises stopped, then quickly picked up again, but were now receding. The car doors opened and shut and the tires squealed. Philo lifted his head, hazarded another peek past the windowless dash in time to see the sedan screech into an about-face fishtail, catch rubber, then whip past them in a hurry.

Whup-whup-whup-whup...

Overwhelming the horizon, a helicopter gunship closed in.

Philo kicked the sweeper door open and rolled out of the cabin, dropping onto the asphalt. He locked his elbow as he steadied his Sig, stiffening his arm as he drew down on the retreating sedan. The Navy gunship roared overhead, blotting out the sky above the crippled sweeper. When Philo fired his weapon, the cracks of his shots were drowned out by the Seahawk's dual M60 machine guns taking their measure, strafing the speeding sedan until it veered out of control, flipped end over end, burst into flames, then exploded. Philo lowered his gun, wanting to believe his steady and precise sharpshooting took out the driver and the men in it before the explosion did, no accounting for the hundreds of expended machine gun shells that littered the highway in the Seahawk's wake.

Police vehicles with piercing sirens pursuing the sedan slammed past him and Patrick, the two of them standing outside the stolen truck. One police SUV stopped alongside them. Chief Terry Koo exited, gave Philo the visual once-over. He directed one of his cops to Philo's side to give him something to lean on, then he spoke.

"You said something about a hostage, Trout?"

His 9-1-1 call.

"Yeah. Back seat, Chief, a woman wrapped in a tarp. They drugged her, then they cut her open. She would have been the next evisceration murder. She needs an ambulance—"

"You have a name for her?"

He looked at the street sweeper, the truck full of bullet holes, all its glass shattered, its engine compartment hissing steam, and one front tire flat. His disjointed conversation with Kaipo was still fresh in his mind. Mostly incoherent, it had been coherent enough, especially the promise he made to her.

"Yes. First name is Aiata, last name Hauata."

35

Ella Waumami's husband Ben pushed the small, overburdened buckboard wagon out of the storage space in the rear of the church, then closed the double door, not bothering to padlock it. He guided the wagon outside the church, where Ella's horse Kumu awaited him. Full moon; Ben didn't need a flashlight. He spoke to Kumu in a soothing tone, then hitched her up to the wagon, her disposition changing as soon as Ben climbed into the buckboard seat, with her becoming all business. She met his command for her to pull with eagerness and determination. They made a stop at the settlement's community garden to retrieve bushel baskets of gathered vegetables: squash, cucumbers, onions, some sweet potatoes. Ben deposited the baskets in the back of the buckboard, filling in whatever empty space remained around a tightly tarpaulined payload.

A yacht coasted quietly into the sleepy Miakamii lagoon, no running lights, almost no wake, under moonlit skies. The engine shut down. Six men climbed overboard into an inflated skiff and motored away from the cruiser. They beached, climbed out, and assembled on the sand, overdressed in dark business suits, and over-armed, on so peaceful an island, with AR-15s. One man took command, said "Follow me" in Japanese, and they filed in behind his lead.

They entered the interior scrub on a dirt path, the leader demanding they stay quiet. A clearing spread open before them, the island's school, church, farmland, vegetable gardens, and smelly, decomposing livestock carcasses, and the crashed helicopter halves strapped and chained on large sleds, ready for transport to the beach, closer to the ocean. The dead copter pieces generated muted conversation, the men grabbing parts from tables and large canvas bags, winging them in all directions into the jungle, snickering at their cleverness, their disdain for the investigation and for this island full of backward, simple, vulnerable people. They dragged cardboard boxes off folding tables, tipped them over and spilled them out, then urinated on the littered helicopter parts.

Another path led to a new clearing. Volcanic ash underfoot gave way to a furrowed dirty rut that was fifty, sixty yards in length, at its end a memorial plaque in English on a concrete stand. The event the plaque commemorated: the crash of a WWII Japanese Zero in this very space after its Pearl Harbor sneak attack, its rusted hulk hauled away decades later for research and to validate the wartime historical event. The men gathered around the plaque, bowing in prayer, offering thanks to their pilot and other Samurai heroes in *kami-no-michi*, or Shintoism. Their prayers and the clearing left behind, they reached their destination: the settlement with the island's only population, its defenseless houses and huts peppering this elevation and northward, up a gentle sway of a hill. They began their ascent.

A front door exploded behind vicious leg kicks, two Yakuza men leading with guns and flashlights, the living room unlit, unoccupied. They kicked through brittle wooden chairs and tables, shoved a parlor sofa aside, stormed the dining room, the kitchen, the two bedrooms at the rear of the house, found no one inside. The hut across the path faced a similar assault, a residence furnished for occupation by simple, indigenous people, the other two men strafing the entire interior with semiautomatic fire when finding no one inside to execute.

Two more small, simple, dust-laden, cobwebbed homes, two more residences obliterated with gunfire, neither with any people in them.

The lead executioner found a phone signal and made a call, began speaking in Japanese. "There is no one here in these homes, Oyabun. No one to kill..."

"You are wrong, you idiot!" Mr. Yabuki said. "Search every house in that bung-hole of a settlement. There are still many people on that island! The census says so. Find them. Exterminate them. Restore your country's honor. Honor the Samurai...!"

The Yakuza leader assembled his men outside, eyed the higher elevation in front of them. More homes at intervals, four, five plus, a little larger than the ones they'd checked already. The largest homestead in the settlement, a farm, sat atop the hill.

"There," he said, pointing. "The one at the top of this ridge. Our next target. If anyone is in this backward, scrub-fish shithole of a village, it will be there."

The path opened up. At the end of it was a barn, a two-story house, a grain silo, and multiple fenced yards. Squealing pigs, sheep, and two horses roamed a corral outside a stable, the horses breathing heavily. The six men each caught their breath while checking the magnificent moonlit view and sightlines at this altitude: the lagoon with their moored cruiser, the beach with the inflatable outboard, a starry-starry night, the moon aglow. Across the channel and seventeen nautical miles away sat Kauai, the island illuminated and sparkling with nightlife. Breathtaking.

Barn first. Roaming, clucking chickens squawked at their arrival, each man tempted to blow them away in a flurry of bullets, but all were kept alive by the leader's finger to his lips, demanding silence. Next, the house. On quiet feet they moved from room to room, the home basic but comfortable, with an old sofa and tufted but worn side chairs in the living room, a hand pump for well water in the kitchen, and a dining room with a china closet, the house's entire contents about to be obliterated by indiscriminate gunfire. Two men cradled their long rifles near their hips, wrapping their fingers around their triggers.

"No," a Yakuza warrior said, "look! Shadows in the horse stables, a flickering light..."

The six Yakuza marched across the dirt yard, guns by their sides, alert but giddy, about to participate in the slaughter of the innocent, God-fearing, and unarmed Miakamiian farmers that this property supported. The flickering candle threw shadows on the inside walls, shadows that were on the move.

"This is the place," their lead said. "Someone is in there. Time to restore Japan's honor, and the honor... of the Samurai."

They entered the horse stable. Many stalls, no horses, a side-wall paddock door open to the starry evening, the horses wisely outside, in the corral. Hay on the floor, in the hayloft, and in all the nooks and crannies and corners. Baled hay in piles, singles and doubles. Hanging farm tools: sickles, scythes, steel leg traps for the occasional wild boars who wandered too far up the ridge. One man grabbed a pitchfork and started poking, speaking in English to the stable's unseen, shadowy occupants.

"You must show yourself, you American worms."

He wandered farther into the stable, jabbing, poking, grunting while he thrust the prongs of the pitchfork into the scattered piles of hay.

"You must pay for the murder of Oyabun's grandfather eighty years ago. Come out, take your medicine. I will use my tantō, and I will make it quick, just like I did to your pilot before I rode the air to safety while his helicopter crashed into your despicable island. Hel-*lo*-o (*jab, poke*), where ar-*r-re* you...? My tantō is preferable to this pitchfork..."

No movement, no giveaways anywhere. "Very well then, you give me no choice." He raised the pitchfork overhead, was about to come down hard into a hay pile.

Ben sprang from behind two nearby bales, his knife in his hand, an antique handgun in his waistband, startling the speaker, overcoming him. Ben's short, sinewy body subdued the loudmouth Japanese Yakuza with a knife to his throat.

The other five men lifted their long rifles, trained them on him and his hostage, in the ready. Ben sized up his enemies, dropped his knife, replaced it with a handgun to the man's cheek and an arm around his neck for a chokehold. He wandered to one side with his hostage.

"Leave my island now, without this man," Ben warned. "Chester's murderer! I get to keep him. Go. No questions will be asked. I implore you, man to man, be smart. You need to go. Now."

His captive tried to speak. Ben jammed the gun into his mouth and started shoving it down his throat while tightening his chokehold.

"*Roujin*. 'Old man!'" a different Yakuza said, stepping up, flexing his bravado for his peers. "The Bushido code of the Samurai reigns supreme! This warrior does not care what you do to him. He will die an honorable death, in battle, and will be honored by his family for generations. You, *roujin*, have no chance of survival. You call that rusty handgun a gun? It probably won't even fire. And I thought guns on the island were against the Logan family rules—"

The Yakuza chuckled, as did the other henchmen, all presenting mocking laughs and wide smiles, all of them still flashing their long guns. "These... what we are holding... now *these* are *guns*..."

The speaker raised his weapon and his associates did likewise. The AR-15s erupted, began spraying the interior of the stable with chaotic automatic fire, aimed not at Ben or his hostage but rather at everything else: the roof, the stable walls, the floor, the windows, the stalls. The gunfire stopped, the laughing beginning again, with Ben still in command of his captive.

"Now. Back to you, *roujin*—"

From deep within the rear of the stable came a disembodied female voice. "Big fucking deal," Ella said.

The Yakuza speaker turned up his nose at this revelation, did a visual sweep of his charges, the men now snickering, chiding him for letting a woman speak to him that way. He played along.

"Wow," he said, aiming a flashlight deep into the shadows protecting the rear of the stable, where they'd heard the voice. "Guns on the island, and now their women are cursing at men! Mr. Logan wouldn't like that a bit, you gutter *gaishō*..."

In the tense silence that followed, Ella poked her head through the large pile of hay against the rear wall, the Yakuza's flashlight glinting off her eyes. In one motion she swept a tarpaulin back, exposing the old buckboard kept in church storage. Visible in its payload was a black 7.7mm type 97 aerial machine gun cannon, the one removed from the Japanese Zero eighty years earlier, fully operational, and able to feed and fire nine hundred rounds per minute from a tripod mounted inside the buckboard's bed.

She spoke in a defiant tone. "You consider those things guns, asshole? *This*... is a *gun*."

With the forty-one-inch machine gun chest high, she depressed the trigger, feeding the ammunition on a belt from a black box on the air cannon's right, decapitating her targets, shredding limbs, severing torsos—"This is for Chester!"—the tinny noise of the ammunition belt the same as she heard while sleeping on the beach, her beloved Ben taking the heavy-duty artillery piece through its paces once every year or so, making sure the air cannon remained operational.

Chicka-chicka-chicka-chicka-chicka-CHICKA-CHICKA—

Ben held the last Yakuza in his arms, the man's squirming plea for mercy so unbecoming a Samurai, Ben's knife now against his throat just like the thug boasted that he'd done to Chester in the helicopter, and like Ella's grandfather did to the Zero pilot in 1941. Ben told his hostage as much, told him what he was about to do to him, then slit his throat ear to ear.

36

"We're in position, boss," Magpie said on the phone to Wally. Wally rubbed his brow, at a loss. A lot on his mind.

He exited a different chicken slaughterhouse building on the farm property after having his men toss room after room in an exhaustive search, no Kaipo inside. He'd moved from anger to grief with each passing moment, but the hate and the need for revenge still drove him.

Their casualties from the post-fight skirmish: the number of Ka Hui dead, zero; number wounded, three. All would live. Yabuki's casualties, from what Wally could tell: many more wounded, two dead. Neither of the dead was Yabuki, which was all Wally cared about.

"Tell me what you see, Magpie. Your surroundings. I want to feel this."

"One dead Japanese yacht guy, boss, draped over the con, a rifle shot to the head. My doing when we boarded from the Navy outboard."

More description from Magpie, wearing night goggles: a well-appointed bridge, even for a yacht, a nervous U.S. Navy commander standing next to Magpie, eager to get on with it, and the island's calm lagoon, lit by the moon. Some monk seals were on the beach, sleeping, paying no attention to them.

"Raising my binoculars, boss."

He mentioned the view of the channel separating Miakamii from Kauai, leading to the lagoon, with a soft chop and moonlit whitecaps. Mentioned the whine of an outboard engine, moving slowly across the channel, Magpie seeing two people aboard.

"It's Yabuki, boss, closing in. Fifty yards."

He again mentioned the Navy commander on his left, who now raised the rocket launcher to his shoulder. The launcher's red laser dotted the chest of one of the outboard's occupants.

"Is Commander Malcolm ready, Magpie?"

"I believe he is, boss."

"We owe this to him."

"I know, boss."

"Anything else, Magpie?"

"Yabuki sees the laser on his chest, boss. Now he sees me in his binoculars, looking at him."

"Take him out."

Magpie's final description was his tap of CO Evan Malcolm's shoulder, the commander's face drawn into a fist, his depression of the trigger, and the release of a screaming projectile traveling something short of Mach One that struck the bow of Yabuki's approaching outboard and raised it ten feet out of the water while halving his body, showering the channel with sheet metal, nautical gear, a Samurai sword, and human body parts.

A knock at Wally Lanakai's hotel room door. Wally's armed man looked through the peephole, called behind him to his boss.

"Mr. Lanakai? Sir?"

"What?" Wally sat slouched on a sofa in front of a TV, sipping a bottle of beer, anywhere from his sixth to his tenth.

"It's a hotel staff person with a package."

Wally stumbled to the door, swept it aside, and grabbed the small cardboard box out of the delivery man's hands before slamming the door in his face. He turned the box over and over, looking through bloodshot eyes for the return address, then read return-address-sounding words somewhere on it that meant nothing to him. Fumbling while peeling off the paper, he found a white Styrofoam container inside, the size of a meatloaf, double-wrapped in mailing tape. He dropped the unopened container to the floor like it was contaminated and pulled back. Tears formed, further compromising his eyes, him unable to pick up the package.

His unsteady voice demanded that his man open it.

The lid aside, Wally peeked in, saw a reddish-brown internal organ the size of his hand, packed in dry ice.

The human chemical factory. A miracle organ. The cure for Alzheimer's.

A full liver, not a partial. Wally had never taken a full liver from any living person who hadn't deserved to die, had even walked away from a million and a half bucks from a cop who threatened to close him down.

"Kaipo…"

He didn't want this one.

Wally sobered up enough to call Douglas Logan, who answered immediately. In a few short words, Wally retracted his offer for the purchase of Miakamii Island or any of the island's businesses. He'd lost Kaipo for good, and he wanted nothing to do with that fucking island ever again.

37

They settled into the chairs as Douglas Logan's guests and would be fed a nice brunch when they were through talking to him in his ranch office.

"Commander Malcolm—Evan. Mr. Trout, and Mr. Stakes. So glad you're able to join me. So let me begin with a confession."

The Kauai Police Department had been overwhelmed physically with the carnage and multiple investigations in progress. Exploded cars with the bodies of local Yakuza redistributed along coastal Highway 50, near the U.S. Naval base's Howling Sands Airport. A stolen sanitation department vehicle on the same highway, ready for the scrap heap after its decimation at the hands of mobsters. The street sweeper operator's revised statement that said no, he didn't know nothing about no body parts in no cooler, he'd been mistaken, it was his ruined lunch-bucket he was complaining about on his 9-1-1 call. An abandoned chicken farm that had more blood, all human, no fowl, in its slaughterhouses than the place had experienced in decades, but no bodies to attach to it. An abandoned yacht registered to a Japanese corporation left floating in the channel, no one on board. A midnight report of a fire in the channel, but no vessel to attribute it to. The NTSB and Terry Koo's hounding of Douglas Logan because someone had monkeyed with the evidence of the helicopter crash on Miakamii, with Logan unable to provide an explanation.

And a woman named Aiata Hauata, former Yakuza hostage, her location unknown, who had checked herself out of Kauai's Veterans Memorial Hospital in Waimea a day after she'd been ambulanced there, treated for an abdominal laceration.

"Miakamii is a relic," was how Logan began his admission. "A beautiful gift to us. We're able to see the majesty, and listen to the language, of a Hawaii of hundreds and hundreds of years past. It has struggled to remain a way of life for its people, and for my family as its curators. But it is in incredible decline, and the island's natives..."

———

Ella carried pieces of a broken dining room table out of the thatched cottage at the foot of the ridge, tossed them into a fire, and headed back inside. Ben was nearby in a different home, using a crowbar to knock out a window frame shredded by bullets. He tossed a Victorian stationery desk through the empty frame, two legs of the desk gone, severed by the gunfire. Ella put her back into a vintage armoire carved with Hawaiian royalty figures in plumed headgear, the doors of the chest splintered. She shoved the antique piece out the front door of the cottage toward the roaring flames, the fire calling to all the empty homes, its flames waiting to taste the hundreds of years of island history being fed to it piece by piece, defaced heirloom by defaced heirloom, artifact by artifact, home by empty home.

They were determined not to be sad, determined to embrace the good of it. A new beginning for the island, and for them as a couple, and as individuals, one female, one male, from a long line of native people who rarely got sick, preparing themselves for whatever the other islands, and the mainland, had in store, for whatever miracles that could be found in the volcanic ash, the gentle waters, and in their own flesh, and blood, and organs.

———

"—its population, gentlemen, numbers only two now. Ella and Ben Waumami. The charade needs to be over. Twelve hundred residents per the 2010 census, eleven hundred ninety-eight fewer people ten years later, some gone for good, to heaven, but the rest living modern lives elsewhere, enjoying visits back there to rekindle their inner Miakamii.

"So Evan. I understand now, because of your fiancée Miya's research, the island's importance to medicine. Starting in a few days I'll have other research doctors brought in to pore over Miya's work. To move the island into the twenty-first century. And to recolonize it. My family has agreed, but more importantly, Ella and Ben have agreed. It's time, Evan."

"Copy that, Mr. Logan."

"'*Douglas*,' son. Please call me Douglas."

"Copy that, Douglas."

"Mr. Logan, sir?" Patrick said.

All eyes went to Patrick, someone who usually spoke only when spoken to.

"What is it, Patrick?" Mr. Logan said.

"I want to stay here on Kauai, Mr. Logan sir. My identity, my home, it's here. Philo sir, you and Mr. Logan helped me find it. I want to learn more. I can't leave yet. Can you give me a job, Mr. Logan?"

This could only be an incomplete discussion at this point, but Philo understood, had no choice otherwise when considering the mindset of the former Patrick Stakes—the current and former Patrick 'Ōpūnui—painful as it might be to Philo and his business. Patrick, and his dented noggin, needed to explore more of his roots, to discover more about himself. Mixed feelings swelled Philo's heart to see his employee near the end of his quest, but in the process losing one of his closest friends.

"Your call, bud. A lot to talk about, but one thing's not negotiable. There's no chance I'm breaking the news to Grace. You're on your own there."

First leg, she splurged on a business class ticket for her nine p.m. flight. Eight hours of pampering and rest ahead of her. She kept on her sunglasses, leaned back, and melted into the seat that turned into a bed. The doctors in the hospital, or probably the nurses, had undone her cornrows, needing to scrub her head before she went into surgery, where they'd determined there'd been no harm to her internal organs, liver, the intestines, stomach, only muscle damage. The incision made by the Yakuza doctor had been the only damage. She'd lost a lot of blood, but every organ that should have been in there was still in there. Twenty-four hours later, she bolted from the hospital.

She had incision tenderness and pain, and had been prescribed meds for it. Non-narcotic, per her request. Fading into dreamland...

Wally Lanakai. Her mob patron, her cheerleader, her

lovesick suitor. He'd gotten her sober. He'd kept her that way, made her think that way. She'd always have him to thank for that. But unless she was willing to sacrifice everything, her independence, morals, and freedom, she could never be with him. Her only choice was to return to anonymity. To allow the news of the demise of one Kaipo Mawpaw to be gruesome, sensational, and final. To let him think he'd lost her forever, and in so doing, break his heart.

And to have her wonder if another person would ever love her that much again.

Binge Killer

National Indie Excellence Award Finalist

A FEMALE BOUNTY HUNTER TRACKS A SERIAL KILLER TO A RURAL MOUNTAIN TOWN

A town with its own dark secret...

After serial killer Randall Burton is diagnosed with a terminal disease, he decides to jump bail and go out in a blaze of glory.

One woman stands in his way.

Her name is Counsel Fungo, and she's an exceptionally talented bounty hunter, if a little eccentric. Officially, her two canine companions are therapy dogs. But she considers them partners. Counsel will do anything to stop criminals from preying on the vulnerable, and she's intent on stopping Randall Burton.

Randall's trail leads to sleepy Rancor, Pennsylvania.

Named one of the "Safest Towns in America," it's a quiet town tucked away in the Poconos. Its citizens are mostly widowers, bowlers, and bingo players.

But there's a reason no one in Rancor has reported a major crime in the past 50 years.

Get your copy at www.chrisbauerauthor.com

JOIN THE READER LIST

Never miss a new release! Sign up to receive exclusive updates from author Chris Bauer.

Join today at ChrisBauerAuthor.com

YOU MIGHT ALSO ENJOY...

Blessid Trauma Crime Scene Cleaners

Hiding Among the Dead

Zero Island

Scars on the Face of God

Binge Killer

Jane's Baby

Never miss a new release! Sign up to receive exclusive updates from author Chris Bauer.

Join today at ChrisBauerAuthor.com

ACKNOWLEDGMENTS

My apologies and thanks to the people of Niihau in deference to the Hawaiian island's history fractured in this novel to better fuel the plot and protect innocent parties. Apologies and kudos to the heroes from the actual Niihau Incident, December 7–13, 1941, including Niihauans Benehakaka "Ben" Kanahele (1891-1962; U.S. Medal of Honor and a Purple Heart) and his wife Kealoha "Ella" Kanahele (1907-1974). Third, apologies also to the Robinson family who have owned the island since the 1860s and continue to steward its progress. I appropriated your island proprietorship and used it as a jumping-off point for the sake of some hopefully worthwhile fictional thrills. You continue to do great work for the people of Niihau.

Author/physician Bill O'Toole, whose suggested revisions made the medical malpractice I perform on these pages somewhat more practical. I listened to you and incorporated your feedback, Bill... kind of.

Rerioterai Tava and Moses K. Keale, Sr., authors of *NIIHAU: The Traditions of an Hawaiian Island.*

Jason Kasper, thriller novelist and mentor with a number

of successful thriller series in progress, for feedback and encouragement in completing this project.

JJ Hensley, thriller novelist. Thanks for your last-minute help with this, JJ.

The Severn River Publishing team of professionals headed by Andrew Watts. A great publisher to have on an author's side. Cara Quinlan, professional editor, for your fantastic edit.

Actor/producer/writer Paul Hogan. I thank you for the screenplay earworm you gave me that produced the fan-fic climax paraphrasing of your most wonderful, momentous, iconic line (IMHO) of *Crocodile Dundee* dialogue. Well done, sir.

Past and present members of the Bucks County (PA) Writers Workshop chaired by Don Swaim, including Lindsey (LCW) Allingham, Candace Barrett, Beverly Black, Bobby Cohen, William J. (Bill) Donahue, Natalie Zellet Dyen, Jim Hamill, Jim Kempner, Wil Kirk, Ashara Shapiro, John Schoff-stall, Alan Shils, David Updike, and workshop alumni Jim Brennan, Daniel Dorian, Tracy Grammer, and George MacMillan (aka H.A. Callum).

Additional beta readers and peer novelists Al Sirois and Grace Marcus Sirois.

The Rebel Writers of Bucks County (PA) writers group of Russ Allen, Martha Holland, Dave Jarret, Jackie Nash, and John Wirebach (1943-2020). John, my friend, I wish you could have seen this novel in full. You would have liked it. We miss you big-time, bud.

Albert G. Christian, 299th Infantry, the KOA Regiment, Hawaii National Guard, for a memorable WWII quote. A posthumous thanks to you also for your service during so momentous a time in American history.

ABOUT THE AUTHOR

"The thing I write will be the thing I write."

Chris wouldn't trade his northeast Philly upbringing of street sports played on blacktop and concrete, fistfights, brick and stone row houses, and twelve years of well-intentioned Catholic school discipline for a Philadelphia minute (think New York minute but more fickle and less forgiving). Chris has had some lengthy stops as an adult in Michigan and Connecticut, and he thinks Pittsburgh is a great city even though some of his fictional characters do not. He still does most of his own stunts, and he once passed for Chip Douglas of *My Three Sons* TV fame on a Wildwood, NJ boardwalk. He's a member of International Thriller Writers, and his work has been recognized by the National Writers Association, the Writers Room of Bucks County (PA), and the Maryland Writers Association. He likes the pie more than the turkey.

ChrisBauerAuthor.com

facebook.com/cgbauer

twitter.com/cgbauer